LOVECRAFT'S NEW YORK CIRCLE

George Kirk, as sketched by Clark Ashton Smith c. 1921.

LOVECRAFT'S NEW YORK CIRCLE

THE KALEM CLUB, 1924-1927

Edited by Mara Kirk Hart and S. T. Joshi

How often, brothers, shall we meet
With hearts that still serenely beat?
How many years are ours to stay
With minds as cloudless and as gay?

—*Rheinhart Kleiner, "The Four of Us"*
Double "R" Coffee House, February 15, 1925

Hippocampus Press

New York

Published by Hippocampus Press
P.O. Box 641, New York, NY 10156.
http://www.hippocampuspress.com

Cover design and illustration by Barbara Briggs Silbert.
Hippocampus Press logo designed by Anastasia Damianakos.

On the cover: George Kirk, H. P. Lovecraft, Samuel Loveman, and Frank
Belknap Long are seated in an automat, a Manhattan cafeteria frequented by the
Kalems where food was purchased from a wall-sized vending machine.

Photographs owned by Arkham House on pp. 154 and 208 used by
permission of April Derleth.

First Edition
1 3 5 7 9 8 6 4 2

ISBN 0976159295

For Nicholas and Natalie

May your hearts ever beat serenely,
your minds remain cloudless and gay.

PREFACE

Early in 1991, I had the pleasant, if somewhat unsettling, experience of
receiving a letter from the daughter of one of my characters. That is
to say, Mara Kirk Hart, the daughter of H. P. Lovecraft's friend and fellow Kalem Club member, George Kirk, had read *Pulptime*, my apocryphal
tale of Lovecraft and Sherlock Holmes, in which George plays a supporting role. I was relieved to discover that Mara wasn't writing to object to
my portrayal of her father. Instead, she wanted to know if I was in touch
with any surviving Kalems. Since I'd derived the background for my no-
vella from secondary sources (primarily Lovecraft's letters), I had little to
offer other than an acquaintance with the frail and elderly Frank Belknap
Long, whose younger persona serves as my narrator.

Mara and I exchanged a few letters, and within a year or so she and
her sister came to New York and we met for lunch at a place in
Greenwich Village, not far from the site of her father's old book shop
and the brownstone where he lived briefly that provided the setting for
Lovecraft's "Cool Air." Horror writer T. E. D. Klein joined the group,
and as I recall it was a convivial get-together in the best tradition of the
Kalem Club. We've seen each other a few times since on subsequent
trips she and various family members of hers have made to the city. On
one of them Mara was lucky enough to have the unforgettable experience of visiting Frank Long's widow, Lyda, at her Chelsea apartment.

At some point I referred Mara to S. T. Joshi, who would publish in
Lovecraft Studies her touching essay, "Walkers in the City," based on the
voluminous letters from the mid-1920s that George wrote to his fiancée
back in Cleveland. One must credit Mara for suggesting that, despite the
blessings of a wife and two daughters in the post-Kalem years, her father
perhaps "lived life to its fullest" among his male pals in New York.

Now, with the editorial assistance of S. T. Joshi, Mara has gathered
all her father's relevant letters from those halcyon days, along with
sample writings, many rare and obscure, by the rest of the Kalems.
George Kirk, Rheinhart Kleiner, Sam Loveman, Everett McNeil et al.
were little more than names on the page in *Pulptime*. Here they come
alive as real human beings in their own words.

PETER CANNON

New York City

CONTENTS

INTRODUCTION

In August 1924, when my father George Kirk arrived in New York to establish himself as a bookseller, he immediately contacted H. P. Lovecraft, whom he had met in Cleveland two years earlier. Lovecraft soon introduced Kirk to writers Rheinhart Kleiner, Arthur Leeds, Frank Belknap Long, Everett McNeil, and James Morton. Then— within weeks—Samuel Loveman, from Cleveland, resettled in New York also. Little did Kirk realize to what extent these new friends would sustain him during the next years and influence his entire life.

These eight men were to form a close friendship, at first calling themselves "the gang," and, several months later, naming themselves officially "The Kalem Club." The Kalems are well known to Lovecraft fans. These men—in various configurations—became all but inseparable during the next two years, when Lovecraft's return to Providence in April 1926 drastically altered the circle.

This story takes place in Manhattan, over eighty years ago—before the Empire State and Chrysler buildings, before the Holland Tunnel, when men wore bowler hats and bow ties and carried canes; when flappers wearing short skirts and long pearls danced the Charleston; when double-decker buses down Fifth Avenue and subways to Brooklyn cost only a nickel. Prohibition was in force, and speakeasies were rampant.

In 1924 Yankee Stadium had recently opened, Coney Island boasted its Ferris wheel, King Tut's tomb had been discovered, and Macy's held its first Thanksgiving Day Parade. The Metropolitan Museum of Art, the Museum of Natural History, the New York Public Library, the Bronx Zoo, and the Flatiron Building were well-established landmarks. Household names included Gershwin, Stravinsky, Chaplin, O'Keefe, Valentino, and Will Rogers. Mussolini, Chang Kai-Shek, and Stalin, were in power; Coolidge was president, Al Smith New York's governor, and Jimmy Walker the city's popular mayor.

Who were the Kalems? Adventure writer Everett McNeil, 62, originally from Wisconsin, had hitchhiked and walked to New York as a young man. Columnist and fiction writer Arthur Leeds, 42, originally from Canada, was in New York to find lucrative work and absolve his debts. Essayist and lecturer James Morton, 54, originally from Massachusetts, lived in Harlem, where he espoused Negro causes. Poet and fiction writer Frank Belknap Long, 23, and poet Rheinhart Kleiner, 32, were New Yorkers, born and bred. Poet Samuel Loveman, 37, and Bookseller George Kirk, 25, were drawn to New York as a literary center. And fiction writer, poet, and essayist H. P. Lovecraft, at 34—recently married to Sonia Greene and living in New York—was from Providence.

They ranged in age from twenty-three to sixty-two, and in education from high school dropouts Kirk and Lovecraft to Harvard M.A. and Rhodes scholar Morton. Most were poor, although Long still lived with his affluent parents. Most were single, and the married ones—Leeds and Lovecraft—exercised the freedom of bachelors. Kirk, engaged to Lucile Dvorak of Cleveland, wrote her almost daily.

Soon Kirk entertained them all in his room at 50 West 106th St., brewing coffee and serving crumb cake, Kleiner's favorite. He wrote Lucile: "I have fallen in with a crowd I doubt that one could duplicate anywhere else in the country. . . . Our adorable seriousness in debate about this, that, and everything else—our air that it really was very important—gave me a pretty kick."

These men, who grew to love one another and to hold one another in mutual esteem, were almost courtly in their behavior toward their fellow members. They helped the others find employment, encouraged them in writing and publication, celebrated their birthdays and their cats, and helped them decorate their rooms. Their friendship was a most remarkable phenomenon, perhaps unmatched in twentieth-century American literary history.

No occasion was too small for a celebratory evening with commemorative poems. They met in one another's rooms, especially Kirk's, Lovecraft's, Loveman's, or at the Longs' spacious apartment. Voracious readers who drank in the arts, they introduced one another to books, music, the visual arts, and architecture. Because the Kalems could not afford the city's rich cultural offerings, most of their entertainment was free: the zoo, the aquarium, museums, an occasional movie, much walking and hiking. Theirs was a world of coffee houses, ice-cream parlors, and automats. Although a few smoked, took snuff, and sipped muscatel when they could afford it, most were abstainers.

Kleiner, Loveman, and Leeds were—as we say now—"underemployed." Morton became director of the Paterson (New Jersey) Museum in 1925, the same year he married Pearl Merritt. McNeil researched diligently and wrote slowly, a few pages a day. Although Lovecraft worked hard at free-lance and ghost writing, generally Sonia supported him with her millinery business, his aunts in Providence also contributing. Kirk tried—but not too hard—to make a living in the book trade. Long had no pressing need for employment.

They were unfettered by familial or religious restraints, limitations on what they could think, read, or say, set times for meals or sleep, or fear of the night. Lovecraft and Kirk—sometimes joined by Kleiner or Loveman—thought nothing of walking from 106th Street down to Greenwich Village, lingering to pet stray cats and to admire colonial doorways. After stopping for coffee in the morning, they separated, often only to meet again the next evening. After one such night, Kirk wrote Lucile: "Girl, if you ever give me a more pleasurable time I shall hand you the skid-proof banana peel."

In December 1924, when Sonia took a job in Cleveland and Lovecraft moved to 169 Clinton Street, Brooklyn, Kirk rented rooms directly above Lovecraft's. During the next few months, with Kleiner and Loveman nearby, these four formed a special friendship, immortalized by Kleiner's rondeau, "The Four of Us." Kirk writes of this time: "I am entertaining—and altogether too much. . . . Less than four hours of sleep a night." In Brooklyn their favorite haunts were the Cairo Gardens, Tiffany's, Tontini's, and various ice-cream parlors. These men, with fancy dress and canes, promenaded each Sunday afternoon down Clinton Street, as described in Kleiner's "Bards and Bibliophiles." (See Appendix.)

On February 6, 1925, when "the gang" met at Kirk's, "The Kalem Club" was officially formed. Kirk wrote: "Because all of the last names of the permanent members begin with K, L, or M, we plan to call it the KALEM KLYBB. Half a dozen friends are to be here tonight."

The Wednesday night Kalem meetings had no set agenda. They were evenings of scholarly interchange, with more questions asked than problems solved. The Kalems were concerned with ideas—and no subject was too wide-ranging for them. Talk included—besides books and writing—metaphysics, astronomy, and atomic theory. Like most of the Western world, they were fascinated by Einstein and Freud. Kirk considered these widely read, erudite men "the finest chaps in the world."

In August 1925, Kirk opened the first Chelsea Book Shop in the front room of a two-room parlor suite at 317 West 14th Street, with his living quarters in the back. This bookshop, which became a frequent meeting place for the Kalems at all hours of the day or night, hold special interest, because Lovecraft's story "Cool Air" is set in this building.

Alas Kirk's landlady soon sold the building, and in late October he settled into a new home at 365 West 15th Street. (Kirk's Chelsea Book Shop remained at West 15th Street until February 1927, when it moved to its permanent location at 58 West 8th Street.) On West 15th Street he adopted the first of his beloved cats: "OY! The darlingest kitten vot I've adopted! His name is Edgar Evertson von Saltus Kirk and Oy! You otta see him! . . . What a joy he is to me!"

At this bookshop Kirk entertained the Kalems for his twenty-seventh birthday, November 20, 1925. Lovecraft brought maple sugar candy and Kleiner brought a record of Caruso and Shumann-Heink singing "Home to Our Mountain." Lovecraft, Kleiner, Loveman, and Morton all commemorated Kirk's birthday with poems to him. Describing the party, which lasted until 5:00 A.M., Kirk signed himself "the great GK, one, only and supreme." He adds: "He's a prince of a fellow and is going out after coffee and the papers. . . . Here I sit, take me or leave me—that's my motto." I see seeds of trouble in the marriage, caused by this cavalier outlook.

Wilfred B. Talman, who attended some meetings but never became an official member, called the Kalems "square pegs in round holes." To some degree, I have to agree. Certainly they were far from the cutting edge; in a time of modernism, they loved tradition. On the whole, they were impractical nonconformists who scorned conventional middle-class values, which they labeled "Babbittry," to such an extent that some were unwilling to write for pay.

In a time when much of the literary world praised Eliot, Joyce, cummings, and Hemingway, the Kalems' reading, with few exceptions, harkened back to the nineteenth century or earlier: Edgar Saltus, Swinburne, and Poe, their idol. Although new and important periodicals began publication in the mid-1920s (the *New Yorker*, the *New Masses*, the *Saturday Review of Literature*), Kirk's letters mention only *Weird Tales* and H. L. Mencken's *American Mercury*. At a poetry reading evening, who did they choose? Shelley, Keats, Wordsworth, Hardy, Yeats, Shakespeare, Lander, Swinburne, along with Alice Meynell, Fitz-Greene Halleck, Thomas Lovell Beddoes, and Edmund Gosse.

Why was this? I believe the Kalems, although skeptical and disillusioned with much that was modern, remained incurable romantics and optimists, who continued to honor tradition. I find that a good part of their charm.

And what of their writing? McNeil's adventure tales for boys were based on historical characters and events. Loveman and Long wrote formal poetry using classical, Elizabethan, and romantic subjects. Kleiner, although writing in light verse, used formal meter and rhyme. And Lovecraft's weird fiction was romantic and his verse stilted and rhymed.

This group, although bright and interesting, was not destined to capture the public imagination as were their contemporaries, the expatriates, and the members of the Algonquin Round Table. They were not self-promoters. They neither exemplified the swinging 'twenties nor were they out of the Wharton or Fitzgerald traditions of wealth and privilege.

In April 1926, Kirk wrote, "HPL—Alas!—has returned to his native and beloved Providence." Then the Kalems substituted long Sunday hikes led by James Morton and the Paterson Rambling Club for their all-night walks. They continued to meet, but rather desultorily and without a center. Individually, they visited Lovecraft often, and as a group delightedly entertained him on his frequent visits to New York.

I have grown very fond of the Kalems for their kindness, love, and support of one another, their playfulness, and their generosity. My heart goes out to these men—enthusiastic, articulate, and optimistic, most dreaming of a better future, some remembering a better past. I want them to be successful in their literary and bookselling endeavors. Unfortunately, very few dreams materialized, and the days to come did not necessarily "kindly greet" these men. Ill health, exacerbated by poverty and poor nutrition, shortened some lives; alcohol dependence later affected others.

Only after death has Lovecraft—who died young and in poverty—become famous. The recognition Long achieved during his lifetime was unaccompanied by financial rewards, and he too died in poverty. Morton became well known in Paterson and in reform circles. Leeds, in later years, achieved a modicum of success writing for the American Guidebooks series. McNeil, once widely read by boys, has long been out of print. Kirk and Kleiner remain all but unknown. Loveman's poetry, fortunately, has recently been collected and published by Hippocampus Press.

It delights me to see young Kirk's generous spirit and enthusiasms, and the esteem in which he was held by his friends. How I wish I had known him before marriage, children, financial difficulties, depression, and dependence on alcohol clouded his vision. During these bachelor New York years, with a mind still "cloudless and gay," my father had the most satisfying male friendships he would ever experience. From that time he kept letters, poems, postcards, dedicated and inscribed books, and happy memories indelibly etched in his heart. But I knew almost nothing of it during his lifetime.

Whatever happened to these friendships? Why didn't we, as a family in New York, see Kleiner, Morton, Loveman, or Long? It's a mystery I wish I could answer. Was there a falling out? Was Lucile jealous? Were family responsibilities overwhelming? I have no idea.

Although Father loved his wife and daughters, and although Mother made a nice home, I doubt any happiness quite equaled that twenty-seventh birthday high, when he was fêted with poems and tributes; or the exhilaration of an all-night walk with Lovecraft, lingering to pet stray cats, exploring Minetta Lane, and stopping for morning coffee in the Village. Although the Kalem years were short-lived and intense, they were his halcyon years.

The Kalem friendships crystallized many of Father's traits: kindness, generosity, love of hosting, love of classical music, respect for ideas and for the arts, but also an indifference to money and to material things. How will an eighteenth-century gentleman who scorns philistinism and work for pay support a wife and children? He was a Democrat through and through, an NAACP member, and an Esperanto enthusiast. Father was happiest without responsibilities or expectations laid on him. He continued to love formal verse—especially Shakespeare and Marlowe—and often brought a book to the dinner table. All his life he loved cats, and Aphra Behn, Tobermory, and Macavity replaced Edgar, Prisky, and Oscar.

We, Kirk's daughters, discovered these letters only in 1992 after Father had been dead thirty years, and Mother could no longer live alone. Without the help of Peter Cannon and S. T. Joshi, they would have remained unpublished.

These letters are the only contemporary documents—beside Lovecraft's letters home—describing the extraordinary friendship among these eight men. They are of enormous help, as S. T. Joshi says, "in filling in gaps in Lovecraft's own letters and in rounding out the general picture of the group [and] rival Lovecraft's letters to his aunts in their detailed vignettes of 'the gang.'"

In addition to Kirk's letters, this collection includes representative writings by the Kalems never before published in one volume. Whenever possible, we have included poems they wrote to each other, along with a sampling of their significant work. These representative writings, along with the letters, photographs, and calligraphy, offer the reader an intimate, fascinating glimpse of the Kalems, and of New York during these years.

—MARA KIRK HART

Acknowledgments

To April Derleth for permission to reproduce photographs owned by Arkham House; to David E. Schultz for supplying original material; to Kenneth W. Faig, Jr., for supplying photographs; to Joel Ness and Jean Vileta for freely offering technical help; to Catherine Koemptgen for her support and encouragement; and to my husband, Bob, for his patience and enduring love I extend heartfelt thanks.

—M. K. H.

THE KALEM LETTERS OF GEORGE KIRK

INTRODUCTION

From August 1924 until their marriage on March 5, 1927, George Kirk wrote almost daily from New York to his fiancée, Lucile Dvorak, in Cleveland. The Kalem Letters contain excerpts from the letters that relate to the Kalem Club and its members during that period.

In 1992, my sister Kitty and I discovered them—among many other documents: manuscripts, poems, and calligraphy included in this volume—when we cleared out our mother's apartment after her entry into a nursing home. Fortunately, Mother—a sentimental woman—felt the written word was sacred. Thus these letters remained in sealed boxes almost seventy years. George Kirk had died many years earlier, in 1962. Lucile Dvorak Kirk died on October 26, 1994.

Although they have never before been published, portions of these letters appeared in the essay, "Walkers in the City: George Willard Kirk and Howard Phillips Lovecraft in New York City, 1924–1926," *Lovecraft Studies* No. 28 (Spring 1993): 2–17.

1924

AUGUST 1. 50 W. 106th St., NYC. Am in room with litter about me and soiled laundry to count and take to laundry down the Ave. Am both delighted and worried about the room. It is large with three good windows, a fair closet, a good bed and other furnishings are good enough. It is on the corner of Manhattan Ave—50 West 106th St., NYC is the address—and is but a block away from Central Park, a short walk to 5th Avenue busses or 7th Avenue El, though I know of no subway about here. All kinds of junky stores are about and a good-looking drugstore across the street, the Museum within walking distance and the pond—o hell!—I probably shall hate it well enough within a month. I pay more than I intended but I have a two-burner stove and can cook breakfasts and make tea or coffee.

AUGUST 3, Sunday. NY is much as ever, though I have never before been here at this time of the year when things are quite so quiet. The famous Wrigley advertisement has given way to a very pretty collection of colored lights and moving figures extolling Clicquet Club. Have come across a few buildings which I never before had seen although I really have spent very little of the daytime in sightseeing. I do love NY and believe that I shall love it still better when I know it better—as I intend to do. Spent yesterday morning with the secretary of the *Publishers' Weekly*, the booksellers' trade journal, from whom I received many valuable tips. . . . After making sure that all the bookshops were closed I took a boat to Coney Island and returned by bus. The subways are hot; waiting for trains is especially uncomfortable. Think I shall go out to the stadium tonight. . . . Ye Gods! It is almost three o'clock Saturday morning and I need to get lots of sleep even though I have been usually unable to sleep because of heat. Understand that Sam expects to be here soon. Ed,[1] of course, expects to come. I should like to work up a plan to make a living in England.

AUGUST 10, Sunday. Met a poet and book-collector named Rheinhart Kleiner. We already call each other by our first names. Another new acquaintance is Arthur Leeds who does free lance writing. He has just finished a scenario in collaboration, which *Cosmopolitan* has under consideration and which is about, I believe, Peter the Great. Kleiner works in an office, Fairbanks Scales Co., Broome and Lafayette Streets.

AUGUST [undated]. Think I shall phone Kleiner—he is of the crowd tonight—whether he can dine with me . . . then to Morton's for the evening. I believe he is some relation to John Seigler, who printed for me. He is said to be very erudite, bookwormish, and likable. . . . An adorable note from HL, next to yourself the most lovable creature on this or any other universe known or imagined. The salutation is "Georgius Rex." He is 18th Century English—English to the core—though he has become more and more interested in American colonial houses, furniture, and times. He has been interested in and knows quite well both Roman and Egyptian histories and living. But all that is secondary. I believe I had rather I had met him earlier in life, that I might have less

---

1. Edward Lazare (1904–1991), a Cleveland friend who came to New York in September 1924.

GD[2] and more HL. But you love me as is, so I complain not at all.

AUGUST 11, Monday. A fat letter from ums. It reminds me of Mrs. Lovecraft. She is not terribly so, but she continually bewails her avoirdupois. Or is that a system of weights? Moreover, I started to write about last night. If I like it, and I think I shall, I shall offer it to Howard L. for amateur publication. Shall enclose a copy if I do it.[3] . . . Will you like the Lovecrafts? How should I know that? I should like you to like Howard but if you do not happen to, well, it will be nothing serious.

AUGUST 13, Wednesday. Want to start book but have been quite unable to get time. Think I shall go to library tonight. Tomorrow night I go to James F. Morton, Jr.'s place. Shall tell you about it. Hear that Sam is coming in about one month from date.

AUGUST 15, Friday. Went to a party in black belt last night. If Lovecraft is a prince James F. Morton Jr. is a king. Have fallen in with a crowd I doubt that one could duplicate anywhere else in country. For one can look for a long time in Cleveland, San Francisco, etc. without finding a certain type of person. How many do I know? Starting from west—one in SF if he is still in SF, one in E. Auburn CA,[4] two in Akron and S in C and Bill Sommer[5] in between, then two of the five of the group. Others are Rheinhart Kleiner, near poet, more or less indiscriminate collector of books but taking himself, his work, and his collecting very seriously, who has somewhat attached himself onto me; Arthur Leeds—last traveled country in stock, done work with movies, does free-lance writing, one McLean,[6] an oldster—lovely purely white hair, writes books for boys and does not need to write down to them, he's quite equal mentally. I do not say this of McLean from my own short acquaintance but in agreement with judgment of others. Our adorable seriousness in debate about this, that, and everything else, our air that it really was very important, gave me a pretty kick. RK told a story, which I have a vague recollection of having heard before.

---

2. Kirk would sometimes refer to himself condescendingly as GD (goddamn).
3. Apparently a sketch to be called "One Enchanted Night."
4. Clark Ashton Smith.
5. William Sommer, a Cleveland watercolorist and draftsman.
6. I.e., Everett McNeil.

AUGUST 17. Don't know about Samuel. Have not heard from him except through HL.

AUGUST 18, Monday. Spent a very pleasant evening with RK—cooed over his books—he has about a hundred good ones out of a thousand, a fair average—over his poetry, and talked much. He would have me open a shop in Brooklyn. He really has renewed my intention of living there. As to the shop, I dunno.

AUGUST 19, Tuesday. HL is Howard Lovecraft. He writes: stories, etc., and rewrites: Houdini's stories, poems for one Hoag, something or other for David B. Bush,[7] etc. Heard something about Morton, which makes me honor and revere him. He is a Harvard MA, has had good opportunities, and has chosen to devote his life to working out his ideals, even though it entails personal discomfort. Am glad that I finally got away from C. All whom I've met here are so delightfully conservative I'm certain 'twill do me much good. I told you of group. Rheinhart tells me that, though it has never been organized, it still consists only of original members since applicant is kept out by one blackball. R tried recently to get in a friend, but vainly. I asked whether I should be voted upon and he thinks not, since they accepted my invitation to meet here, thereby recognizing me as a member. I noticed, but had not thought of, some hesitation in accepting. I did not know that I was taking the bull by the horns. I greatly fear that there will be trouble before so very long.

AUGUST 22, Friday. 9:00 a.m. If I cannot recapture, I shall at least try to picture to you, some of the charms of the last twelve hours.

Called for and ate with RK who seems to be trying to rush me. I eat with him again tonight. Sunday afternoon and evening I am to hike with the Blue Pencil Club.[8] McLean did not appear. Thus I am rid of inconsequentials. We were here till after one. As I've said before, I believe Lovecraft and Morton vie for the honor of being the most erudite man I have ever met. No one ever wore even the slightest knowledge more lightly than either. They are, on a great many points, at opposite poles. The resulting confab, with RK and GK coming in occasionally

---

7. Kirk refers to the amateur poet Jonathan E. Hoag (1831–1927) and HPL's persistent revision client David Van Bush (1882–1959).
8. An amateur journalists' group in Brooklyn, affiliated with the National Amateur Press Association.

for shorter or longer periods, was very pretty. But aside from that the coffee was better, and the fruit very good, little made the night differ from a week ago. Morton lives on out and took the El at 104 and Columbus. RK lives in Brooklyn, and took the subway at 103 and Broadway. HL, Arthur Leeds, and GK had a pleasant walk to Leeds' place at 8th Ave and, I think, 49th St. Then, at about 2:15 or 3:00 the time really started. We walked down 8th Ave to where it turns into Hudson and where Greenwich Village begins. Perhaps you were not aware that GV was a village a long time ago and became part of NYC a little less than one hundred years ago. It was at one time connected with NYC by a narrow, unpaved road about three miles long.

I have mentioned to you HL's 18th century craze, also his love for American Colonial architecture, furniture, etc. That I felt no particular love for either I need hardly mention to you who know me so well, but I do enjoy H's company. Girl, if ever you give me a more enjoyable time I shall hand you the skid-proof banana peel.

I should like to give you some idea of the impression in my old bean, so bear with a poor old man who has been up and on his feet most of twenty-six hours, with the prospect of about seventeen more. I confess to having before been shown colonial types but never before did I get any kick therefrom. But H's enthusiasm, the age and imagined romance of the houses, and, gradually as I came to recognize the types, a slow realization of the beauty like a faint and subtle perfume crept over me. Houses which lived through the Revolution; houses such as G. Washington, Alex Hamilton, etc. knew and, for a while lived in; houses where hundreds of feet for a hundred or more years had worn hollows into the steps inches deep, houses which were almost exactly as they were many years ago and about which hangs ineffable mystery: the repetition of these began to affect me as does a heady wine.

Not that they were alike in condition. No. Charlton St. is known as the show street for colonial houses. On Grove and a number of other streets were many examples in practically perfect condition. Others were remodeled and ruined. While still others were falling to pieces. At places the doorway had been replaced, at others only the door. Some windows were changed, while many of the delightful dormer windows were ruined for studios. More and more as I write this I realize how dull it must read: would that I could recapture the joy of the hunt and of discovery, the excitement of seeing a perfect specimen between a row of modern apartments and, perhaps, a church. But don't think that was all.

On Minetta Street and Lane—the latter delightfully short, crooked, and useless—we saw the places in the worst state of repair of anyplace on the west side that we visited. Dirty, squalid, miserable. And then we saw some very pretty examples. A pair of cops came along in a Ford, passed us slowly, stopped at the corner for some time to watch and discuss us. No one else did we see there. And that's not the half of it, dear.

Rupert Hughes[9] recently said that Batavia St. is the most Dickensian St. in NY. I don't believe it. But aside from that, listen to this. I doubt that I should care to take you to some of the places we visited, at least not at 4:00 in the morning. But this a.m. the occasional element of quite real danger added much to the gist of it all. Well, #1 Howard knew, had discovered, a few days earlier, and when he suddenly pushed me into it, 'twas like another world. I stood speechless and almost breathless for minutes. The place, as finally revealed to me, is like this:

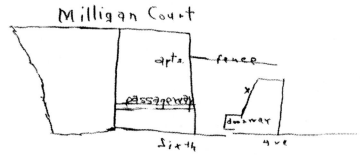

"X" is a set of swinging square lamps, which was claimed to be the only one still in existence in NYC. H and I proved otherwise before morning was over. That inner court! Next to one building a hole with weird running water; the moon eerily peeping down, the silent solitude and seclusion of the place! The outer court has less of the eerie but more actual beauty. Really lovely! Patchin Place is quite good, but PP is well known. We decided that we are two out of not more than 1,000 persons in NYC knowing of this place by experience. Another place was very good but had a detestable odor, which I claimed was Colonial, but that was denied by H. He tells me the odor, which is almost unbearable even in NY where one becomes more or less accustomed, if not acclimated, to unpleasant odors, is ever-present.

---

9. Rupert Hughes (1872–1956), once-popular American novelist, playwright, and biographer.

It was on Minetta Lane that we came upon a narrow passageway alongside an old house. We went through and came upon a *most* delightful little old-world place, court, or whatever one calls a little cluster of houses connected with the world by only a passageway about two feet wide and five high. Then, a graveyard, unused since 1705. The other alleys, byways, anyplace to go through a passageway in a house or to climb and flights or two of stairs now daunted us not in the least. I remember our standing within a little yard, watching pass a man tall, stooped, who clumped down one foot as if he had a wooden leg, and who rubbed his arm as though he were a 'dope.' And the worst was only half of it, o[ld] d[ear]. But I must rush as 'tis late and I have yet to shower.

Vandewater, Ross, Jacob, all the little streets up to or through the Brooklyn Bridge and near the waterfront, all of them are delightful. In one, one of the most dilapidated, where all the doors into the passageways were open, we went into them, examined the stairways, and looked for a court or place. Once we found a court with two houses facing it, terribly ramshackle things. In this court or place we found the other square-bracketed lamps of the city. Then we entered the place at the end of the place, climbed a flight of curious, winding stairs, and examined the view of the whole. And I am tired and I know this is dull.

AUGUST 23, Saturday. Do not think RK Jewish, though possible. He works in office, Fairbanks Scales Co., Broome and Lafayette Streets. Party Okay. I am assured it was the best in a long time. Nice? Cannot go into Morton now. You'll meet him at the Blue Pencil Club here. . . . Met HL in Cleveland somewhat over a year ago. Met RK through him. . . . We leave Dykman St. ferry at noon tomorrow and are not back till late. . . .

AUGUST 25, Monday. Have been to Doc Stile's with such of the Blue Pencil gang as showed up. Became interested in Esperanto and I walked the 2½ miles to the ferry with a Mr. D.A. Kalgin who speaks fluently eight languages and gets by with eight others . . . organizer of the Harmonia Society. James Morton is president of another Esperanto group, and teaches it at a fashionable young ladies' school. Mr. Marney of Danville, VA, also a Blue Penciler, is an Esperantist and is the only one I care for. Doc Stile's is a place on the other side of the Hudson and on top of the Palisades, a very beautiful spot. Blue Pencil invited me to come along on their annual outing to a lake up in Joisey. Oh yes,

RK was so kind as to ask me to accompany him to dinner and the theater tonight, but since Thursday night is at his place and I shall see him then, I declined. I rather feel, if you know what I mean, that I've seen RK before.

AUGUST 27, Wednesday. Did I mention that Alfred Galpin, Madisonian, friend of Lord and L (whatshisname) and myself, incidentally, went and got married some time ago?[10] Hully gosh! He, Howard! Next I suppose CAS, SL, RK, and even JFM and perhaps even GK will join ranks.

AUGUST 28, Thursday. I have not written about FBL yet because I am not yet certain whether I like him. As for GW, it becomes harder and harder to get any kick out of existence. What oh what is next?

OCTOBER 1, Wednesday. The meeting is here tonight. Sam [Loveman] is still here. So is GD. Ed is with someone in Brooklyn . . . with whom I know not, nor know I why he has left his things here. Nor care.

OCTOBER 3, Friday. HPL is an old dear. So are you. I felt quite important yesterday. Received four telegrams and one long distance call. . . . Met another person who knew Saltus[11] and heard more nice stories.

OCTOBER 11, Saturday. Last evening I sat at table thinking of you, only entering conversation when forced to. I missed little, however, since chaps were merely airing their usually absurd ideas about your sex. One was a homo, one an avowed fetishist, one quite nothing where sex is concerned, and your GW with whom you are usually acquainted. I tire of half-baked ideas and people, of old-fashioned and antipathetic prejudices, of raw geniuses, and, when I happen to consider him, of GW. However, in many ways, his sole company is the most bearable of them all.

OCTOBER 12. Thought for a while yesterday that I was about to be ill, got over it, came in about five this morning and slept till after noon. Since when I have been bathing, drinking coffee and tea, reading *Purple*

---

10. Galpin (1901–1983) married a Frenchwoman, Lillian M. Roche, on 23 June 1924.

11. Edgar Evertson Saltus (1855–1921), once a highly acclaimed American essayist and novelist.

and Fine Linen,[12] looking over papers and working at certain records. . . . GW well enough knows that he is nothing, that he is a cheap poseur in his little circles, that he knows nothing about books, music, literature, painting, architecture, nor is he often unconscious of this fact. But to get by in business and to gain and to keep certain of his friends, and in the often vain effort to relieve his knowledge of his rather sad deficiency, he must keep up the pretense, which so frequently is merely ludicrous. . . . Had a pretty fight early this morning, all on account of L. Too, it was partly your fault, although I rather overrode you in the matter.

OCTOBER 14. I am having lotsa fun etc. and know very well that I am getting sick of it all and either something will change or I will leave or and or and. So! That, in the words of dear GW, is that!

OCTOBER [undated]. I walked with Leeds and Howard from 138th St. to Times Square. Howard then took the subway and I saw Leeds to hotel. Then I started home. First I started to walk along Central Park West, watching the changing colors in the sky over the trees of the park and the buildings beyond. However, that sorta lost its kick, and I went on west to Riverside Drive and walked to about 103 along the pretty ol' Hudson with the beauty of the opposite bank, the morning light playing on it as it did a long, long time ago when I first came to NYC on the NY Central. . . . And so home, more or less seven o'clock. I hope I have more to read than is here. And I *hope* I don't have to rely on Rheinhart's taste for reading. Ugh! Guess I shall have Rheinhart out to sell him a few books. He hasn't much but I don't need a lot. Did I say I've asked them here for next Thursday night? Must buy some more cups.

OCTOBER 24, Wednesday. Got you a copy of the complete "De Profundis" today.[13] Bought a copy of Dante bound in vellum, which the dealer had more or less ruined, by washing off the painted design and the gilding in trying to clean it. Also the second edition of *The Phoenix* by Thomas Middleton, 1630. Spent a very enjoyable evening (last) at Lovecraft's. Got lost going over. They both are in better health than I ever before had seen them (bad to woise). I go over again tomorrow to meet some friends. Would tell of them, but you will meet them, and I

---

12. *Purple and Fine Linen* (1873), a novel by Edgar Fawcett (1847–1904).
13. *De Profundis* (1905), Oscar Wilde's posthumously published account of his imprisonment in Reading Gaol.

become wobbly.... By the way, I had a discussion with Mrs. L about Jude.[14] She thought him a likable character and I remember him as being otherwise. Must look at the book again.

OCTOBER [undated]. Friday evening and Saturday morning. HPL hanged himself the other day because of Sonia's leaving him. RK is in the tombs for picking pockets. Poor Leeds shot his daughter, strangled his son and his wife to death (don't you dare to say I'm naughty—that's nil to what I *could* say!), and leapt from his hotel window. FBL is to get the chair because he shot a man who dared to stand next to him in the subway after plentifully imbibing garlic spaghetti. Our next meeting is scheduled for the third pit in the eighth hell (they've dug a new and special one for us). You want to know how I'm to get there? Why, my bargain with the old boy ends tonight and he'll be here anon.... I should like to read and must work, for I probably will soon have someone or other on my hands and I'm not wholly sorry, for even such misanthropic chaps as am I occasionally can almost enjoy the company of a not quite senseless friend for a while at least, although they frequently stay too long, except Howard, who frequently stays longer than the rest put together, but never too long to suit me, for he is a wonderful chap, probably the best intelligence in the crowd, although Jim gives him a run for his money in intellect, but of course Jim has the advantage in schooling and Jim has been about the world much more: Europe twice, free love colonies, news reporter, socialist speaker, dead broke several times in several places—in Boston he lived two weeks on the broken crackers from the bottom of cracker barrels, but then again. But Howard has the advantage of genius, while Jim has gone a bit stale.

FALL [undated]. Sunday. RK has all of us taking snuff. Ever try it? Sneezemydamnheadoff. HPL brought for me some cigs from Allen Street. Sorry I never took you there, but didn't know the street then. They are quite peppy.

OCTOBER 20, Monday. Samuel is Samuel. Saw Sam and RK for a while in the afternoon (yesterday). Talking about our respective youths and GW said that although he had at that time no particular love for himself and realized only too well how little reason he now has to es-

---

14. Kirk refers to the central character of Thomas Hardy's novel *Jude the Obscure* (1896).

teem himself, he feels that he was quite something about four or five years ago; that during that time came into being much of the little that is worthwhile in him, but which he has gradually been losing ever since. Sam agreed. But the statement was only about as true as such statements are in a conversation. . . . Tomorrow night I'm invited to the Writer's Club, where Pearson of P[ublic] L[ibrary] speaks, and should be interesting.

OCTOBER 22. Too many thin people are simple to let one say that simplicity makes them fat. And Jake Falstaff is not simple.

Mrs. Lovecraft went to the hospital the night before last because of another breakdown. Upon which my comment is that I make none. . . . RK is tied up with an Irish damsel at office whose hair I dislike.

OCTOBER 31. Have two boys here this evening but told them that I only returned home to work, and am doing this instead.

FALL [undated]. Wednesday. Centaur of Philly is to issue Sam's book in January or February.[15] Sent a poem to FPA[16] but it has not been published.

NOVEMBER 2, Monday. Spent some time recently with Mrs. Munds, Saltus's daughter by his first wife. At least I think it was his first. . . .

No, I do not read H. L. Mencken.[17] He has done a real service for reading America but he has had his day. He has ever been terribly conservative, a hopeless puritan, and is now even more apparently the exact sort he has always raved and ranted against.

FALL [undated]. Going over to Lovecraft's this evening at 8:00.

FALL [undated]. Sunday and Monday. I spent several hours in the pm with RK, HPL, SL, and GK in evening ending up here in my room. Went out with them at midnight and went alone to Village joint. Met some friends and got home at 5:30. Tomorrow I shall meet Halsey, the

---

15. Loveman had written a treatise on Edgar Saltus. It was never published.
16. Franklin P. Adams (1881–1960), American journalist who had a long-running column, "The Conning Tower" (1913–41), in the New York *Tribune* and (later) *Post.*
17. H. L. Mencken (1880–1956), leading American critic and founder and editor of the *American Mercury* (1924f.).

eccentric bookseller of Church Street. RK is to be here this p.m. . . . My coffee is becoming quite famous. But I must be careful. Next I may say that I've once washed dishes or swept a floor. GD be praised, I've never sewn a button but once, and it came off a day later. . . . Have been having an orgy of Swinburne, Keats, Francis Saltus, Edgar Fawcett, ever since I arose. RK still wants me to open a shop. Well so do others and so do I, but not at present. Got to bed at 4:30 this morning. Up at 8:00 and ho! for 47th . . . I'm glad you're enjoying life, even without my company, since I have been having some very pleasant times and expect many more.

MID-NOVEMBER. Election Day. Am supposed to go to a party tonight, which will get returns by radio and stay together until decisive reports are received. I intend getting out of going; I amn't suited for this sort of life, at least so I enjoy telling me. Perhaps I shall get used to it in time.

UNDATED. Wednesday. Scarcely know what I am doing this morning. Arthur was here until 2:30, I read a while, tossed around in trundle a few hours and have been trying to enliven myself for the past few hours . . . But I am but an ill old man who should die and perhaps will, for once, do as he ought. If he does not within a reasonable length of time, I believe he will at least leave this country. Never have anything to do with anyone who has an artistic, or in any way unusual, temperament. They are terrible creatures.

NOVEMBER 18. Would it not be simple and prevent complications if I should merely pass out . . . Seacrest of Washington[18] was here and desires that I visit him and wife. He is not much, but has lived several years in S[outh] S[eas] Islands and talks very interestingly of them and has a fine and an only too unusual viewpoint of their morality. . . . I dread awaking again—that is the worst of sleeping.

NOVEMBER 20 [George Kirk's 26th birthday]. Twenty some years ago, at some time between midnights of this date, there first did yell a youngster who came to be known, among other ways, as GWK. What else he may have done then I do not know—that he did not yell for

---

18. Edward Lloyd Sechrist (1873–1953), amateur journalist in Washington, D.C.

Lucy would surprise me. Of what he has done since we had, perhaps, better keep a grave and solemn silence.

NOVEMBER 21, Friday. Think I shall become a first-class drunkard if ever I am well enough. I can't get drunk now—stuff merely puts me to sleep . . . Friends again argued about women. They make me ill. I took a nap. One b[oy] f[riend] said 'twas criminal for a woman and man to lie together if not married to each other. I claimed 'twas criminal (which, to be sure, is too strong) for them to lie together whether or not they were married unless they loved each other, and if they loved each other, they were foolish if they didn't lie together.

[Thanksgiving eve, a meeting of "the gang" at Kirk's lasted until after 2:30 a.m. While Lovecraft read, Kirk and the others worked crossword puzzles. Afterwards, Kirk and Lovecraft walked all night, down to Greenwich Village, where they stopped for coffee. Then they revisited their favorite haunt, the Minettas. When the sun rose they were in Washington Square. After separating for some hours, Kirk and Loveman went to Lovecraft's for Thanksgiving dinner. Kirk praises Sonia's fine cooking and Howard's warm hospitality. During this dinner, Kirk and Loveman ask Lovecraft to join them the following Saturday, when they will spend the evening with Allen Tate. I have these notes from George Kirk's letter, but cannot locate the original.—M. K. H.]

NOVEMBER 29. Am anxious to get out of NY. Am tired of all things living. . . . At one period of my life I feared that I should never really live. I wanted to be intense: to have strong hates and fears and loves, etc. Well, if I live long enough, I shall have something to think back upon. Don't quite forget.

DECEMBER 1. So much to do and so little heart for it! How terrible is age when it comes, not slowly and peacefully, but as do certain loves. Suddenly you realize that all is not as it has been and that this has been coming on for a long time without your being aware. I am about ninety-five winters old today.

DECEMBER 2, Saturday. Our Wednesday meeting was last night. Only a small turnout: HPL, Leeds, RK and your GK—why does your super-scription (if that's what it is—the LD and address)—always become wet and rubbed?—But we had an enjoyable (hope I get well soon so that I can get some new pens—guess I'll try the Waterman) evening (it is rather stubby but will do, at least it doesn't root up the paper), which lasted until 4:30 this is. . . . Shall have this sent SD, and hope you get it on the gentile's Sabbath. . . . Phoned Belknap yesterday. He was born and bred in Manhattan, but speaks a broader Brooklynese than anyone else I know. He had a cold and could not rise to even his usual grade of distinctness. I said that I could not understand him. He said, "Can't you hear my verse?" "Every stanza of it now," I replied. But alas! He didn't get it.

DECEMBER 8. I determined when I came to NY to make more of an effort to create and hold friends than I had done, but when I must stand, lie, or sit while noisome nuts tell me about this and that and such I wonder if it is worth the trouble of repressing the numerous sarcasms and ironies which come to mind.

WINTER [undated]. Was told last night, "You'll end yet by blowing out your brains." "I doubt it," I replied, "I have naught but a large rifle and a .25 automatic. The rifle is too clumsy and the .25 would not blow out even my few brains." Oh well, what matter such squabbles?

DECEMBER 10. HPL is the greatest 18th Century gentleman in these parts. He was here, talking, from 10:00 Saturday night until 8:00 Sunday morning.

DECEMBER 16, Tuesday. RK showed up his true cockney colors at a gathering here a few nights past. He would—figuratively—twirl on his nose for sparkling burgundy, do the French act for red wine, and would lick anyone's buttocks for chartreuse. I say this not to be improper but to show the way he actually degraded himself. He had earlier shown me his ability to crawl. One of the strangest happenings I have seen in NY was RK at a Writers' Club meeting saying "I am a *libertine!*"

DECEMBER 25, Christmas Day. Some band is playing Holy Night or whatever's the name of it and I feel that I've heard it before. It is cool and dry but neither white nor green. If the day must be given a color I should call it a yellowish gray—a smoke shade that Persian cats sometimes attain. Am invited to Sheepshead Bay, but it's only the Denches.[19] . . . I have eaten one grapefruit, four oranges, some stale rye bread with butter and marmalade—but, because it is what it is (if it is and it may

19. Ernest A. Dench, an amateur journalist, and his family.

be) I decided you would pardon a bit of indulgence and so have been partaking somewhat liberally of my Muscatel.

DECEMBER 26. Ed Lazare has found an angel and intends opening a bookshop in Flushing if I will go in with him—which I doubt that I shall. Here's a joke, which I must repeat to RK—he detests such: Don't cross a bridge even when you come to it: you may find yourself in Brooklyn.

DECEMBER [undated]. If ever you think that I don't like to write to you, recollect that on Christmas of 1924, when I had planned having the Chinese restaurant send me a fancy meal, I preferred writing to L even though I had already scribbled *pages* to her. . . . Oh yes. I want to move. Am told of an attractive corner room on Gramercy Park and of others in Brooklyn Heights at the same rents as this foolish noisome hole. Wanta move. Wanta be well, and shall be shortly. I like assonance. I like HPL. I like the Jumel and the Van Courtland mansions.

NEW YEAR'S EVE. I am tired of being cooped in and soon will be either well or dead. That is final. . . . If I leave my toil I read at beloved old Michel Montaigne as Englished by one John Floris, whom I dare to like, even though Shakespeare didn't.

1925

JANUARY 2. Believe I mentioned the gang here on NY Eve. Had a fair time and would tell you more of it if I could. Would that you could have heard W. Dryden[20] sing his adored papa's immortal "The Miner's Dream of Home"! His 'leading part' in "White Cargo"[21] consists of appearing for about two minutes in the first act and then being led off the stage. [Kirk encloses a typescript he's written about "The Miner's Dream of Home."] I amn't beginning 1925 exactly as I might have chosen to do. Just noticed in the N.Y POST that Sir James George Frazer has been given the Order of Merit by his king, and dear

---

20. Wheeler Dryden (1892–1957), Charles Chaplin's half-brother and, as an amateur journalist, tangentially acquainted with the Kalems.

21. *White Cargo* (1923), a three-act play by Leon Gordon.

Edmund Gosse is now Sir Edmund Knight.[22] How I came to be reading the paper you may imagine. It is one of those dread secrets which I shall never disclose. Have a dill? Or some New Year's cakes? Should like to tell all about the interesting meeting which lasted until five, but I cannot, dare not, take the time just now, nor tomorrow. And I fear I shall have forgotten all about it by Sunday.

JANUARY 6. Belknap came in, then left, as I had to get off certain things. Guess I'll read a half hour, and bathe, and hit the holy hay. Have heard high praise for the picture, "Peter Pan."[23] See it if you can. Galpin is in Galveston or some such hole, instructor at some university in French. He's a gdsb of a clever kin—ask HPL. He treated three of us rather scurvily—but I take those things easily. Except when, several days ago, I got wind of a dealer's lying about me—or at least stretching a partial truth into a lie—I became angry. Phoned him and had him come out. Sold him some worthless books for more than they are worth at retail. But I'm afraid he's still ahead as I've shunted him off some bad deals. More gossip tomorrow.

JANUARY [undated]. Wednesday. Meeting at Belknap's tonight, and I shall not go. If I am strong enough to go anywhere, I shall go to the sale of Currier and Ives at Anderson's. But I doubt that I shall go out. Have a bit of food and a bit more whiskey so I probably shall soon be either well or dead. . . . Shall send a "Weird Tales" with magazines. It contains "Hypnos," a very fine short story by dear old H. P. Lovecraft. "Imprisoned with the Pharaohs" is also by him, but it is much too long and not very good. Do not try "The Latvian" because it is by Herman Fetzer (Jake Falstaff, you know), for it is very poor. But "Hypnos" is little short of being a masterpiece.[24]

---

22. Sir James George Frazer (1854–1941), British anthropologist and author of *The Golden Bough* (1890f.); Edmund Gosse (1849–1928), British critic and biographer.

23. *Peter Pan* (Paramount, 1924), directed by Herbert Brenon; starring Betty Bronson, Ernest Torrence, and Cyril Chadwick.

24. Kirk refers to *Weird Tales* for May–June–July 1924, containing HPL's "Hypnos," his ghostwritten tale (for Harry Houdini) "Imprisoned with the Pharaohs" (i.e., "Under the Pyramids"), and his ghostwritten tale (for C. M. Eddy, Jr.) "The Loved Dead."

JANUARY [undated]. Thursday. Are you interested in knowing why I have not made a success in the commercial world? I believe I know: I believe it is because I have thought too well of myself. Do you get me? No? Well, that I was unwilling to be like the others, to really get into the game, because I know that I must lose a part, at least, of my identity should I do so. Had it been a case of leaving life to make you happy, I really believe I should have done so, but to continue to live and to love you but to become other than I was anyway, although I had not then thought out the matter, was probably more than anything else what stood in my way. There was, too, a certain fear which I more clearly understood: you had loved the chaotic, curious, strange GD; would you love the commonplace, placid GD? HPL, RK, and I talk of a walking tour through part of New England in the summer. Only two persons are there in the world with whom I have spent any amount of time who have never bored me, L and HPL. The rest may go blah and blooey.

JANUARY [undated]. Sunday Afternoon. I must bathe and shave and care for my various digital nails and dress before RK comes, which I presume he will by four or half-past and I rather wish he weren't but having once asked him for every Sunday afternoon and not going out, I don't know how to break off the thing without hurting his feelings, and I certainly would not do that since, although I am not at all certain that you would like RK—who walks Broadway with rubbers and umbrella, although he might amuse you with such ways—while I am not extremely fond of him, I respect him for what he does and because he doesn't pretend to do more, but I do not like certain traits in him, into the details concerning which I shall not go, as if there is anything I amn't it's catty, at least that's what I try to tell the scroot down the way when he barks at me. (Should not take more time but shall be in bath when he comes and he can wait, huh?) Why do you think me 'so damned ungracious'? My! Of all the gracious persons I know I am the most.... Why couldn't I become commonplace? The only circumstances which could infallibly prevent it would be being already so. I think of myself as strange and chaotic.

JANUARY [undated]. Sunday, 11:00 p.m. I, too, am sorry I don't feel better. Several friends have been here and just left for W. Houston Street joint for chicken dinner and much fair booze. But I felt for neither. Can it be that I'm in love? ... I am really sorry about your mother.

Whenever any misfortune strikes me I can trace it to some foolishness of my own—but cannot, to be sure, so successfully do so for others. If there is anything I am, it's careful. Gossip has it that we have been secretly married, at least so it's come to me at third or fourth hand. . . . You don't deserve more, but I enjoy writing, and few things interfere with the enjoyment of the eminent gentleman and NY bookseller, GWK. Must soon be better and able to work or shall starve. Wouldn't that be exciting? Quite Chattertonesque.

JANUARY 9. Tuesday Morning. HPL, RK, ARTURO, they came upon me singly, and tomorrow will be here in a group. I wonder if this friendship stuff is so much after all. I do like to be alone. The difficulty is in dates. If it were a case of telephoning me and then coming out if I had naught handy to plead would be more or less okay, but, almost always when an engagement is made several days ahead, I dread it by the time it comes to pass.

JANUARY 12, Monday. I tell RK that one should not cross a bridge *even* when one comes to it: one might find himself in Brooklyn. . . . Writ by RK after reading GK's copy of Brantome:

> My little love, I would not have you shy,
> Nor coy, nor clod to arts that love will try!
> That little mouth of yours were wrong to miss—
> Since life and love are brief—a small bliss!
> I would not have you hide that tender breast
> Whose swelling white was made to be caressed!
> Nor be too careful of that middle zone
> Where greater joys abound than you have known:
> In short, be always kind and true to me:
> To others be as cold as cold can be!

JANUARY 14. Don't you *adore* the idea of being the wife, clerk, bookkeeper, cook, housekeeper, sweeperupper, and factotum of a bookseller? Or don't you? The thing of greatest import, no matter what I am to do otherwise, is that I get well immediately. If only my well-meaning friends would leave me in peace and quiet—my illnesses are usually as much mental as otherwise—I am certain I should be chipper within a short time. . . . You ought to come for the eclipse. Cleveland has only 97% while NY has 100%, and while that may seem to make little difference, it does mean much. 3% is ample light to prevent seeing the much-advertised corona of the sun: the stars and planets will appear; Bailey's Beads, the last rays of the sun through the canyons of the moon are visible, strange and curious color effects are seen, and it is said that to be on a hill in open country and see the rushing shadow thrown to Miss Moon is to marvel. Few people have seen one—that is, a total eclipse—and it is unlikely that any of us will be in the right corner of the world at the right time ever to see another. Line between part and full is four blocks from here, 110th St., Yonkers. I rode it on a bus. Do come here and we'll go up to Yonkers and take glasses along and walk up on an aqueduct, and my! Won't it be fun?

JANUARY 17. Why don't I be a columnist? Why don't you be a fashionable dressmaker? Sam is working in a bookstore. The Saltus is promised for early spring.

JANUARY [undated]. Tuesday, isn't it? We have had no snow to amount to anything—not even enough to cover the streets. But cold! Five above today, which is not enough. I shall have an all night party here tomorrow eve; stag of course. And I hope to be able to sleep through most of same. Would you were here for eclipse. I believe there isn't another in the U.S. for several hundred years.

[According to Lovecraft's letters, after he and Kirk helped decorate Loveman's rooms, they shopped for Kirk. After redecorating his room, Kirk entertained "the gang" to celebrate. This festive evening inspired a celebratory poem by Lovecraft, "To George Kirk, Esq., Upon His Entertaining a Company in His New-Decorated Chambers: 18th January, 1925" (see p. 184). Afterwards, Lovecraft, Long, Kleiner, Loveman, and Kirk adjourned to the Double R Coffee House on 44th St.—M. K. H.]

JANUARY 19. When I haven't been tied up with a mass of work I am entertaining—and altogether too much of the latter. Even though I have been able to sleep when in bed I have been unable to spend more than four or five hours a day or night therein. Shall have an all night party here tomorrow eve; stag, of course. And I hope to be able to sleep through most of same. We have had no snow to amount to anything—not even enough to cover the streets. But cold! Five above today, which is not enough.

JANUARY 20. Allow me to quote from my Bible:

> To burn always with this hard, gemlike flame, to maintain this ec-stasy, is success in life. While all melts under our feet, we may well grasp at any exquisite passion, or any contribution to knowledge that seems by a lifted horizon to set the spirit free for a moment, or any strange stirring of the senses, strange dyes, strange colours, and curious odours, or work of the artist's hands, or the face of one's friend. Not to discriminate every moment some passionate attitude in those about us, and in the very bril-liance, in their gifts some tragic divining of forces in their ways, is on this short day of frost and sun, to sleep before evening. . . . Great passions may give us this quickened sense of life ecstasy and sorrow of love, the various forms of enthusiastic activity, disinterested or otherwise, which come naturally to many of us. Only be sure it is passion—that it does yield you this fruit of a quickened, multiplied consciousness.

Let us love beauty wherever we see it, and make it a point to see it, shutting our eyes to what is sordid or ugly. Let us carry on the cult of Marius the Epicurean.[25]

[Wednesday January 25 Lovecraft, Morton, Leeds, Kirk, and Ernest A. Dench traveled to Yonkers to see the eclipse and then spent the night partying at Kirk's.]

JANUARY [undated]. Monday Morning. Things are very quiet. Half a dozen places ask me to come around in four or six weeks. Everyone tells me I am very foolish to give up my own business. Don't you want to come in with me? If you do not, I may ask Sam to. I dunno. . . . You would have been amused to see me fifteen minutes ago buying house-hold utensils. Shall have to have some friends in to try them out soon as I buy commodities such as coffee, tea, etc. It will be very meager as I shall have no ice. . . . Who are we who went to Coney Island? All the gang. Shall tell you more of traveling proposition later. 'Tis an unusually good chance for a beginner, a good line of exclusive job jots (remain-ders), good art books, and a line of ten cent crap which should sell, in fact, I know that it does.

JANUARY 27. Here I am at 169 [Clinton], Brooklyn, more or less laid up, and tired of trying to continue my existence. From now on the af-fair will be wholly in the hands of others; I don't care. Would that I

---

25. *Marius the Epicurean* (1885), a novel by Walter Pater (1839–1894).

were religious, such nonsense can really help one at times—but I fear that in me reason is stronger than poetry.

JANUARY [undated]. Think I can get in with Harry F. Marks, 187 Broadway, if I care to, but would rather be with a more reputable dealer. He disclaims the honor, but he has the reputation of being the largest dealer in the country in erotica. He is not too honest but he handles an interesting line of firsts and has the best copy of *Pickwick Papers* in the country. The death of Joseph Conrad makes me sad. Marks wants me to take out fine books to call on stockbrokers, etc. Scribner's tells me to come in in about a month, as do Thomas & Eron and not a few others. Must look for a garret or storeroom in Brooklyn or Harlem or anyplace which I can get cheaply enough to keep books, etc. All of the shipment has not yet arrived.

JANUARY [undated]. Tuesday Morning. Mrs. Healman, landlady, today informed me that I might have another man in the room without additional cost. Imagine Brooklyn will prove at least to be Oi! Old Harry Marks wants me to work for him. Phoned me this morning. Said I'd be in to see him. He's a little beast and I like him not.

JANUARY [undated]. Friday. If I vote I most assuredly would vote straight independent—Rheinhart has been here and left. R would be okay if he were not such an ass and didn't talk women so damned much. Apologized for not taking me to house tonight—said he was hard up. I assured him he need not trouble himself. Says he will find me a female. Told me his life history. I'm to go to his place Monday night. Would that I might be soused. Walked along Ann Street where a pretty kitten meowed hungrily. Wished there was meat store there that I might get it some liver. Was not.

JANUARY [undated]. Not like the 4th Ave. shops? Girl, what would you have? What we call a whorehouse bookshop? Atmosphere can be caused in plenty most anywhere, unless in stores such as Brentano's, Scribner's, etc., which are too large, with the right books and the right personality. And if I opened, which I shan't now, I'd plan a shop to dispense books and dispense with atmosphere.

JANUARY [undated]. Had a pretty time with a Fourth Avenue bookseller the other day. I much dislike him. He is about forty-five and has a young and attractive wife. I paid her marked attentions and hoped he would try to throw me out of store—he didn't, but was much peeved and will from now on dislike me as heartily as I do him. . . . 'Tis easier to take time from work than from pleasure.

JANUARY [undated]. 'Course I shall be glad to critique your work. And can, if you want me to, show it to HPL, who rewrites books, etc. and shall set to work all the staff of the extinct "Elite Type and Revising Bureau" for you.

JANUARY [undated].

> "This is the rule of the traffic squad:
> East is even, otherwise odd."

Which explains *so* much better in pure poetry what I could *never hope* to express in my prosiest prose and was it not a good saying, "Meredith is a prose Browning, and so is Browning"?[26]

JANUARY [undated]. I am *not* like the dear old dame who was recently characterized: "She enjoys ill health." But I do think I have a right to be discouraged without being reproved by even you. . . . How long in Washington? HPL and I want to go there again, also to Baltimore.

JANUARY [undated]. Met a girl as claims to have known MS, that is, my late, lamented father. It makes *lots* of difference to me. Iante. J'ever hear of him? Of him does McLean write a book at present. He was one of the Frenchmen exploring U.S., I believe with LaSalle.

FEBRUARY 2. Was up all last night and intend staying up tonight even though I sleep for a week afterwards. But that's naught to brag about. There are so many fools in NYC that being one is not in the least distinctive. I am rather tired even though 'tis but eight o'clock in the evening. Wonder how I shall feel twelve hours from now? . . .

I fear I have too hearty a hatred of business to ever be much of a success at it. . . . Wouldn't it be pleasant if all were only as intelligent as you and I? . . . I have noted several rather attractive she's in the house. RK's in love with five of them, by his own count. Am in a large house on the late 'Fifth Avenue of Brooklyn,' which was until quite recently owned and used by a famous actress (so I am told, although I cannot

---

26. The quotation derives from Oscar Wilde's *The Critic as Artist* (1891).

discover her name) and the section is really quite pleasant—though not of NY—being quiet, clean, and with a distinctive atmosphere. If you have your NYC guidebook, read what it says of Brooklyn Heights. The Spanish, Syrian, and Arabian slums approach it, but are still a comfortable distance away, and of course they in themselves are colorful and interesting to such a one as I.

FEBRUARY 3. Shall have some company soon and must clean up the room and myself. Damn you, anyway. Would that I cared no more for you than I do for the remainder of your sex. Then I might heartily damn you and wholly forget you. But! . . . Later. Hot, tired, and sleepy. Had a pleasant evening with crowd. Might, but shall not, tell you about it. Am to call another friend tomorrow who is going Saturday to Atlantic City for three weeks. Have a great many things to tell you, but cannot spend all of time writing to you. Want to get books started.

FEBRUARY [undated]. Don't read any Maupassant other than the Ernest Boyd translation. It's all there is. Any other is junk.

I enclose a poem writ by two friends while with me at Tontini Coffee-house last evening:

> Greatest of bookmen, since the world began,
> Evolve for me some yet untested plan
> Of purchasing your wares sans self, sans price,
> Regardless of the fall of fortune's dice!
> Give first editions, many a famous dame,
> Entrance into my pantheon of fame
> Kindred that perished long since unknown
> Indecently interred beneath a stone.
> Reptile you may be but within your heart
> Kinglier friend and comrade ne'er bore part.

"Reptile" was because of my 'reptilian laughter' a bit earlier.

FEBRUARY 5, Thursday. Just a week before Friday the Thirteenth, however, since neither of us are of the 140,000 chosen to exist after tonight—or have we a chance of a day or two? I understand 'tis to take at least three days to demolish the earth—we need not fear that, at least. . . . That drawing of Bill Sommer's is the most beautiful object in the room. The painting of his which is near the door comes next. Then the exotic, unhealthy, greenish-yellow vase on the mantle. Those dark purple glass candlesticks, tall and plain, with high dipped orange candles are a not unimportant bit of decoration. I would have you with naught on but a flowered dressing gown only partly covering your nakedness, reading on the couch—rather in a half-recumbent position—like a drawing by Degas. . . . These rich Arabian pastries will be the death of your GD. I just *can't* use any so-called common sense. That's what comes of drinking so much coffee, but I was up all night talking and reading and had to drink it. Those two delicate silver vases over the door are not terribly terrible. Two of my friends dislike the steins, but I like them, and it's my room. Must replace—someday—those green vases at this end of the plate rail—they don't belong. Haven't yet decided about the Ricketts-Hardy thing. It is a huge lithograph and is the only piece between the two doors on the east wall and over the couch—which is what I call a synthetic bed. It tends to dominate the room and it doesn't wear any too well. Charles Ricketts did it for the first presentation of Hardy's "The Dynast" and it is a proof copy, signed by both. Need a different clock on the mantle. Want an old mahogany or walnut with a gable roof and a picture in the lower panel of glass. Isn't it a shame that the use of walnut coincided with the most terrible of Victorian taste? . . . Because all of the last names of the permanent members of our club begin with K, L or M, we plan to call it the Kalem Klybb. Half a dozen friends are to be here tonight. Mostly they're bores. All but me; and that I am much of a friend to GD is doubtful. Why is it?? Who is your favorite Poet? Novelist? Essayist? Biographer? Man? Girl Friend?

FEBRUARY 6. Dear Mrs. Kirk: "Though I have relinquished a portion of the large stock I had in Cleveland, my intention is to lose no degree of contact with my former patrons." This is the first of these gdfls for today, and I am scarcely awake yet. I have not even done, as yet, my daily dozen cigarettes. But my cigar helps bring me to (what?). Dear Jim Morton will be curator of the new museum at Paterson, NJ, about one hour's ride from town. Write me in what manner I can serve (sic!) you. I am at your command in any bibliopolic or literary capacity. How am I? Why am I? Ought I to be? . . . I regret to have to inform you that Mr. Kirk died December 23 1924.

FEBRUARY 11. How I am is a moot question. You see, Lucy, it's like this. Sometimes it's peppy and sometimes it isn't. Sometimes I am unable to sleep. At others I cannot walk. At still other times I am unable to lie down. And I am never capable of sitting. And usually I can't stay awake. I never can eat. Although frequently I eat too much and am ill thereof. If it were not for such matters, I should be quite well, I do assure you. . . . If you are in Cleveland, and I hope you are, you need not bother about the old 'Erster Stew' poem. HPL is getting a copy he sent his aunt. Am in a twenty-five-room rooming house and I like it well. Am not staying with RK, although he comes here, at times, reversing that—he came over last Saturday evening, stayed overnight, Sunday, and until two o'clock Monday morning. I was not sorry to see him go. Sam is on the Heights and expects to move this week, though he is not certain where. . . . I don't blame you in the slightest for wanting me to have my teeth repaired, and I shall as soon as I find it possible, though I cannot just at present. I should write more but that old friends are coming in for a bit of a bite and a wee nippie and I must make preparation. Am tired of this social whoil and am really trying to halt it, or at least slow it up a bit. I hate women who have any sexual appeal. Don't you?

FEBRUARY 17. If you had been longer in NYC you'd know that there are many boys and many girls both male and female. My dear Double R is claimed to be a hangout for these half and halfers. Why don't I be a columnist? Why don't you be a fashionable dressmaker? Sam is working in a bookstore. The Saltus is promised for early spring. I enclose a poem by Kleiner ["The Four of Us (Rondeau)"; see p. 128].

Am about to take a step in business that I have planned for about a year. It may make me and it certainly is sufficiently expensive to break me, but I believe it's worth the trying. I don't, at any rate, care to continue playing along as I have been. Wish me luck, kid. . . . Have had little opportunity to write of late, but have thought of you and us considerably, and decided that on several points I have been deceiving you when I really had not intended to do so. While I began by spoofing you along a bit, I carried it too far until, as it now seems to me, it became absolute deceit. Shall rectify the same anon.

FEBRUARY 19, 4:20 a.m. Last evening I entertained the Kalems on to two this morning.

FEBRUARY 25. Do you know what it is to be tired? If I told you the length of time I've worked fairly steadily, with never more than five hours' sleep out of twenty-four and not infrequently zero hours of sleep. If I dress one day and must be dressed the next I never bother to take off clothing—*ain't* that *terrible!*

FEBRUARY 26. I have started reading Addison and Steele. Dju ever? Had a poetry reading fest last night—HPL, SL, and RK and Belknap were over. We read from Shelley, Keats, Wordsworth, A. Meynell, J. Davidson, E. Goss, Griffith, Hardy, Yeats, Masefield, Shakespeare's sonnets, F. G. Halleck, Landor, David Gray, T. L. Beddoes, and, naturally, Swinburne, and kept at it until 3:30 this morning. GD has been up since and is oh! so tired! Why don't you oftener tell me what you read? I'm very interested. For all you tell me I might suppose you read nothing but the daily sheets. . . . If you can catch up with the ancients you can let the moderns go hang. . . . What's the longest I ever was in love with the same person? Five years. Whom? GD.

MARCH 11.

> Pious Selinda goes to prayers
>   If I but ask her a favor;
> And yet the silly fool's in tears
>   If she believes I'll leave her;
> Would I were free from this restraint,
>   Or else had hopes to win her:
> Would she could make of me a saint,
>   Or I of her a sinner.—William Congreve

Hate the rush business keeps one in. I frequently meet persons who claim they would not care to live if they could not work. Why can't such do all of it to let such as you and I take our leisure: love, read, and enjoy life as we see fit—and I was once a Socialist—Heigh ho! Well a-way!! 'Tis good to be home and alone again. Talked of everything under the sun as well as several things not under the sun. Friend even desired to talk of you, but I was not interested. The two most exciting discussions were on very dissimilar subjects: which is the greater art, music or literature? Is rubber contained in chewing gum? I chose literature for the former question, and affirmative on latter. Have been sitting around over an hour scribbling and playing Chopin.

MARCH 14. Oriental pastry is delicious! A strange somewhat porous little pancake, soaked in syrup, and filled with ground walnuts. A crisp very thin cookie covered with unknown nuts. I use up my spare time

wondering why no one has popularized them and made a fortune from
them. There are about ten varieties, but I care only for three or
four. . . . Read *The Cloister and the Hearth* most of the night.[27] Strangely
enough I never before had looked into it. Wednesday I was up the
whole night. Thursday I slept about ten hours. This morning reading, I
looked at the clock and saw that it claimed that four and one-half hours
were shot out of the day by Mr. Reade, so I says, says I, what the hell's
the use o'goin' to bed now anymore, and I suits the action to the woids
and stayed where I was, which was in the big easy chair though it ain't
so very without pillows and why does one speak of sleeping Thursday
night when one never goes to bed until the next morning; it's such a
funny ol' woild, huh kid? NYC is no place for theaters; it is too much a
one itself. How can one go to a show and expect to see anything as
thrilling as Broadway with its thousands of free comedies and tragedies
and in a glorious setting that is seldom the same?

MARCH 16. Was up all last night, am beginning to get tired, and have a
good evening's work ahead of me. . . . What have you of Yeats? Rose
Macaulay? Why doncha read something decent, or indecent? Life is too
short to waste it on trash. Finished *The Cloister and the Hearth.* Had a
witty gang here last eve and should send you some of the gags if I recollected them and had time to write them and thought they'd bear writing. Yes, I dote on mushrooms. Do you like oriental pastry? . . .
Haven't been out of the house for a week and think it would be rather
pleasant to die here.

LATER. HPL tells me that the current *Subway Sun* (#10) merely
copies an editorial from the *Brooklyn Citizen* re Hylan and 5¢ fare. I am
not certain that various ones I recall to mind are *Sun*'s or the BMT
placards.

MARCH 29, TELEGRAM. Sunday night I shall start a long deferred
trip to Providence, Boston, Albany, and various other towns. Shall be
away about a week.

MARCH 30. Sunday. On Steamer "Lexington" to New England. I am
going to Providence, Boston, Marblehead, Salem, Albany, and where
else I know not. Started from Christopher St. at 5:30 p.m. (scheduled
for 5:00), have rounded Manhattan's point, and am going up the East

27. *The Cloister and the Hearth* (1861), a novel by Charles Reade (1814–1884).

River—past Bedloe's and Ward's—and just where we are now I know not, but shall soon see. Girl! If I ever give you such a thrill as I got from seeing the dear Shelton from the bow of this worthy Lexington I shall not have lived in vain. Good old Brooklyn Bridge from the south is well worth seeing. I've taken no berth and shall spend most of the night at one of these tables writing letters to you and to some of the boys who seem to like me (strange) and of whom I am fond (naturally, for they're the finest chaps in the world.) Have been testing my strength by trips to Staten Island, Elizabeth, Queensborough, Jamaica, and such like places in the vicinity of NYC. Really marvelous. Would you believe that in NYC you can walk for half a mile or more without seeing a house or a human being? No, I don't mean through a tube, but in the open air. . . . Look forward to seeing Marblehead and Salem. Also Providence, the birthplace and hometown of my good friend, HPL. Also Boston, and strangely enough, Albany, through which I've passed I know not how many times but have never been off the train.

UNDATED. Hotel Garde, opposite Union Station, New Haven, CT. Want to go to Philly and to Harrisburg but I *must* learn more about Americana.

UNDATED. Thursday a.m. New Haven. Just before going down for shower. Wonderful, rolling country, some of the loveliest in the U.S., dear colonial houses and, usually, pleasant and English-speaking people.

LATER. Had little fun on the bloomin' trip. The best was the bus from Springfield to Hartford, some of the most beautiful scenes and houses in America; quiet, you know, but the sort that touches the heart without causing it to stand still, the sort of which one can never tire. Came back sooner than I expected because New Haven had nothing for me in the way of business, and I decided the intervening points were too close to NYC to be important. The Harkness Tower in New Haven is the most beautiful building I saw.

APRIL [undated]. I have struggled, so far in vain, to get out of the Kalem and the Sunday gatherings because of the time they take from letters and work (though I've worked through most of the recent and of course have been (until recently) unable to attend the KK when it meets anywhere other than at 169. Tomorrow I'm to hear Rachman-inoff. Oh to be with Lucy, now that April's here.

APRIL 4. Next Sunday I go to Washington with the gang on a pleasure trip, but while they return I shall stay over and *do* Washington, Baltimore, Philadelphia, and Harrisburg.

APRIL [undated], Wednesday. Must make two stores and the bank before going to the meeting, where I'm supposed to be at 8:30 and it's now 6:45. Oh well, no one expects GD to be on time anywhere anyway. Did I tell you that Sunday I go to Washington and shall be nearly a week returning? There will be some high jinks in DC next Sunday, which is given over to pleasure. . . . Haven't been any too well, either, and only hope I am not again confined. Sympathy, kid, I crave Sympathy. Got the Bierce letters[28] from Frisco today, but must forward them immediately though I should like to read them. At a glance, they seem very interesting, and I've little doubt they're all of that. I've so much to tell you of Boston and New Haven and Springfield and Hartford and I dare say you are glad that I probably shall forget it ere even I can write it to you and after all, it will save much time and how's that?

APRIL 7. Working very hard. Have OH so much to do ere Sunday when three others and myself go to Washington whence they return S eve, while I shall spend two or three more days making my way back.

APRIL 12, Sunday. Tonight begins the grand migration, only Howard and I make up the whole and we don't start until tomorrow morning, 12:03, and I would we were there, and if I can get a table I may write to you, but then again, I may not. Howard and I, under such circumstances, always talk metaphysics and the beginnings and end of the universe and I should be calling on James F. Drake and I didn't rise till 10:00 but I shan't sleep much tonight and we both converse as little as possible upon human life for we both at least affect to hate it. Started to pack, and I find my two pieces of luggage insufficient for the books I must carry so shall forget the appointment in Manhattan and try to discover to whom I loaned my suitcase while still at 50. I'm glad to get out of here for a while. The social amenities of Brooklyn bore me to distraction and only when I'm out of town can I count on an evening to myself.

[According to a Lovecraft letter, the evening of their departure "the gang" met in Greenwich Village for dinner. After packing and dressing,

28. Apparently *The Letters of Ambrose Bierce*, ed. Bertha Clark Pope (1922).

Lovecraft and Kirk went out with Loveman and Kleiner for coffee before their 12:03 train from Pennsylvania Station.—M. K. H.]

APRIL 13. Washington. Ain't got no desk or table or bowth or nuthin'. Most hotels filled up and had to take the only room in the only hotel I could get. Next to Los Angeles and Canton, at least one time, and certain towns in the West, this is the naughtiest town in the US and this *must* be one on the naughtiest hotels. But my door is double-locked and so I guess the boy will be introducing no more nine-tenths naked females to tempt my virgin purity. I have given up the day to pleasure, but didn't sleep last night. I *hate* this sort of thing and—more and more as I grow older—want to settle down in some quiet little place like NYC and marry L and live more or less happily ever after. I spent the day in a Buick—public grounds, Mt. Vernon, Alexandria, Arlington, etc. Had a very good time, and I should like to tell you all about it, but I must hit the hay very soon. Should like to finish Washington tomorrow, but rather doubt that I can. Had a wonderful chicken dinner and I have just finished a good cigar. Never have anything to do with a man who smokes only cigarettes or only bum cigars. Never have anything to do with any man but GD. Breakfast in a nice, home-cooking place that I intend patronizing hereafter and while here. Much to do and another coffee to drink and I could become very tired of ever seeing the capitol dome.

APRIL [undated]. Washington's a little place, good enough to die in, but less pleasant for that recreation than Berkeley. After duly admiring a dimple on my knee I am almost ready to leave for Baltimore, and 'tis 8:30.

APRIL [undated]. Baltimore. This pen and paper (bad) are truly Baltimorean. Only they rather balk at saying so. I shall write more later, but guess I'll have some Baltimore chicken, the proper variety.

APRIL [undated]. Baltimore. Baltimore's not so bad. Had a pleasant hour with Janvier[29] and though I did no business with him we promise to be of mutual assistance. Either tonight or about noon tomorrow shall go to Wilmington, then Philly. If you want to send me any special word, send it to the Centaur Book Shop, Philly.

---

29. Meredith Janvier, a well-known bookseller in Baltimore.

APRIL [undated]. Am at "The China" and have ordered chicken chow mein. Went into another restaurant but it had hard top tables and I felt for jazz and comfort. This is the only paper present on which I can write, and I feel like writing, only here's a meal, and I haven't had time to eat since breakfast. . . . Report: Usual total absence of chicken at least in the chow mein, though there are several in room. Coffee unusually good. Don't care for the Southern habit of hot biscuits. Wish I had eaten again in sweet little hole in Washington. Fine bath, though I was to be disappointed till I found that the cold water was the hot. Baltimore talks horses, women, and such stunts as second-hand jewelry (buying it of those who go broke at the races) and the like. A curious admixture of N & S.

APRIL [undated]. Am in Room 301, The Rittenhouse, and am in love with the room. Shall cruelly tear myself away in the morning, stop off only at Trenton, and reach the Penna Station sometime in the p.m. Felt, this evening, bored with Penna, so I took a car and a ferry over to Camden, NJ, an ugly place. Shall be glad to get out of here. I wasn't cut out to be a traveling salesman. "George" denotes "homesteader." But I *do* like this hotel.

APRIL 21. Poor HL. Still, nothing west of C is worse: only Pittsburgh and C. Did I tell you how happy I was to be back, see the buildings and nicely painted females and my friends? At about five in the afternoon at Trenton I wired a friend I'd be at a certain restaurant at seven and would he be there with the gang. I walked into the place and found two of those I expected but not the one I'd wired. He had been out doing the town with a chap from England and had not received the wire, nor, naturally, notified the boys, who were there by chance. The other came later, and we had a glorious time, what with two lovely kittens and the quite as pleasant muscatel. Tonight I go to the wonderful George Barr McCutcheon Sale of modern firsts at the American Art Galleries. To think that I actually considered buying a store in Brooklyn—and still may buy it.

APRIL 25. This is a replica of the Sunday in Washington—the first such we've had here. The sort of day when one must be eighty years old and feel twice his age or be madly in love. Last night meeting at Belknap's. 'Twas more interesting than some. Home about 2:30 and did work until 10:00 a.m. Saw, last night, good old Jim, and he is now getting settled at Paterson. He wants me to open a shop there, says he could throw considerable business my way. I shall go out to investigate. Am taking a very important step, which is not taking a store, but which will, instead, prohibit my doing so, for it will take all my cash and gets underway tomorrow. It may go big and it may go slightly, and it may not go at all. It will take time to get it well under way but—oh hell! Why am I so damnably serious and earnest? Imagine! Tried Dunhills again. I couldn't finish even one. Shall keep to 'erbs, pipes, and cigars.

APRIL [undated]. What do I do when I sit up all night? I sit up all night—talking, reading, or working. No, I don't sleep until the following night—usually about twelve or fourteen hours. Did I find RK interesting? How could I? HPL I'm very fond of, and spend more time with him than with any other. See next to naught of Sonia.

APRIL [undated]. Saturday, 7:00 a.m. HPL visited me and read while I toiled over cards. He is now sleeping over on the lounge with *The Ghost Girl*[30] open before him—no compliments to Saltus. When I've finished scribbling shall get ready and go out for the day, mostly in town. Am invited to a Blue Pencil Club meeting tonight, but shall not go; am frequently enough bored without going out of my way for it. HP awoke—uttered "Avernus!" and went back to Nirvana. . . . About midnight we went to Tiffany's restaurant where I had a beautiful shrimp salad and coffee, while H had a slice of cheesecake and two coffees. We sat around for one and a half hours over the meal and the morning papers, looked for somewhat to clip, but naught amusing to be found.

APRIL [undated]. I read *The Forsyte Saga*.[31] Not much of literature, but a good picture of life. Slow. What's the longest I ever was in love with a girl? Lemesee. One Jeanette, I believe, from four to fifteen (my ages.) What if you did accept and came here to live and gosh! Wouldn't that mess things up? Look at the bird downstairs: can't go out when he wants to and must go out when he doesn't and can't have in his friends but on occasion and can come up here only when she chooses and has with him ever a fat old female who should have passed on years ago.

---

30. *The Ghost Girl* (1922), a novel by Edgar Saltus.

31. *The Forsyte Saga* (1922), a series of novels and tales by John Galsworthy (1867–1933), comprising *The Man of Property* (1906), *In Chancery* (1920), "Indian Summer of a Forsyte" (1918), *Awakening* (1920), and *To Let* (1921).

APRIL 29. Have taken another room, at 52 Orange Street, Brooklyn, and must move as soon as possible. . . . 'Tis now 7:30 and the gang comes here this evening and I've neither cleaned the room nor prepared the refreshments; you can see that I have little time for another trip to Manhattan. Nevertheless, I shall make it to 59th Street, even though I miss the early part of the meeting. LATER. Have no time to tell the whys and wherefores of the move—they are quite sufficient. New York is a wonderful place and strange things are done here. Probably I shall sell the Hardy thing; I never liked it, and shouldn't have room for it at 52. Perhaps the Poe too, which I don't like, and a book or two. LATER. Worked all day Sunday and gave up yesterday to pleasure. Further details regarding which I shall give you later. Auction this evening and a guest after that.

MAY 2. So busy! Sunday Ed Lazare came in from Bayside—rather, he came in Saturday eve and stayed with me overnight, and Martin Kamin is here from Cleveland. Martin wishes to open a bookshop and I promised to go in with him—not in investment of money, but with time, energy, and knowledge. P.S. I am not moving at present.

LATER. Why do you say it's gd hot? It's gd cold and friend HPL is sleeping before my electric heater while I write. 'Tis now 5:30 a.m. Goil, I suppose I'll bore you terribly. There's only one person with whom I spend any time here who never bores me and he's with me now. H and I have more in common than any other two I've known of: and he doesn't smoke, is on a diet, doesn't care for the majority of the books I love, has no belief in an absolute in beauty: still we get along wonderfully. As for you and me, I've no doubt the only time we won't bore each other is when we're fighting. Lucy mine, I have much respect for reason. I hate jealousy. Reason is all that keeps us from being beasts—when it does. Beasts are all right when they're cats, but when they're humans—ugh! In my spare time I'm planning a trip to Albany and various points in NY State, perhaps again going over to Springfield. Am anxious to get to Harrisburg PA, but guess I'd better let that go till I come West.

LATER. Some day I shall take Jim's advice, if I've a thousand or so at the time, and open a shop in Paterson or some such place and rest and probably make more money than I do at present.

MAY [undated]. I shall be extra busy from tomorrow on. We open June first, no matter what happens: of course we want to be in the best possible position as to fixtures, stock, etc. Martin comes in the morning.

MAY 16. Only a few days ago one Miss Allison—remember Allisoun? Chaucer?—offered to teach me to dance. Ought I? In her "back rooms?" Told her I hadn't time because of the store. You are *not* to go to dances! Tell me whether or not you shall continue. Please. Otherwise. Martin was here to sign the lease and returned to Cleveland for several weeks. I'm furnishing the store with fixtures and a half-dozen thousand volumes for stock. Sorta keeps me sorta busy.

MAY 30. Worked from eight this morning until ten tonight and am, to put it mildly, gd tired. Nevertheless, I think of my S[weet] L[ove] nearly continually, and am crabbed and sharp with my friends if they try to make me talk. Never knew before what it was to be busy. Store plans come on. Yours in anguish, GD. LATER. Dear Miss Dvorak: Please send me your special portfolio of spring wood stove advertising. Have so much to do that I'm now afraid to go to bed. Am going out for coffee and perhaps a sandwich or fruit salad and shall try to work all night. LATER. Worked all day Sunday until 4:00 Monday morning preparing the shop for the opening Monday and haven't had more than four hours' sleep any night since. Shall be busy tomorrow and the first of the week since advertising begins Sunday and will take up all my time. I am going to The Russian Bear again tonight and perhaps to the beer garden afterwards.

JUNE 10. Martin's Book Store, 97 Fourth Avenue. 'Tis nine and several books have been sold off the stands and I got an order for a three or four dollar book from a poor Russian whose twelve year old son "goes to the toilet and holds his—you know—his man, and there must be some book in English which will keep him from it—there is in Russian." Ignorant fools. Here's hoping his son becomes a whoremonger, if you'll excuse your GD's saying so. . . . Love, I know I have done various things in a business way that were not wholly straight. Ere very long I intend to do another. But my friends find me honest in the slightest detail. You know that the form of marriage is little or nothing as far as I'm concerned. Believe, if you can, for it's as true as that Bryan[32] is either an

32. William Jennings Bryan (1860–1925), American political and religious

ass or insincere or both, that as long as I love you I shall be as true to
you as you could wish. I love you, and am working hard to make this
store a success, for as soon as it is assured I shall come to C, overcome
any possible qualms, marry you, and bring you to NY. A sweet young
thing just brought in a Kipling marked 80c which she found on the 5c
table. It was laid there by mistake last night when Martin and I worked
over some fiction. I could have refused to sell it for 5c, but she was so
petite that I could not refuse. Forgive me if I don't write often: I am
putting in from ten to fourteen hours a day, either in the shop or out
buying for it or attending to some of the many details connected with it
and the thing MUST succeed. Telephone: Stuyvesant 1605.

JUNE 12. Business is fair for the weather and considering the general
depression in the book trade. Am told it is the worst in eight years—
but I have a faint recollection of having been told that before, that is,
last year and the year before and the year before that. Am now in
smoking waiting-room. Good old pipeful of Blue Boar tastes good this
morning. Am becoming very Babbitty, if you get what I mean. Rather
like the island. That such a meandering small town, undeveloped section, should be part of NYC is still a marvel to me. It is well to have
something to marvel at. Last night on subway I marveled at the richness and beauty of Milton's prose. J'ever read any?

JUNE 16. You see I can write and do nothing else. Must bring in
stands and leave for old Brooklyn soon. Just recollected that I hadn't
certain addresses I need and spent three-fourths of an hour looking for
them. Martin is a wonder at putting things away. Must pull in stands
now and go. More, sometime. A lazy Monday morning. Much to do but
all outside, and Martin is out about an apartment. May move this week,
though I sure dread the task. It's a sad, sad world, old dear.

JUNE 21. Didn't leave 169 as yet because had no time to move. May
this week have a free day for the task. Tomorrow and Tuesday are tied
up, but don't know what will be better later on. Sara, Martin's wife, is
here for good.

---

figure. The Scopes evolution trial, in which Bryan represented the prosecu-
tion, would begin in early July.

JUNE 22. 617 W. 115th St. The store takes so much time I have been unable to get away for a much-needed haircut and manicure. Saltus's *Jurgen*[33] put me to sleep Friday night at a new apartment at 617 W. 115th St. 'Tis very nice, in Columbia College district, between Broadway and Riverside Drive. It's midnight and very soon I shall leave you and sleep, and I hope, dream of you. I could sleepily argue on and on. M[artin] and I and Howard L and I have talked from eleven to three; ten to noon. But let's have a rest, huh kid? . . . How much do I love you? Oh, after my books and my booze and my tobacco, and me, I love you. Enough? Why pick on good-natured, muddle-headed, weak little me? Do you ask what is "Babbity" or what is "Babbittry"? Babbittry is that which is like Sinclair's Babbitt:[34] Cleveland and Rotarians and such are Babbitty.

I somewhat doubt that Martin's Book Shop would come to use your kindly proffered services. Thank you heartily, however. The work turned out by our present advertising manager who is, I have good reason to believe, well known to you, has been eminently satisfactory, and we see no reason for any radical change.

JUNE 24. Just a word before I close the shop and go to Kalem at the new apartment with Martin and Sara, to which I move [officially] tomorrow. Ma Burns[35] hadn't cleaned my room for a month, but did so yesterday. She'll think I am leaving because I don't like it clean. Such ain't the truth.

LATE JUNE. Thursday. Go to Stadium tonight to hear the Philharmonic Orchestra with little Miss Warren. I know her well and like her, but you need not be jealous; I have known her for years and have never had the slightest desire to make love to her. I think you will like her too, if she remains here, but she thinks of returning to her parents in the South, who are tremendously wealthy: cotton. I am about two blocks from Broadway and three or four from Riverside Drive and, of course, the Hudson. Must get a coffee pot and coffee cups and teapot and tea and what else? It's a long time since I have kept house. 'Twill be fun to

---

33. Kirk's error for *Jurgen* (1919), a controversial novel by James Branch Cabell (1879–1958). It was the subject of a celebrated trial in 1920–22, when the New York Society for the Suppression of Vice attempted in vain to ban it for obscenity.

34. Sinclair Lewis (1885–1951), *Babbitt* (1922).

35. Mrs. Burns, the landlady at 169 Clinton Street.

unpack books. I always get a kick out of unpacking boxes or trunks of books and the like which have been out sight for a long time. These were left here the last time, and I know there are some junky art books, some Saltus stuff, some nice naughty books, but just what else I don't know.

JUNE 30. Certain things about Martin's Book Shop irk me. Firstly, I have not a definite interest in the shop, although I am, when the shop is going, to be able to draw one third of the profits. Then, M is not exactly as I would have him, and Sara, though I like her well, continually annoys me by questioning this and that. I don't feel like enumerating my troubles further. I have worked hard to make this place go, and it will! If I stay with it. But I shall never be fully satisfied until I have a place of my own. I plan that it will be in your name, since I have various suits and judgments and debts that I should prefer to pay at my leisure and not when the court decides to take over the store. I rave. Martin has really done very well; the shop is going to be a success—not only to the degree to which he plans it to be—but as I plan it, which will make it a rather decent business. There is much work to do. I do it for your sake. Were it not for you I should, oh well, you can imagine how I would be living. Not working twelve hours a day, at any rate. LATER. One must live in Brooklyn at least six months to be an acquaintance of RK, as long as one can get that "Yes" with quite the correct inflection. Went last night to a Blue Pencil meeting. Dull! Ye Gods! I have no patience for such gatherings. Kalem, frequently, is plenty bad enough. I dislike being bored.

JULY [undated]. Without that incentive to toil (LDK), I doubtlessly would be less or not at all ambitious, for I am not so by nature, but am rather an elderly gentleman of the old school, or perhaps even more than that, I would make a better gentleman farmer than anything else.

JULY 3. Meet tonight at RK's. He went with me last night when I went after a library (that I didn't get) and we walked for hours discussing, as ever, architectural styles, and the history of our times as it will be written five thousand years from now, and education and such. . . . Got to bed about four this morn and to work only about an hour ago. Not a very wild affair—and stag. Have just a tinge of a headache. I have not eaten today, not, at least, since I got out of bed, and shall go out for a bite when Martin and Sally return. One pleasant part in staying out at night and in bed in the morning is that I see nothing of the Kamins but at the store. I like them, but Martin with his continual compromising wears on me. Shall have a talk with Martin tomorrow or Sunday and, if I do not gain certain points, I shall make him a gift of what I have put into the store, that is, I put all except my most personal books into stock, and those still there I shall remove, but as for the money for those sold, and as for my services thus far, at about two dollars a day, he is welcome.

JULY 5. Spent most of the Fourth in a solo walk. Went up Riverside Drive. It started to rain and I went to Broadway at about 160th St.. Went into cinema and saw Menjou and B. Bronson in "Are Parents People?"[36] 'Twas fair. Walked on Broadway to about 204, then crosstown to old Fordham where Poe once lived. Took 3rd. Ave L to 116th thence across to here.... Do you, by chance, mean "Rheinhart" by "Reinald?" He spent most of last week—the first of his vacation—at the store. Next week he tramps the wilds of NJ and Penna with Jim Morton, the museum curator. Is it possible that my writing in this pose is even worse than possible? Read anything by A. Symons, J. A. Symonds, Hardy, Dowson, read all of Poe—if you haven't—the early James—if you can—too sleepy to think of others now. HPL's wife is in town and I see but little of him.

JULY 9. Went to meeting last night and had a fine time, partly, perhaps, because I had a few glasses of sherry at my new joint, only two blocks from here. Tonight I go with a friend to see *The Dove* with Holbrook Blinn.[37]

JULY 11. Shall be in Cleveland on Sunday, the second of August. That M's and my little semi-partnership will flop is apparent, but I care not.

JULY [undated]. Am somewhat shamefaced today. Not that I did anything very terrible, but quite foolish. Went to John's with a crowd and spent a little over twenty plunks—my only splurge in months—and became too drunk for my own pleasure on the delicious German port wine. Now, at noon, I am OK. Martin is making overtures toward my

---

36. *Are Parents People?* (Paramount, 1925), directed by Malcolm St. Clair; starring Betty Bronson, Florence Vidor, and Adolph Menjou.
37. *The Dove* (1925), a three-act play by Willard Mack, based on a story by Gerard Beaumont; starring Sidney Toler, Josephine Deffrey, and Holbrook Blinn. At the Empire Theatre.

staying, but I see that it would be only temporary. I can make no money here for several months and just now I cannot draw sufficient for expenses: the earlier I can break away the better.

JULY 20. Am ill and disgusted with NY. Will leave tonight and be in Cleveland Thursday.

JULY 28. A good time at Howard and Clara's.[38] Am fond of both of them. We go to Akron Friday. I think I shall keep the mortgage unless they refuse to meet our terms and go to a bank. . . . It would have been easier to have brought about your trust by lying to you about certain things. But this is not quite like life. Life one gets through as one can. This is a game, and a major and essential rule calls for absolute and full truth and honesty on both sides. We made our rules and have no right to object to them. I enjoy—get a kick out of—following them.

AUGUST 21. Am hungry. Ho! for breakfast. It rains. Damn! Me with a room to find and no slicker. Waited at Penna Station for RK, and looked up frequently, expecting you.

AUGUST 23. Sunday, 1:00 a.m. Hotel Martinique, Broadway at 32 and 33 Sts. Took a 2:00 train to NY where I phoned RK and Sam and we went to hotel and I bathed and we ate and walked up Broadway and I said 'twas good to be home and did think much of my darling L and had a quarrel with Sam which I should probably not have done, at least I should have been less vindictive, had I been less tired and sleepy. Finally to bed, whence I arose not until noon and found room through the Telegram and bought suit which I get Wednesday. Got trunk at station and bags at hotel and brought them in a cab. After getting out laundry I telephoned Sam and found that Belknap had just returned and was anxious I should come to the house, as the rest of the gang were to foregather there. Went to PO for mail and found none from you, alas! Thence to Long's where I did have a very pleasant evening with B, HPL, McNeil, RK, discussing a variety of unimportant but interesting topics. Thence HPL, RK, and I went to a cafeteria for coffee, after which RK dropped to subway and H and I walked down Broadway, and in passing a theatre with raffia hanging as decoration, I did leap up for a handful and H and I darted onward, each with an end of

---

38. Howard and Clara Kirk, George Kirk's older brother and sister-in law.

the strand—excuse me while I get into robe and fix pipe and get a drink of water. We came here and sat until four o'clock, talking, and deciding how to decorate the rooms. I am not certain, however, that I shall give this much thought, time, or money. Must, however, take care of certain things. May also buy a folding bed, as I believe they are always usable. . . . Desired to arrange for a phone, but found office closed. Visited several shops and had a Jewish-vegetarian meal and bought a medicine cabinet and glasses and walked through the village and up to 14th St., where I took a ferry to Hoboken and walked there for several hours. Returned by ferry to 23rd St. and walked home, and here I am, in the ancient village of Chelsea, just north of Greenwich, in a two-room parlour suite lately rented by a dancing teacher who was a bit too noisy for the landlady who lives below. . . . Shall I send my cigar bands to you or direct to the kids?

AUGUST [undated]. Today I went rowing at Prospect Park, Brooklyn. Three hours or more. Fun. Would you had been with me. Many people. Walked. Ate two good meals: nice fish; halibut steak. Felt like seeing no one I knew. Didn't. Not so very difficult, even here. . . . Stuff comes at 8:30 in the morning. Much to do tomorrow. Most important is telephone. I cannot advertise nor have printing done until I have a number. Will be Watkins, but would 'twere Chelsea.

AUGUST 25. Worked fairly hard today, until about five. Then I quit and went uptown and saw "The Gold Rush."[39] It is probably Chaplin's greatest picture, and I look forward to seeing it again—straight through, and not from the middle to the end. I walked on down and ate at a little place in the village. Desired something slight but nicely served. The meal was more slight than well served. Then home and: what the hell shall I do this evening? A decision! A pleasant bath, a few minutes more of picking up, and an old-fashioned letter to you. Guess I'll light my big old pipe which I haven't smoked in months—it was at Clinton Street, then in storage. Just a moment, Love, we need all the proprieties for a really good old epistle. I am in the one-time town of Chelsea, [317 W. 14th St.] and I think of calling myself The Chelsea Book Shop. If only the telephone company will give me a Chelsea number. One thing

---

39. *The Gold Rush* (Chaplin, 1925), written and directed by Charlie Chalpin; starring Charlie Chaplin, Mack Swain, and Tom Murray.

especially stands out in my memory of The Gold Rush. His giving the Oceana Roll is the funniest thing I ever have seen. He takes two sweet potatoes, spears them with forks and, sitting at the table, he uses them as feet to mimic a dancer. Wait till you see it. The picture is the saddest, maddest, gladdest picture ever done here.

AUGUST 28. Didn't feel like the Kalem tonight, so stayed at home and worked. Haven't seen Martin and would just as soon not, though I must, as there still are some of my things at his apartment and shop. And as far as I'm concerned he may consider me as he pleases, or not at all, as I do him. Last night I ate with RK and went to the Century and saw the UFA film, "Siegfried."[40] Disgusted with RK and am supposed to be with him Friday evening, but intend to not. Howard has some wine for me, sent by a mutual friend from Paris. What shall I do with it? 'Tis well it wasn't in the house tonight, for I felt a craving for some more or less strong drink. LATER. Mrs. Lovecraft is in Cleveland, which seems to me to be a perfectly delightful place for Mrs. L to be. She is with some millenary concern in, I believe, the Kinney-Levan Bldg. Stopped in at Martin's this evening and I was more cordial than was he. When I get out my belongings I shall see very little of him.

SEPTEMBER 2. Took, last night, a look at *Ariel*.[41] Why read that? It tells nothing that every Shelley reader doesn't know and not as much as most know. I, for one, would get much more pleasure and knowledge from the letters. Why should I go to night school? If I knew more than I do know, none of my friends would find me bearable. . . . There is but one period for the drama in English. It is the greatest in the world, and so great that any other period is tenth rate beside it. And who, who wants to study tenth rate periods when they don't really know the Elizabethan? The shop probably will be open until eight. If in some sections, 'twould be later. Have so many desires and ideas and thoughts—not so much that I have so many, but such wild, foolish ones. Kalem tonight and probably I will go, though shall first need to discover where. Am reading again. Conrad, France, *The Beardsley Period*,

40. *Siegfried* (UFA, 1925), directed by Fritz Lang; starring Paul Richter, Margarete Schoen, and Hanna Ralph.
41. *Ariel: The Life of Shelley* (1924), a biography by André Maurois (1885–1967), translated from *Ariel; ou, La vie de Shelley* (1923).

A Passage to India, H. L. *Mencken* by E. Boyd,[42] and am still on the book
about Broadway, NYC. Would you had told me why you sent the
Emily Dickinson. Did you read it? Besides, I cannot care much for her.
She has a fine poetic quality, yes, but both some inner feeling and her
half rhymes irritate me. She, perhaps, was not a puritan, but her form
and manner show that repression so obnoxious to the whole-hearted
Rabelaisian spirit known to a few choice and chosen friends as GD.

SEPTEMBER [undated]. Telephone is installed—Chelsea 10461—and
ads appeared today in Jersey and Brooklyn papers. Your grand-dad
must be a card. I have a very slight and dim recollection of mother's
father. I remember better the house, small, white and green, through
the trees, set in the truly American style. Haven't seen a dentist. Haven't even decided whom to visit. Probably Belknap's father, at least for
advice. Sam and I are good friends when we see each other, which has
been seldom. Asked him over frequently, but he really hasn't been in
good health. Shall be with Kalems tonight. Belknap's. An Arthurian
meeting.[43] The next two are here. Didn't really want them but am easy
and excuseless. LATER. Meeting was interesting and lasted until 1:45.
HPL, Arthur, and I walked to A's hotel at 49th St., whence H and I
walked to here, stopping on the way to admire London Terrace, which
I had never seen, and various cats *re* which I probably was in the same
vicarious predicament. We sat till six, when I lay down till ten while H
read on, nodding occasionally, as he admits, over his varied books. I, up
and cleaned, read the mail, and took H to the Fr-It joint for my first
and his only meal of the day, where we played the Victrola and de-
plored the absence of a cat. Then back until ten in the evening, while I
worked at various things and read *Serena Blandish, or The Difficulty of Getting Married*, and *Cuckoo in the Nest*, the latter by Ben Travers.[44] Also a

<hr>

42. *The Beardsley Period* (1925), a study by Osbert Burdett (1885–1936); *A
Passage to India* (1924), a novel by E. M. Forster (1879–1970); *H. L. Mencken*
(1925), a study by Ernest Boyd (1887–1946).
43. Kirk refers to the fact that the Kalems were forced to have separate
"Leeds" and "McNeil" meetings, because of a minor financial dispute between Arthur Leeds and Everett McNeil.
44. *Serene Blandish; or, The Difficulty of Getting Married* (1924), a novel by Enid
Bagnold (1889–1981); *A Cuckoo in the Nest* (1925), a novel by Ben Travers
(1886–1980).

new *American Mercury*. *Harper's*, *London Times Literary Supplements*, etc. Talked. At H's departure I hurriedly retired and, upon arising, did go forth on some business, return, to town, to dinner with RK, here with RK, and, sure enough, there, with a cigar and the *American Mercury* and his ever-present pleasant smile, sits RK in all the glory of a gloriously contented man.

SEPTEMBER 8. Take, by all means, the modern drama course, if you think 'twill interest you. Congreve is Restoration. He, Wycherley, Farquhar, and Vanbrugh are the highlights of that period, and he is the cleverest of the lot, perhaps of any in English drama. Shakespere (he spelt it so) one *must* of course know thoroughly, though I don't, and I've read all the plays at least twice and favorites a number of times, and the apocrypha once.

SEPTEMBER 14. Went to bed early last night but didn't sleep well. Awoke for good at 2:30, read till 5:00, tried again to sleep but couldn't, so I walked to the Battery, ate breakfast and read papers and watched boats and took the El home. And so here we are. . . . Shall open a shop as soon as I gather a sizable stock. Craven is not nicotineless. I dislike the implication. Nicotineless tobacco, caffeinless coffee, alcoholless wines, and all such denatured and unnatural products are to me Babbittry, shoddy, and disgustingly American. How'd I happen to break my vase? I happened to knock it off the mantle ledge, whereupon it happened to strike the marble slab before the mantle and then happened to crash into a number of pieces. It was not my cherished yellow treasure. As for the drawing, I intended writing about it, but didn't. I, GD, I did it with my little pencil (or did I borrow it from RK?) 'Twas thusly that it chanced. He had been here. Later we walked to Union Square, from whence he was to take his subway. We talked. There, my Lucy, is the story of the picture. . . . Read and liked Leon Vincent's *The Bibliotaph and Other People*, a book about books and bookish people.[45] Essay on Keats' letters excellent. It is like old times, and I love the past. It reminds me of a younger and more living GD to once more feel what is left of a torn and tattered and leaking heartache once or twice again because of a beautiful woman. LATER. Haven't much time as I momentarily expect friends to call and shall then go with them to eat. Hungry,

---

45. Leon H. Vincent (1859–1941), *The Bibliotaph and Other People* (1898).

too, since I've had nothing but a pear today. Up until six this morning, talking, walking, theatering, eating, drinking—no, I didn't forget my promise—and such. Arthur has come, alone, so we must wait a bit longer. He I leave to his own devices: he seems to be interested in *The London Times Book Supplement.* He is Canadian of English parents and has spent considerable time on the other side. Arthur is out of work now and I may ask him to help me. He is far from being an ideal assistant; he talks too much, much too much, and I couldn't merely ask him to do something but should have to tell him how and why. Shall think it over, however, and may speak to him this evening.

SEPTEMBER 17 [on Chelsea Book Shop Stationery, 317 W. 14TH]. I distressed RK last night, when I kidded him about a word in his poem, "To Dickie." He rhymes "awaits you" and "surfeits you" and does not believe in poetic license. He erased the word but has not yet replaced it. Have, and intend to, tell no one of my engagement. Laukhuff[46] note is interesting. No. 1 letter is real as two Kalemites know the writer, and claim he's that sort.

SEPTEMBER 19, Saturday a.m. Had a curious dream of a stepfather and we three children in a strange land. Helen and I laugh uproariously and I play cruel practical jokes on a little man who is almost mad with his fear of the terrible cloudburst and thunder and lightning. We are on a porch, but a sudden change in the wind drives us into the house. In a few minutes I ask Polly (Pauline Hall, our Akron cousin), "Where's Helen?" She stood there dumb and blanched and pointed outside. I go on the porch and take her up in arms and up to bedroom and start to undress her. Here—I'm too fast. On the porch she knelt on corner, head down. Now—family came and women chased me from the room. I was much chagrined and disappointed—sorry, too, for her very physical condition, very wet—but more so because of what I considered her moral weakness.

SEPTEMBER 21. Working hard and still the catalog isn't started. And it must be a good one from the sales standpoint. Otherwise I care not. Would you were here as my set-up, make-up, etc. expert. I know the shape I should like to have it, but doubt its practicability for certain possible inserts. However, I've several days for that as it isn't yet writ-

---

46. A bookseller in Cleveland.

ten and all of books are not even selected. Looked around in section I should like for shop but saw no inviting vacancies. Rents are high: $225 for a small unheated hole with a "wonderful basement." LATER. So you think it's about time you change your job? You ought not be so damned fickle. Be quiet and steady like your GD. Such a nuisance not having an efficient aide. Consider getting Arthur a temporary job of which I know (campaigning, and he *can* talk!) and getting in a girl. Would that I had the kid I had in Cleveland. A. spends too much time saving stamps on foreign mail and looking at books. Not that he really spends much time at that, but he's slow, and that irritates me. I may have been slow once, but NY's the cure. Got, yesterday, a copy of *The Art of Love*[47] for customer, but haven't time to reread it myself. It's a good book, but not for dear Lu as yet.

AUTUMN [undated], Monday. Quite an exciting affair this morning. Thought I was to get a thrill, but 'twas denied me. Have always wanted the opportunity to jump into a net from four or five stories. This is only three, but if one can't get what one wants, etc. Nice fire and lots of smoke on first floor, much noise, and many firemen and jumping and the fire was discouraged and went out. This is the *perfectest* autumn I have ever seen or known. Don't dislike Mrs. L. She is, as I have said, at hospital. H more than intimated that they would separate. . . . Don't know just when divorce became effective; perhaps thirteen or fourteen months ago. Don't know that I was 'nicer' five years ago, but I was a different GW. Friday, with Howard—I was with him from Friday midnight to Saturday noon—this was one of the many subjects under discussion. We also talked astronomy, Dunsany, Pater, Wilde, de la Mare, atomic theory (when I discovered that all matter and all force—such as electricity—is naught but motion), the curious aspect of the moon, boys, books, friendships, certain aspects of the sex, et cetera. May write a paper on same some future day. Even at seventeen I thought my autobiography would startle the world, and thought of writing same.

SEPTEMBER 24. Didn't go to Kalem last night though it was at McNeil's only half an hour away on Third Ave. El. Didn't feel for it and so instead I worked and read "The Lay of the Nibelungs," a frightfully dull thing which I've intended reading since childhood. . . . Per-

---

47. Presumably a translation of Ovid's *Ars Amatoria*.

haps, besides being more than ordinarily selfish, I'm more (if that's possible) than ordinarily vain.

SEPTEMBER 25. RK phoned to ask me to eat with him. Consented. Water's hot and I must have my bi-annual bath. Read until 6:30 a.m. this morning: *Some Do Not* by Hueffer.[48] Rather interesting; shall tell you more of it when I've finished it, and didn't rise until ten. Even now, at two, I'm feeling none too good, and haven't yet been out to eat, though I let A bring me some apples and pears. . . . You ask about Sam—I hadn't seen him for considerable time, but he called last eve for a while. He's now with another bookshop on The Avenue (when speaking of books that means Fourth) and has a cold and tires of NY; he never really liked it. Many don't, you know. LATER. Mrs. Eisert (landlady) expects to lease the house to a banker who'll make the basement a restaurant and the upper floors a hotel, both Spanish, and promises to let me stay. She, however, wants me to go with her to a place she will buy if the deal goes through, on 15th St. I have little desire to move, however, and shan't unless I've good reason to distrust Lago, the Spanish banker. 15th is a much pleasanter street on which to live: cleaner, quieter, and a few Americans. Had promised to hike with Paterson Rambling Club tomorrow, but dare say I shall renig. Nice thing about 15th St. is that I could have the whole lower floor (parlor), its two rooms, for the same price as here. No more space but, I imagine, pleasanter to be alone on floor with windows at both ends.

SEPTEMBER 26, Saturday at 6:00. A lazy day. Read this a.m. until almost five, slept till nine-thirty, fooled around doing mostly nothing until noon, took your parcel to X company and had a chunk of chicken at the rotisserie, chatted with A, had him write some letters while I finished *Some Do Not*, ordered some printing, marked some catalogs.

SEPTEMBER 27. Up about 11:30 and amn't even dressed by three. Terrible? Cats and papers. Had a bit of a fire—do love an open fire, do you? Have another fireplace in other room, but haven't used it yet. Ma E says she has much wood in the basement for which she has no use. Guess I'll have boy bring some more up for me. Didn't rise for hike at 5:30. Didn't retire till 3:00 and thought it unlikely I would be satisfied

---

48. *Some Do Not* (1924), a novel by Ford Madox Hueffer (1873–1939), later known as Ford Madox Ford.

with two and a half hours' sleep. Would that I had taken that Akron three thousand in cash instead of leaving it in mortgage.

SEPTEMBER 28. Would, if I may say so, I had an assistant such as I was to Martin.

SEPTEMBER 29. Your first letter to GD was sent on Christmas Morning, 1923. Do you remember that it hadn't arrived when I left 1625 to call on you? Was it that evening that we went to hear Padereski?[49] Hereafter you must write me an anniversary letter every Christmas day. I shall cherish each as I cherish this, the first. Have to help both Arthur and Sam out of troubles besides taking care of my own. Hope to get my black kitten soon.

SEPTEMBER 30. Got to bed finally at 2:30 this a.m. Don't know how interested you are in when I retire or rise, but it is of some importance to me. Sam I fixed okay I believe, but A's affair still hangs fire. Kalem tonight, but doubt that I shall be there; at least, if I go, I shall be late.

OCTOBER 1. Am enjoying my Galbas. They are a tiny cigarro, no more than half the thickness of a cigarette, but longer and much stronger, stronger, in fact, than some cigars. Shall I send a box to you? They're imported from Portugal. Sam is to come over to talk about a certain business move I contemplate. Should like to go through with the matter, but it takes a lot of money and much time, and the return seems problematical. A. has been a bit more satisfactory in the past two days. Guess we'll manage. Gave him a bit of a scare on Monday and a harder one yesterday a.m.

OCTOBER 3. HPL, SL, and RK were here until one this morning helping A and me. And the job is just begun. Me practical? I dunno! Is staying up all night to do stuff one has been unable to do during the day and so having a naughty headache practical or not? I confess I know not. Fire is pleasant. We had fun last night with old songs; man in back room glared at me as he passed my window a few minutes past, and I stared back. EA Poe is a pun, and his name is AllAn, even though they had an 'e' there on a notice at the Poe cottage, and have not corrected it. Shall never again live where there is no working fireplace. See

49. Ignacy Jan Paderewski (1860–1941), Polish pianist and composer.

Gold Rush whenever you can. Shall see and probably fight with Martin shortly. Feel for a fight.

OCTOBER 5. Arthur hasn't shown up and unless he has a better excuse than I assume he has, today will terminate our arrangement. LATER. Here's Arthur. Must give him some work. Shall send chocolates soon. Or would they be fresher and better if Mac's delivered them? Am going uptown tonight—sale of American Art Association, and shall look around. Worked last night until four, but wasn't up till nine. Usually get to bed by 3:00 a.m. Called at 7:30, but frequently too gd tired to rise.

OCTOBER 7, Wednesday. Went to auction and bought a few books yesterday—bought a topcoat and hat on the way—both gray—and worked until two this a.m. Later I go to see prospective residence. Meeting at HPL's, and I'm undecided. Should enjoy going, and missed last one there, so guess I will. Am framing a number of things for walls.

OCTOBER [undated]. Saturday. I fear I must move. I hate doing so, and must pay, it seems, at least half again as much rent, but shall take no less than three years' lease that I may fix up a semi-permanent place. If I take the place I imagine I shall go with Ma Eisert to 15th St—I shall have the whole parlour floor, a very much pleasanter place to live, but, alas, less space. Tues. I do or don't sign the lease. I must be moved by Friday. I shall get out of doing as much as possible, but fear that even so I shall be able to care for little else. Expect to see Chaplin for the second time next week. Most of the Kalems will go. HPL, RK, SL and A were here helping me address envelopes last evening and we had much fun. Fireplace is a joy and a comfort.

OCTOBER 20. Am at 365 W.15th St. Didn't see mail for a week until Sunday. Moving, cat, carpenter on job here, electrician, printing, etc.

OCTOBER [undated]. OY, My Lu. The darlingest kitten vot I've adopted! His name is Edgar Evertson von Saltus Kirk and oy! you otta see him! White mostly, with a black tail and enough black on his head to go from around his left eye and just cover his left ear. such a affectionate Ket. Oy! What a joy he is to me! Should like to have a cattery. Would you marry into a cattery?

OCTOBER 21. RK here last night and was up until 3:00. Am still sleepy—though I wasn't up till 9:00. Man is rolling about on curb—has tie in one hand and alarm clock in other. Man has trouble holding him up. Prohibition would be a wonderful thing if only we had it. All men should have Lucys, eh kid? Damn Kalem! Should miss it were it not at my place. LATER. Priscilla is the latest of our cats. They ran: Edgar, Oscar, Algy, and P. Prissy, we believe, is in an interesting condition. HPL was in for a short time last eve. He likes the place much. Didn't like the carpenter, and Arthur is doing shelving with an occasional assist from boss.

OCTOBER 26. Last night I walked to the subway with RK and intended sending a night letter to you, but found Western Union closed. I have between two and three thousand catalogs to mail. To prove that it is not unwillingness to write I pass on the information that I don't even indulge in decent meals but almost always either have food brought in or go to cheap cafeterias for speed.

OCTOBER 28. Hoped to go to Paterson tonight, meeting at Jim's, but doubt I can make it. Should get in more help were there more room and were I not afraid it would add to bedlam.

OCTOBER 29. Tomorrow paint will be dry and the place will begin to take on a semblance of order when books are put on the shelves. Fire in each fireplace—very desirable, as cold is omnipresent, if not celestial.

NOVEMBER 5, Saturday afternoon. By the moving to the wall of two large unpacked cases we have made the place look twice as large. Don't recall whether or not I gave you the ghastly details regarding my interviews yesterday. Haven't time now as I must keep a dinner appointment down in the Village. Had more or less of a fight with Arthur today. Felt for one and was very nasty.

NOVEMBER 6. CBS [Chelsea Book Shop] is now better known. An ancient French lady is on the top floor. Her mail is sent to "Miss Jane Heap, Chelsea Book Shop, New York, USA" and it comes. I think F. Sullivan the best newspaperman in the US.[50] LATER. Enjoyed the rest, early this morning, of lying in bed with my old pipe in face, and a pile of books beside me. Pipe was never better and may Shelley never read less well. A rainy day. . . . Have recently again been drawn to the unpleasant habit of thinking. I thought of the long fight I had to gain

---

50. Frank Sullivan (1892–1976), journalist for the *New York World*.

mastery over what is called a soul. Now that I can say I have it, can command it at will, can caress it or damn it, I prefer to forget it. I think, too, of the persons I hurt in varying degrees, with the dull pain one feels over such things, irrevocable and past.

NOVEMBER 7, Monday morning. My sympathies for the loss of your grandfather, dear. I'm sorry I never met him. Went with a friend last night to see "Don Q."[51] Since I had had no recreation for months I was not very critical, and enjoyed the thing considerably. Marveled at the beauty of the Shelton as though I were seeing it for the first time. Went inside too, and while it is not startling, it satisfies. Little Abraham Auerbach, the latest addition to the CBS personnel, stands before me posing gracefully in his Oxford bags. Abe is likeable—is now rather vainly trying to use Underwood. LATER. Rather expected to get together a gang for dinner tonight, and then hadn't time. . . . So sorry you don't care for cats. They are, to be sure, sensuous, but there is more: they are frequently almost psychic in their understanding. I should send my copy of Repplier's book on cats[52]—the best I know—but that it might be trouble for you to return it and I like to have it around. . . . Sam is coming over tomorrow night to help me out. STILL LATER. Have a nice pile of orders. Note one is from Carl V. Vechten and another from Thomas Streeter.[53] Have had them from various personages throughout the country.

NOVEMBER 11. Abe is rather good: not aggressive, but desirous of pleasing. He is doing some addressing. Arthur is downtown. I haven't been out since breakfast and can't get away until late. Kalem meets here this evening. Arthur has been buying things I need for entertaining this particular gang—my reputation hangs upon my ability to make the best coffee any of the crowd has had. I fear they are more kind than sincere. . . . Remember the EBB verse I sent or brought to you in very early days?

NOVEMBER 12, Friday. Kalem lasted until after three in the morning. I was up at 6:30.

---

51. *Don Q, Son of Zorro* (Elton, 1925), directed by Donald Crisp; starring Douglas Fairbanks, Mary Astor, and Jack McDonald.

52. Agnes Repplier (1855–1950), *The Fireside Sphinx* (1901).

53. Carl Van Vechten (1880–1964), American novelist and critic. Thomas W. Streeter (1883–1965), bibliographer.

NOVEMBER 13. Will I bring coffee to you every morning? Huh? With all my aides, assistants, help, etc., I do naught for me. Clothes, laundry, dirty dishes: such things never enter my consciousness. . . . Had to leave you for some time while I got Abe started on a job new to him.

NOVEMBER 17. [The Knickerbocker Lunch, 84th St.] Prisky, who left me for a while, has returned. Howard and A were at place when I wrote before. Together we came here after I finished with letters and I have stayed here drinking coffee and checking catalogs. . . . I desire that the atmosphere of the CBS be a bit precious. My personal taste would be to make it a bit more cheery than it will be—the shelving and wood-work will be a light cream—the walls a light yellow—no, I dunno, tan, perhaps. Am not yet decided *re* furnishings. A couple of bookcases. Either a settee or a sofa or large table to dominate with everything to radiate from that. If winter and fireplaces were continuous, that would be the thing, but 'tis not so, and I fancy they would be bulky in warm weather. Dunno. . . . Scarcely room to turn around in until shelves receive the last coat of enamel and are dry. Had a number of pictures framed, and like some much, others less. I like my taste and am almost always sorry when I follow another's advice. . . . Wed. I go to Kalem meeting in Paterson at Jim Morton's place. When next you use *Who's Who*, look up James F. Morton, Jr. the original joiner. He's now curator Paterson museum. A fine character—Bill Sommer without Bill's genius. 8:45. A. is here. So's Prissy. Such a pretty pussy! HPL calls her 'Cilla.'

NOVEMBER 18. Arthur agreed to deliver a 50¢ book on the other side of town. Abe had to go, and I had to pack. I hate to pack. Hate to do anything anyone else can do for me. Usually don't.

NOVEMBER 20. Such a pleasant time I had later! Sorry I can't tell you all about it. Really am. But can't. Promise. Must go. Rather expect some changes in CBS personnel. Not certain yet.

NOVEMBER 22. [Kirk's 27th birthday.] Haven't even started with the dentist, and shall not until I have someone who is more competent than they whom I now have.

NOVEMBER 26. Am in so that Abe can go to lunch and see what's doing—nothing much: a few store sales, two orders, many catalogs, and missed a salesman I want to see and would I had missed a bore I didn't care to hear. Window cleaner here and had to clear windows; shall let Abe replace the books.

NOVEMBER 27. Thanksgiving Day. Had a bit of a party last night in my own honour—nothing like doing that when others don't. Friends were here until five this morning and I wasn't up till three this afternoon. Here are some verses or extracts from poems—I quote them for their interest, not their truth: [Kirk quotes Rheinhart Kleiner's "To George W. Kirk, Upon His 26th [*sic*] Birthday" (p. 132), James F. Morton's "To G. W. K. on His 27th Birthday" (p. 210), and Samuel Loveman's "To George Kirk on His 27th Birthday" (p. 194).] I shall enclose Howard's, as it is too long to copy. Please either return it or keep it for me; which, I care not. I toasted you but mentioned you not. Then and only then, did I drink, so I feel that I can safely crave your pardon. Had two invitations to dinner today, noon and evening, and refused both; at one I feared a girl, at the other boredom. Took Al to Pappas for a really passable dinner. . . . Have just finished the last piece of maple-sugar candy HPL brought for me. De! Oscar is a pretty puss. [Enclosed: "To George Willard Kirk, Gent., of Chelsea Village, in New York, Upon His Birthday, Novr. 25, 1925" (see p. 185). LATER. Yes. The first step has been taken towards decorating the place. Want all new furniture and furnishings. Have the accumulation of today's work and pricing of a few hundred books and must prepare another *Times* ad tonight. Tired, too. Going out with A. He'll eat, but I shall have only coffee and return.

NOVEMBER 29. Arthur came in and awakened me at 5:30 by playing the recently acquired record: "Home to Our Mountain: Caruso and Shumann-Heink"[54] and, as I had not heard it for years and was half awake, I thought it a majestically beautiful thing. . . . I would willingly give everything I possess that I might take joy in the things that once did please me. Shall we become banal? Better death.

DECEMBER 2. Business is rotten and if it doesn't pick up soon, why, Bye, Bye, CBS. . . . I become more and more the old GD to whom all life is a rather dull game. You with your loved personality gave him an

54. A recording by Italian tenor Enrico Caruso (1873–1921) and Austrian contralto and mezzo-soprano Ernestine Shumann-Heink (1861–1936).

interest in what he calls a game. He is still sufficiently your GD, meaning the GD formed by you, to prefer to remain so rather than return to the chap—I am too tired to make clear the rather intricate thought. Anyway, at present, as for considerable time past, dear, I want to be as worthy of you as possible. But I am tired, tired, of this twelve to fifteen hours-a-day stuff seven days a week, and ever being so far behind in work. . . . This, my dear, whom you see before you, is the GK, the great GK: one, only, and supreme. He's a prince of a fellow and is going out after coffee and papers and the clock claims that while I left you to look at some things two hours passed.

DECEMBER 14. It has been wonderful to have you here. Stopped in at several 125th St. bookstores, and took subway down. Talked with A. about day's biz and did *Times* ad and let him take it out. It has meant much, only you can understand how much, to have you here.

DECEMBER 18. I detest those who bore me and 99% of those I meet do that effectually. Eli Siegel was in—terrible. He is the author of "Hot Afternoons Have Been in Montana," *The Dial* or *Nation* $1000 prize poem on which there were so many parodies.[55] . . . Meeting is at RK's tonight. I go to practically none. Only those at the Chelsea Shop.

DECEMBER 19. Should like to replace both the A's in CBS. Am rather sorry I got Sam the job with Dauber and Pine, otherwise I should ask him to work for me, but just now I cannot offer him anything better than he has.

DECEMBER 24. Monday night I read until six a.m. and was up at 8:30. Last night Kalem was here and got to bed a little after three and up at nine. Tired boy. Sorry I can't be with you tomorrow, but business is too rotten. If it should continue as it is for a month, toodeloo CBS. The only way I can reach my quota is to follow RK's suggestion: lower the quota. . . . If you don't especially like the watch, please, please return it that it may be exchanged. I shall be very sorry if you keep it without liking it. Tomorrow I go to Paterson, NJ and have Kalemites here this evening.

---

55. Eli Siegel (1902–1978), Latvian-born printer and poet. "Hot Afternoons Have Been in Montana" won a poetry prize and was published in the *Nation* (11 February 1925).

DECEMBER 27. Soon a friend will be coming over for a chat. I shall put away the letter and have talk or listen: in this case I prefer to do the former. . . . Were I to tell you of a thing that happened to me a few days past you probably would hate me, still, I in no way broke faith with you. If I told you some of the stories I hear and laugh at, and some that I repeat, you would be disgusted with me. Still, I'm no worse than most, and am cleaner in such things than are many. Still, again, I have such a streak in me and I call it a healthy streak—as Rabelais is healthy, as Margaret of Navarre isn't. I have known few honest women who took much delight in them, that is, in any at all public way. Most of them like spicy stories, but the good old Elizabethan sort, calling a spade a stinking, filthy shovel, delights but few of your sort—and you're all alike. . . . Fear my recent wild dissipations have been too much for my health. Am so angry at Arthur that I've more than a third of a notion to ask him to look for another job, even before I find anyone else to aid me. . . . Coicomstances is curious little critters, ain't they, huh?

NEW YEAR'S EVE/MORNING. Remembering that tomorrow is what it is, and tonight is what it is, I refrained not [from writing you]. I'm really sorry, dear, but I knew I could give you only a few minutes but now find I must go immediately, having made arrangements to be with another than the one with whom I should love to be with. Fate and distance!

1926

UNDATED. I'm reading *Chance, Victory*,[56] Flaubert's *Three Tales*, de la Mare.

JANUARY 3. Saw a very fine picture—"Crainbille"[57]—imported from France and from a story of the same name by Anatole France. In its marvelous simplicity, its humor edged with pathos and its pathos tinged with humor, its freedom from the star America seems to demand and

---

56. *Chance* (1914) and *Victory* (1915), novels by Joseph Conrad (1857–1924).
57. *Crainquebille* (France, 1922), directed by Jacques Feyder. Adapted from the short story "L'Affaire Crainquebille" by Anatole France.

which so often spoils the story, the Anatolian satire made it the best picture I've seen since "Stella Dallas."[58] . . . My knowledge of human nature is based not upon the study of crowds or of a host of friends but upon the study of a few with whom I am, or have been, very intimate, and a constant study at watching of my own acts, reactions, and thoughts—not, so much, the ones one could put often into words, but the subtler, innermost feelings that more often control us than the more conscious feelings. I think, though, that I have told you much more, given you a far better opportunity of knowing me, than you have offered to me. . . . I may not be a Rousseau, and I'm not sorry I amn't a Casanova, and I'm saying no more, but I do try to put myself—*almost* the innermost me, down on paper for dear you and I fondly imagine that I am not wholly unsuccessful. Finished *Chance* at 4:00 this a.m. think his first two stories his best. Always have, and probably. . . .

JANUARY 6. Go to Paterson tomorrow and shall stay for the evening at Jim's.

JANUARY 7. RK last night carried an umbrella and wore heavy over-shoes—he thought it would rain.

JANUARY 9, 4:30 a.m. 'Tis early in the morning. Had, last night, a short vacation from work. Sam and RK were here, and after I had worked awhile I joined them in reading poetry aloud. RK remained till after two. Arthur returned soon after that and is now in bed. . . . Why read Walpole at all when there are so many things I believe you haven't read? If you're not going to read good books, keep to the newspapers, *Mercurys*,[59] *Vanity Fairs,* and suchlike balderdash. . . . Day before Christmas and Sunday after New Year's: two wicked days. Sinning once was insufficient, yet, but must repeat. Well, confession is good for the soul, though occasionally bad for love. Well, here goes. It was like this. Don's boss, Mr. Camellia, rather soused, forced on me a glass of wine—must drink or he'd be insulted. I like him, and drank, both times. No more and no less than one glass. Can you forgive me? Show the largesse of your maidenly heart by the largess of your undeserved forgiveness.

---

58. *Stella Dallas* (United Artists, 1925), directed by Henry King; starring Belle Bennett, Alice Joyce, Ronald Colman, and Douglas Fairbanks, Jr.
59. The reference is to the *American Mercury*, edited by H. L. Mencken and published by Alfred A. Knopf.

JANUARY 12. No. I do not care to be trained for an ideal husband for anyone. Here I sit, take me or leave me—that's my motto. . . . Did I tell you that Prisky has left the CBS? She has. Fear I really should have shaved today, but shan't unless I go out tonight. Nothing especially to do but that I have wanted to hear some good music and if I find there's something I like I may go.

JANUARY 13. Yes, I tend towards agreement with you—that anyone should be able to read *The Mercury* for more than one issue in succession proves that the number of morons in the U.S. is very high. Only bright light is that Alf is losing money on the paper and may suspend. The clip about your boyfriend was in the notorious *Akron Beacon Journal*, and was writ by my good friend, Howard Wolf after his visit to NYC and CBS.

JANUARY 15. Ate last eve with one of the worst Babbitts I know out of C[leveland], where they abound. He *subscribes* to Mencken's *Mercury* and quotes HLM whenever possible. Someday, instead of despising M, I shall come to hate him. Have already thought of writing an attack on him and publishing it in Chelsea Booklets. . . . Damn A. Returning from lunch he said he was tired and would lie down for a minute. Methinks I hear him snore. Hope A. soon fixes shelves: he started to and has left them unfinished. Finished *Victory* ere I went to sleep. It was the third reading and I still think it a fine novel. Started *Jezebel Pettyfer* by MacFall,[60] and like it much. Laughed aloud occasionally.

JANUARY 16. 'Tis ten in the eve and I'm going out for a bit of a walk before some friends come over. Have been working steadily—eating crackers instead of going to a restaurant—and am tired of being and working at a desk. That's a very easy thing for me to be, however. . . . Would that I could get more of a kick out of work, but I never could, and doubt that any work would long continue to be other than drudgery for G.

JANUARY 18. Al Fisher was in when I came in a few minutes past, and I took him on from tomorrow. . . . Damn these fool customers. And if he tries again to look at this letter I'll let him in hopes he sees this. *Curious ass!* Shall drop out of the fight with Marks—fun is over.

---

60. *The Wooings of Jezebel Pettyfer* (1898), a novel by Haldane Macfall (1860–1928).

Have as yet made no effort to get other sets, and can't cut indefinitely.
Forced him from $42.50 to $35.00, and shall rest on my laurels.

JANUARY 20. A bit of scandal from the wife of a fiend. At a salon of
one of our publishers: she, Burton Rascoe,[61] Carl Van Vechten. Carl
with a flaming pink tie. Carl all eve making violent overtures towards
Burt. Burt flees to kitchen, where friend's wife finds him, and from
him: "Can't someone keep that damned fool away from me? The (excuse me) bitch wants me."

JANUARY 31. For me [meeting you] was the beginning of life. Of and
by myself I am as naught. When I love, and I never before have loved
as I loved and love you, I am and she is (pardon the inversion, please)
beauty and love and life and joy and spring and even sorrow, yes sorrow too, deep and poignant, stirring the soul that one may not be dull
or immune to Love's least breath. LATER. Thomas S. Jones, Jr., the
poet whom Mosher published,[62] was here today and we had an interesting conversation. He promises to send me more trade. Very pleasant,
and knows several whom I know.

FEBRUARY 1. But I'm not at all certain that you ought to have the
Burton, dear.[63] It really is the most passionate and plain-spoken book
of which I know, and though I've no prejudice against your reading it, I
do think you should wait till WAM [we are married]. Think it over.

FEBRUARY 8. I'm feeling like a ten year old. Just had a delicious dinner with a freind (Spelling is Miss Austen's, not the original), of cream
of chicken soup, creamed chicken, halibut au gratin, a side of brussel
sprouts, and some fine coffee. Now I'm smoking my long retsina and
am hideously (?) at peace with the world. . . . Did I tell you of Mr. Godfrey and his 'lyric' I'm to publish? He telephoned me about it just as I
was to leave for dinner. He's a real estate operator in Montclair, NJ,

61. Burton Rascoe (1892–1957), American critic and journalist.
62. Thomas S. Jones, Jr. (1882–1932), American poet. Several of his books
were issued by the specialty publisher Thomas Bird Mosher (Portland,
Maine).
63. Perhaps a reference to *The Anatomy of Melancholy* (1621), by Robert Burton (1577–1640).

and he lives at the Princeton Club. His 'Lyric' consists of about seventy stanzas and opens:

> This verse—if verse it be—
> Are drops of life wrung out of longing.

I expect CBS to become famous as the publisher of the poorest thing put out during 1926. . . . Al's OK thus far. He's anxious to learn the business, and why I don't know. He seems to have no knowledge and little judgment and is too much inclined to be flip, but as I say, he's willing and a real aid. The other chap is not with CBS at present, and Arthur still is though I doubt for long. . . . Dear, my love, I wasn't born in December. I wasn't born. I have ever been. Are all that is known, believed, or imagined or was or wasn't, I have been for aeons and aeons. . . . 'Tis after two and I'm inanely tired and sleepy and want to see A. ere I go to bed as I must have out a certain matter with him while I'm peeved and may ask him to leave. I rather like Arthur, also, am sorry for him. If I do get him out I can't imagine what the devil he'll do for himself and while that isn't, I suppose, necessarily an affair of mine, I am, I fear, soft-hearted where I even mildly like. LATER. Arthur is working at the list in the other room, swearing occasionally at a difficult address or merely out of his innate good will. Promised Godfrey to eat with him at his club some evening this week. He amuses me at present, which is well, as it makes playing the game interesting. No telling how long it will continue.

FEBRUARY 12. 'Tis about two, and I'm going to continue working until I've finished all the back work. Al worked until midnight to help. Howard is reading at the NYC books, and seemingly enjoying himself. RK was over. He has lost his job at Fairbanks. Had had it for ten years, and though he takes it very well, it is natural that breaking off old associations and going into a new place should not be pleasant. . . . 'Tis now 5:00 and I am going to bed. H is still here but he doesn't bother me. Arthur is asleep on bed, dressed.

FEBRUARY 13. Have been lying in bed o' nights reading the new volume in the Modern Library of W. S. Gilbert.[64] Like him much. Re-

---

64. W. S. Gilbert (1836–1911), *H.M.S. Pinafore and Other Plays* (Modern Library, 1925).

member the first time I read him. Living in C I visited Akron, walked to town and stopped in at a little shop on the way, now defunct, and bought the first volume scarcely knowing the name, and not at all the series, but liking the rhyme. Walked to Grace Park and bought peanuts which, if I was careful in my movements, the squirrels would take from my hand and stand before me to eat. I read through the book and missed an engagement with a friend, but that is an afternoon I shall never forget. . . . A bookselling freelance was in yesterday and gave me some of the gossip he says is going the round *re* CBS. They are curious.

FEBRUARY 14. On Conradiana, I like best his first two books: *Almayer's Folly* and *Victory*. I enjoy the lack of sophistication in them. . . . Kalem—I haven't been to a meeting for a long time. I may go to the next at Belknap's. B's grandfather died a short time ago, and his first entire book was issued.[65] Very good poetry. . . . RK I haven't seen for a day or two, so can furnish no further detail; nor Sam. HP, as I guess I said the other day, celebrated the return of his wife to C by staying with me until 5:30 in the morning.

FEBRUARY 15. The famous Gutenberg is to be sold tonight but I decided they could get along without me. 'Twould be rather fun and quite safe to stay in up to, say, seventy thousand, for the fun of it, but I've other things to do. . . . Received a valentine today and was quite set up about it. Couldn't quite recognize the handwriting on envelope. Then found, and was not at all disappointed, on the inside, "From Jimmie." Without being romantic, I think I'll keep it.

FEBRUARY 17. Going to Belknap's for meeting tonight. Need, I feel, that much recreation.

FEBRUARY 19. HPL and Sonia like each other, but they disagree considerably; she being of the gushing, superlative Jewish type, while he's a cool Rhode Islander.

FEBRUARY 22. Working with printers *re* the projected book, talking with a chap who would have a half partnership in CBS and move it uptown, scurrying after books for the new catalog, and trying to clear up details that I can have a clear way to work at it, have kept me on the go

---

65. Frank Belknap Long, *A Man from Genoa* (1926), a book of poems published by W. Paul Cook.

continuously. . . . Invited to theater for tomorrow eve but doubt that I shall go.

FEBRUARY 27. [Letterhead: Chelsea Book Shop, 365 W. 15th St., NYC. Chelsea: 10461.] Next few months will tell whether CBS is or isn't a success. LATER. RK was here last eve until one this a.m. Studied catalogs till four and Belknap was here when I awoke. . . . Belknap and his mother go to Florida next week. Sam and HPL came over this eve. RK has been teasing me for a long time to read *She*[66] and I've promised to do that. . . . Have been rather ill with the flu. . . . Would that I might get drunk—having no real escape from business gets on my nerves. . . . I wanta be compromised. . . . Forgive us this day our daily sins, and deliver us to evil, for that is the joy and the reason of life.

MARCH 3. Spent afternoon at the Post Office sale, and go this evening to American, but cannot stay long as I am going this eve to Kalemites. . . . Told Arthur today he is to look for another job and I know he thinks it's because I'm not in the best of health, and not getting sufficient sleep. He'll find out, however, that whatever the cause, I mean it. . . . Good old Peter Drake. Perhaps a monograph on Pete will be the first of the Chelsea Booklets. HPL has done a horror story laid in my 14th St. house[67] and is doing another for this. He's good. FBL's book of poems is out, and aside from the preface,[68] is very good. Copies may be had from CBS. . . . RK hikes every Sunday in Jersey wilds and mountains and wants me to go along. I refuse for the present, but promise when ground is dryer. LATER. So you actually read Dreiser? The third person I've known who could. The first was George Davies! . . . Book is one of near-poems by a sure-enough fool. But wealthy. . . . Auctions come fast and furious the rest of the week. Two tomorrow, but can't well make the evening sale as Kalem meets here.

MARCH 5. I am much put out by a headache and a something that happened last night and about which I cannot let myself go nor hope to correct until tomorrow morning, by a foolish act of my own today and by a rather general and uninteresting boredom. . . . I feel broken. I have

66. *She* (1887), a supernatural adventure novel by H. Rider Haggard (1856–1925).
67. "Cool Air."
68. The preface is by Samuel Loveman.

a deadly rancor because of what look like two dirty deals against CBS that both came to light today: tomorrow I shall try to make both straight: one, by getting what I think belongs to me; the other, by getting rid of what, under the circumstances, I don't want. But, though angry, I am angry without reason. I think continually of Swinburne's "I am tired of love and laughter / I am tired of tears and strife,"[69] if that's the way he wrote it, and I would see a change. . . . I am a tired old man, but hope soon to be better or dead. Until that happy time. . . .

MARCH 7. Did I ever tell you of what is to me the finest love scene (not love passage) in literature? It's in old Boccaccio's *Droll Stories*.[70] Alas, it comes to an ill end. . . . Supposed to go to some fool theater this evening but forgot what it is and little interested and may attempt to shake it. . . . Are you a fatalist? Do you enjoy Conrad? Read more of Hardy? Stevenson? Wonder when Al's coming back. . . . Good old Charles Lamb—I'm re-reading him in essays and letters.

MARCH 12. Weep for Prisky. she is no more. She went away. Bye.

MARCH 15. Want to read some naughty books? You're too young, by far. And too impressionable. Am reading *A Man's Will*[71] and don't care much for it. Fawcett is very uneven—some very fine and some very poor books.

MARCH 16. Saltus's *Ghost Girl* is one of his poorest books. I, personally, rank American writers thus: Poe, Saltus, Bierce. No, I doubt that his stories would be, under like circumstances, in greater demand today than when written. His *Imperial Purple* and *Imperial Orgy* are among the great books in English literature,[72] and are slowly and surely taking their places there. . . . Three women and one or two men are having a wonderful and noisy fight upstairs. Ma Eisert has just come in on it and

---

69. "I am tired of tears and laughter, / And men that laugh and weep . . ." From "The Garden of Proserpine" (1866), by Algernon Charles Swinburne (1837–1909).

70. *Droll Stories* (*Contes drolatiques*) is by Honoré de Balzac.

71. *A Man's Will* (1888), a novel by Edgar Fawcett.

72. Saltus's *Imperial Purple* (1892) and *The Imperial Orgy* (1920) are a series of prose poems about the Roman emperors and the Russian czars, respectively.

seems to be carrying away all honors. . . . The A's, Ma E, and friends, and myself took care of me during my illness. When I ate, meals frequently were sent over from the restaurant. . . . Yes, I had the honor of sleeping through part of *What Price Glory* while my companion slept from beginning to intermission, from i[ntermision] to i[ntermision], and from i[ntermision] to end. Otherwise he drank or smoked or both. . . . I never wish I were back at Martin's. I prefer to be anyplace other than. . . . I have an idea for a series for either syndicate or newspaper such as *Eve World* or *Sun* and could do it, and may try—though I've told it to a friend or two, HPL and Sam, and one may try it. A series of articles on books that were immensely popular in past times, many ran into hundreds of editions, and which are now quite unknown. They should not be so much, perhaps, upon the books themselves, as on the relation of the books to the people to whom they so strongly appealed—comparative customs, habits, etc. The series would not be of great appeal, but I do think they could be sold to certain papers throughout the country. . . . Intend writing a real letter tomorrow if possible—though I want to go for a long walk which I shall arrange with HPL this eve. For two reasons: I like to walk, especially with HPL, and it will relieve me of having to entertain some not very welcome visitors here.

MARCH 17. Go soon to dinner and later have in more friends for Kalem.

MARCH 18. England. Magic, what? Oh to be in England. Alone? Reminds me of a male friend. Ambisextrous. Walking across Brooklyn Bridge with girl and meets a young sailor and takes him in tow. Take both to restaurant and makes girl very jealous. Has just won prize for poem, $1500. Says he will take both to Europe. Asked if he will foster love between his friends says no, he wishes to be alone at the apex of the triangle. He's much fun. . . . God, and perhaps, Good God: do you expect me to tell you of HPL in one short letter that is taken up with so many other things? Try again, when there are fewer other things to write about. . . . Sam's working at a Fifth Avenue bookstore. I see him fairly often. He wasn't at meeting last night. I think he will some day rank high among American poets, slight as a critic, considerable as a writer of poetical prose. He has homo tendencies, as have all the artists I have met, but he is not actively so. I don't know how well you will understand that. Shall I some day send you some books on subject. . . .

I have been too little the old GD, the GD whom once I so highly prized, the GD whom once you loved. . . . [I feared] I was becoming that of which you in your kindness or love or blindness had laughed at the possibility of my becoming, a stodgy businessman. I felt as a shadow the depression that the apprehension of this city can cause; the imagining of the millions of persons, individuals, and their tragedies of loves and hopes and all the many things that fill out each life from beginning to end with the many contacts and influences of each, and in the passing of that shadow I realized as perhaps I never before had realized, how and why men go mad here: why Bierce, Hearn, and almost all of the finer of modern artists in whatever field, have feared or hated New York. Safety lies in the lack of apprehension of the individual. And on the tail of this dragged the wonder if this harmless moment were not proof of a slight derangement. And I remembered that one can be insane and still question one's sanity. And I decided that I should, I would, be GD, the old GD, in spite of prohibitions and without inhibitions.

MARCH 21. Am in a soporific condition induced by a variety of things. HPL failed me because of illness. With an acquaintance I went to restaurant, had roast turkey, a huge baked apple, and accessories, and went to cinema. He was negligible though not unpleasant. Everything, including the walks to and from 86th Street, was pleasant—we enjoyed the cinema, Ibanez's "The Torrent,"[73] and especially the coffeehouse, a new one for both of us, The Black Cow. It was not a memorable evening, but it sufficed for a lazy Sunday. . . . Poetry sings in my head this evening. We talked it much of the time, and I had just obtained and have been reading Gosse's *Collected Poems*.[74] I like him well, and that he is slightly known as a poet perhaps adds to the charm surrounding him.

MARCH 22. Last night ate at Batchelder's and walked with Sam and Al to town. Expect HPL to be here soon—I must be getting ready—to accompany me to the same restaurant. Walked with them to the Battery and took subway back and got ready for bed and read the remainder of

---

73. *Ibañez's Torrent* (Cosmopolitan, 1926), directed by Monta Bell; starring Ricardo Cortez, Greta Garbo, and Gertrude Olmsted. Based on *The Torrent* (1921), a translation of the novel *Entre naranjos* (1900) by Vicente Blasco Ibañez (1867–1928).

74. Edmund Gosse, *Collected Poems* (1911).

Chesterton's *The Wisdom of Father Brown*,[75] then looked over *The Mercury* and, as A had come in with *The Times*, at that, and so to bed at about seven. It's only in New York that such very early hours are kept.

MARCH 24. I am rather pleased with me. Some writing I did about a week ago received high praise from one whose praise means much to me—I don't know him, but I admire him much. Perhaps some day I shall give further details. . . . A. says he tried for an hour to awaken me—from 3:30 to 4:30, as I hadn't brushed my teeth, and he knew I wanted to. But he was unsuccessful. What I get for staying up all of one night and most of the next. LATER. Spring is here. Windows are open and work is difficult. I so continually see broad fields and quiet streams with occasional bathing pools, and unpathed woods with trees towering to the skies and soft moss hanging from the limbs and Spanish moss from the ivy covered oaks. And birds, beasts, and flowers. And, to be sure, dear you. . . . Spring, damn it all, is a dangerous time. As I grow older I realize this more and more. . . . Am reading some of Chesterton's Father Brown stories and rather like them. Think maybe I'll buy some of them from London—I prefer English editions, usually. Their books are more bookish and not so American.

MARCH 25 [Lucile Dvorak's 28th birthday]. What a desire for life and living spring brings. I think only the very young and the very old can live where there is no spring. LATER. Think I shall read old Leopardi, the greatest pessimist I know, to cheer me up a bit. And spring is here and sorrow wanes. . . . Am working at the first of the Chelsea Booklets, a bibliographical treatise, which will be the only one to be distributed free, though I can't tell now the price of those following. The cost of producing this will be the basis of figuring. Have things lined up for the following two. . . . Came for a walk in Central Park. Very pleasant. Walked round the lake where I used to row—the last time was with a friend whom I haven't seen since, and that was several years ago.

MARCH 26. Have about half an hour alone—two friends are coming over. One to try to persuade me to buy a certain shop that's for sale. Need I say I shan't buy it? . . . I shall tell you about HPL, though what

---

75. G. K. Chesterton (1874–1936), *The Wisdom of Father Brown* (1914), a collection of detective stories.

and why you want to know I don't understand, at some future time. Probably about the time I write the essays on Lu and G.

MARCH 27. Got Arthur another job and hope he keeps it. . . . Am reading, backslider that I am, *The Girl in the Golden Atom*,[76] and find it interesting because HPL and I have (discontinued at the time, but taken up again in afternoon) frequently discoursed on the possibility. It is fun to let your imagination run riot with HPL: he is apt to not only keep up with you but may be far ahead of you.

MARCH 29. Did you ever read *She?* I just finished her and like her much. I'll be in Jersey tomorrow and don't know when I shall be back. . . . Arthur is going out to eat and asks that I accompany him.

APRIL [undated]. Saturday Afternoon. Had to answer the phone, and now a customer has dared to enter. Oh well, let him look about awhile ere I pounce on him and force upon him what I can.

APRIL 2. And now I must work hard to catch up on a number of things. I could damn this weather. It makes me long to do anything but stay here and play around with this little business. And my mind becomes so cluttered up with details that I cannot think. So this is the book business in which I once so longed to belong! England beckons to me. So, alas! does the doorbell. And the latter is more easily answered. In comes an old-timer who likes "sperrits." . . . Have been reading poetry much. Old Gosse, Meynell, Levy, French, Shelley, and such.

APRIL 5. Boys wanted me to go with them to see "The Merry Widow"[77] this evening, but I couldn't. Do want to see "HMS Pinafore,"[78] however, which opens tomorrow eve. . . . Had soup, Yankee beans, potato pancakes with apple sauce beau strawberry shortcake, and coffee at Batchelder's a short time past and feel beatific. Should like to tell you of Al's experience with a female patron of CBS but shan't now. . . . RK thinks I should read some of Verne, which I haven't, but I

76. *The Girl in the Golden Atom* (1922), a science fiction novel by Ray Cummings (1887–1957), first published in the *All-Story* (15 March 1919).
77. *The Merry Widow* (MGM, 1925), adapted from the musical comedy by Victor Leon and the operetta by Franz Lehár.
78. Gilbert and Sullivan's *H.M.S. Pinafore* (1878) was playing at the Century Theatre in April 1926.

---

doubt. HPL is to return to Providence without even waiting to go to Philly on a planned Sunday excursion. Hope he waits.

APRIL 11. Want to finish catting by tomorrow—Monday RK starts addressing for a week, and Tuesday comes in a 'semi-delinquent' girl to stenog for a week or so and perhaps to aid in addressing.

APRIL 19. HPL, alas, has returned to his native and beloved Providence. After the last meeting I had a walk with him, from Belknap's (100th St.) to the Battery—visiting all of our favorite haunts and a few new ones. . . . Don't think you'd like *The Girl in the Golden Atom*. It isn't well done. I liked it only because of ideas. . . . You want me to tell you why I denied engagement? I shall tell you in part, at least. Because I was irritated by the kidding of a near-friend. Because our love is a holy thing, not to be discussed with non-believers. . . . I *do* believe all will be okay this year. If only I make no *too* foolish business errors and yet am not afraid to take the right chances. That I am taking chances any dealer in town could tell you. LATER. Managed to sprain my wrist so that I can't type.

APRIL 22. Soon after I came in I got a call from dear old Jake [Herman Fetzer] of Akron, saying he's in town and wants to see me. Naturally, I wanted to see him. . . . Had a gathering for J last night and he held us all interested as long as he chose to talk. He's doing a novel and is seeing Doubleday Page and Kit Morley[79] who reads for them, to determine the chance of its being published as soon as finished. If so he will vacation from job and finish book. His poems are here at last—I think you will like them.

APRIL 23. Finished *Queen of Love*[80] and now I have nothing to read, which doesn't much matter, as I shall be tired tonight, tomorrow, as Jake comes in, in the evening we go to the theater, and I dare say there will be a more or less continuous session here or somewhere. . . . HPL has been doing Boston, he indicates on card.

APRIL 30. I had much pleasure in Jake's company. Think more of him, I think, than of anyone else excepting, of course, sweet you. We mostly talked. . . . Went to a show or two—Sat night four of us went, but I

---

79. Christopher Morley (1890–1957), American journalist, editor, and poet.
80. *Queen of Love* (1894), a novel by S. Baring-Gould (1834–1924).

said I had to wait a while and let them go ahead, thinking to get off a letter to you. I wrote one, then hurried out and took a cab to the theater without mailing it and while there I decided that because of what I had said about a more or less mutual friend I would not send it. . . . Jake left on Wednesday. He's doing a novel in which Kit Morley and Doubleday Page are interested. I think it will be a great one. Soon I shall be able to send you little vols of poetry by three of my friends. . . . Jake wants me to spend a week or so with him this summer, and I'd sure like to. Also, I'd like to go to Providence and be with HPL.

MAY 4. Two other friends are coming from Akron soon, still another—I haven't met him but he belongs to the gang there and Jake thinks highly of him—later. Met, the other day, Galpin's wife: she went back to Paris on the Leviathan, and expects to bring him back ere long. . . . Am reading Trollope's *Barchester Towers*[81] and enjoy it. I have a decided taste for the Victorian novel. . . . I must arise and go now, but not to Innisfree.[82] And I don't care so much for huts made from clay and wattles, whatever the latter are, they remind me of waffles.

MAY 7. Last night Sam and RK here until after twelve and work still to do.

MAY 9. Jake, as I believe I have already said, though I may not, has returned to his native city. The other two boys come Monday but they stay at the Commodore Hotel instead of at the Chelsea. . . . Want to hear "Iolanthe."[83] Shall ere long. But I don't much fancy going with a boyfriend, not at all, alone, and don't know that it would be the thing to do to ask a girl. Would it now? Perhaps I shall go with the Akronites next week. Or with Arthur, he would get so genuine a pleasure from it—he now knows most of the songs and could remind me of any I forget—that perhaps he would be my best bet. . . . You ask again whether or not I am 'double-natured'—ambisextrous—we are calling it here. I think I have already tried to explain the matter to you. If you don't know how and what I am by now—how will you? But that, I fear, is ill-natured. . . . I for long hoped to find an ideal companion. I think I did,

81. *Barchester Towers* (1857), a novel by Anthony Trollope (1815–1882).
82. An allusion to the line "I will arise and go now, and go to Innisfree" from "The Lake Isle of Innisfree" (1893) by W. B. Yeats (1865–1939).
83. Gilbert and Sullivan's *Iolanthe* (1882) was playing at the Plymouth Theatre in April 1926.

but dear Ernest Nelson, alas, died.[84] I have neither desire nor expectation of finding another, being more or less satisfied with my few friends, who even so inspire me not infrequently to excessive boredom. LATER. Think that next Sunday I shall go on a hike with RK. . . . Such an admission I have to make! Last night while I was talking with you there was a young lady in the room. A lady whom I love even though I met her only last night and even though I love her less than I love you, I love her. To say that we slept together is perhaps unnecessary. We did. . . . Not only that, but she's black, all but the white tip of her tail, and we call her Tippecanoe, Tip, or Tippy for short, and she's the cutest kitten you could ever hope to play with, hold, or have share your bed.

MAY 11. Tippy's such fun. Arthur has just put a bit of the tissue wrapping of an orange over her head and she's having so much fun. . . . I believe that Mother in her maiden years lived near Philadelphia at one time. . . . When I started this I thought I was to have an evening alone, but now Arthur's here for the eve, and RK, though just now RK is out after some of his sherry. . . . I'll work at lists: RK may amuse himself with the puss and the sherry.

MAY 12. Would you could see Tippy. We love her so.

MAY 14. Eat tonight, and perhaps theater, with Akronites, who start for Ohio tomorrow. Poor things.

MAY 16. Saw Akron friends until late. Walked with them to the Commodore, which they were to leave at 6:00 this a.m. We had a pleasant meal at the Village Moon and came back here. Then went to Papa's and walked uptown. They're a good lot. Both asked that I stay with them when I come to C. . . . Tippy is missing. . . . Am being sued for $114.00 because I haven't found some papers. Oh well, I have a pleasant lawyer who takes me to the Athletic Club for dinner and conferences.

MAY 17. Have finished good old *Barchester Towers* and imagine I shall read through most of the series. Some of the characters are gorgeous in

84. Ernest Nelson was a member of Hart Crane's circle in Cleveland and a co-worker with William Sommer at Otis Lithography. See Samuel Loveman's poem "Ernest Nelson," *Clevelander* 1, No. 1 (June 1922): 8; rpt. in *Out of the Immortal Night: Selected Works by Samuel Loveman* (New York: Hippocampus Press, 2004), p. 107.

their likable unpleasantness. Old Ed Lazare, of whom you haven't heard for some time, showed up Saturday and stayed with me over-night. He enlisted in the army for Foreign Service because he wished to get away from NY. He went to Panama, to San Francisco on way to Hawaii and was detailed back to Fort Schuyler, the Bronx, NYC. He is still interested in books, but is reading mostly Shakespeare. Have been re-reading *Ulysses*[85] and enjoying it. It's really a great book and will be long ere its influence has passed away.

MAY 19. Everything's so damn rotten, if you get me. But old Trollope, I like. Tippy is missing again. . . . Vrest Orton[86] of *Mercury* was here to-day and copied some of Buffington stuff for *Americana*.[87] Did your bit ever appear?

MAY 20. I am enjoying *A Perfect Day*[88] and shall send it to you as soon as it is finished by your GD. Old Tippy is back again and is now sitting in the sunlight in the window washing her funny little mug.

Of all the foolish things I might have done, I broke my specs. Sat. night four of us worked until 2:00. Yesterday Ed was here and helped me clean up dump. . . . Then the d[amn] f[ool] who was to fix them breaks a lens and I must wait till one for them.

MAY 24. Last *Mercury* is so full of erotica that Knopf and Mencken are frightened and we must all be good for a while.[89] Ah me!

JUNE 2. RK is coming in to eat with me. . . . RK is culling spicy bits and jokes from the *Wall Sex Worship* but I think it and everything about it shoddy and cheap. One sort of thing at least I have outgrown. . . .

---

85. *Ulysses* (1922) by James Joyce (1882–1941). At this time the novel was officially banned in the US for obscenity.

86. Vrest Teachout Orton (1897–1986), a late member of the Kalem Club.

87. Kirk refers to the column "Americana" in the *American Mercury*, a collection of bizarre or humorous newspaper extracts from around the country.

88. *A Perfect Day* (1924), a novel by Bohun Lynch (1884–?).

89. The reference is to "Hatrack," a story by Herbert Asbury published in the April 1926 issue of the *American Mercury*. This tale of a prostitute who practiced her profession among the parishioners of a church was the subject of a celebrated obscenity trial brought by the New England Watch and Ward Society against the magazine, its editor (H. L. Mencken), and its publisher (Alfred A. Knopf). Mencken and Knopf prevailed.

Want to finish work and chase RK out and get in bed with a pipe and read Becke[90] a short while and sleep. . . . Here's RK now, wanting to see what I bought—I got some from the place where he works—on 4th Ave—you and I were in the shop. I believe you asked for a Frank Harris there. LATER. RK is playing the Victrola. I think I shall read another Becke, and then another Vernon Lee, *The Countess of Albany.*[91] I love her. Next to Alice Meynell, I think. RK has the audacity to play "Humoresque." He has ever been passionately fond of music. Took off an hour this a.m. and rowed at Central Park. Couldn't afford it—the loss of time—but enjoyed it the more and got sunburned, which I don't often do. Going swimming soon at a place on Long Island. . . . The hackneyed things RK plays make me sleepier.

JUNE 3. Delivered today, in person, to Stephen Vincent Benet, as I was going in his direction. He was pleasant. . . . Akron friends are not of my childhood. Met them within the past five years. Wolfe didn't come.[92] RK book okay. Bought some from him. *MERCURY* turned down advertisements of curious items because of fear of Knopf and Mencken. . . . Had, this, or to be more exact, yesterday, morning, a not very welcome visit from Mr. Sumner.[93] Just as I finished shaving. Not alone, either, but with two officers and a girl witness and a warrant for Johnnie Doe on which they take Al to Jefferson Market Court for handing circular of Harris to said girl witness. Out on bail until hearing in several months. Shall cut out or down on all funny stuff and sell or ship no more Harris. . . . Arthur is married, has children, and left Sunday. . . . As for Tippy, the darling has left me for other fields. . . . I forgot whether or not I sent a copy of Belknap's book. I want you to have one—there are really some very good poems in it—tho' I dislike the preface. Sam's is being delayed by the printer.[94]

---

90. Apparently Louis Becke (1855–1913), Australian author of several volumes of sea stories.

91. *The Countess of Albany* (1884), a biography by Vernon Lee (pseudonym of Violet Paget, 1856–1935).

92. Presumably a reference to Howard Wolf, the Akron newspaperman.

93. John S. Sumner, secretary of the New York Society for the Suppression of Vice.

94. Samuel Loveman, *The Hermaphrodite: A Poem* (Athol, MA: W. Paul Cook/The Recluse Press, [July] 1926).

JUNE 5. Was busy with yesterday's mail until four this morning and needed a bit of a rest. Al tried most of morning to get me up and was heartily cursed for his pains. Did I tell you I gave him a raise last week? Oscar is roaming about the place. I was just offered a kitten from next door but turned it down. She who offered it suspects the lot to be the progeny of Oscar. . . . Have a letter from Arthur about which I may tell you a bit. It appears, from the glance I've given it, to be one of the strangest I have ever had the honor to receive. He's a strange chap, but gentlemanly, and his quirkiness tends towards making him all the more likable.

JUNE 9. I may go to meeting at RK's for a bit this eve, as I desire a bit of recreation. And may not. . . . Guess I must go to Brooklyn. Have been out all day, mostly, and shall be at court in a.m. and very busy rest of the day.

JUNE 14. Tomorrow my Aunt with her daughter, daughter-in-law, and grandchild, are here for the day, and in the evening they sail for England. Must show them the town. . . . Shall send a Belknap soonly. . . . Gosh, I dunno whether or not prison sentence denotes deprivation of citizenship. And confess that I never thought of the same being in any way an important item.

JUNE 16. Saw "Pinafore" but am still promising myself "Iolanthe." Had rather fun yesterday showing relations the town. Took my aunt and her daughter-in-law atop the Woolworth, went for a bus ride, etc. Now am late for the meeting at Belknap's.

JUNE 25. If things are half decent this fall, love, I want you to marry me. No later than October. Don't know how much I will be making— it's hard telling with such a lack of bookkeeping, but we could manage without horrific hardships.

JUNE 28. Case was adjourned to July 15, which I should not have allowed had I known it was to be done, as I should like to have it over with and also it interferes with my plans in regard to my trip New Englandwards. . . . RK is writing a letter at the table in back of me.

JUNE 30. I am both fickle and constant. I like much more strongly than I dislike. Usually, what I dislike makes little impression upon me and I forget. . . . Since I fell in love with you I have loved only two other girls—rather a good record, what? . . . Shall take on a boy for afternoons to help out. Shouldn't need him if Al were less anxious to read while here, but unless he has such work as he likes he does nothing. Am trying to get a certain chap away from another dealer, but have been thus far unsuccessful. He wants so damn much ere he will change.

JULY 3. Saturday. Tomorrow I shall leave on the night boat to Providence. Shall not be leaving Boston before Thursday at the earliest, so you can get me there. Have more or less of an itinerary but it is not exact as I may go on or stay as the town does or does not promise well.

JULY 6. Am on a nice fast express from Boston. Have had a very pleasant time seeing Providence with old HPL, and just had dinner with him and a chap I met and liked named Tycon. He's a very decent young bookseller and is much interested in local history. Mrs. L was with us much of my first day—very unpleasant at times. HPL loves cats and almost invariably stops to stroke them. She—Mrs. L—several times remarked that cats are the only things H really loves—and once she remarked—in a quite casual way, but looking at me to read its effect, which I doubt she did,—that she believes H would love to take a cat to bed with him. I have heard this sort of thing from her before and can't say I respect her the more for it. This train *do* travel! HPL may come to Boston for a day, which would mean more sightseeing. I rather envy H his quiet life in this quiet place: it is both beautiful and interesting, and he certainly makes the most of it. Saw some gorgeous fireworks last eve, the Parade of the Ancients and Horribles, and after an Italian chicken dinner, we sat at hotel room until three a.m. discussing astronomy and chemistry and their relationship. I promulgated a theory of which I am very proud—that all there is is an atom and that's all there is. Beyond is nothing, not even space. I wonder if you'd enjoy our discussions. I doubt it. I can't imagine any girl's being interested in such metaphysics. Wait till I light a pipe. I liked some of the farthest-fetched ideas so much I would do a dance in their honor. We agreed that light is an electrical force—not a new idea—which removes some of the improbability of the Einstein theory. I don't understand how an object in different positions in space—without physically varying—changes its size in relation to space. I think it interesting—I discussed it with Jim two weeks ago—that they know the number and the proportion of the undiscovered elements. Our final answer to "Is anything?" was "Motion is." And, seemingly, there is naught else concrete. Visited an adorable old churchyard which Poe loved and used to haunt and where he was when he first met Mrs. Whitman.[95] And Mansion House, where he stayed when in town, and the Athenaeum, which he and Mrs. W. visited. While there Mrs. W asked him if he had read the anonymous poem, "Ulalume," in the *American Review*, which she liked. Poe replied that he had, later that he had written it, and still later signed the poem in the magazine. Fairly recently this story was verified by the discovery of the signature in the file of the paper.

JULY 7. I rather like: "Grant it, Father / that I live / always in / Superlative."

JULY 11. SUNDAY. Have been having much fun. Shall tell you all about it after I've answered the letter I have from you. . . . This being written at the Irving House, Boston. . . . I can make a good thing of the CBS if I much wish to during this coming season. About another bad month and things will start again, and I shall have the best stock, the best list of names, and the best chance I ever have had to make a success. But, I confess I have to be driven to work. When I've needed money for a trip or a car or what not are the times I have slaved. . . . My trip has been more of a play trip than I had planned. But I've had *so* good a time. Reached Providence on the 5th, and was shown the town as, I believe, I have told you. The next day I worked in P., and that eve took the train to B. Worked Wednesday. Thursday H showed me B and Friday we went to Salem and Marblehead. Both are wonderful, but I prefer M, and hope to spend from a week to a summer there sometime. M's crooked streets and strange vistas and hills and old houses make the lover of ancient things a lover of M. Salem has one perfect street— the finest row of Colonial houses in Salem, the US, or the world, as they are perfectly preserved and are the best doorways anywhere.

JULY 19. Did I tell you—guess I didn't—that at Worcester Ed Morrill, a friend and customer, took me for a day in his Cadillac coupe into the foothills of the White Mountains in New Hampshire where he bought cloth while I swam in the river. The most beautiful drive I've ever had—green trees meeting overhead, forests, mountains and lovely valleys, old houses, etc. Ed is a prince and even paid my hotel bill after

95. St. John's Churchyard, the churchyard of St. John's Episcopal Church (1810) on North Main Street, Providence.

getting me the best room in the house. . . . The Sumner case came off the other day—fifty plunks fine—but had to give attorney $150. . . . Have been reading some nice horror stories. One I like especially by HPL I may send to you.

JULY 20. I am less busy only because the heat is so abominable it seems I must spend part of the day outside. But then I work evenings and manage to get in a pretty full day. Only, last eve went to see Jannings in "Variety."[96] It's one of the best cinemas I've ever seen. Vrest Orton was in today with about seventeen new schemes for making money, in several of which he is so good as to include me: bootlegging, issuing erotica, publishing popular authors in paper editions: wants to come into CBS as a partner, or wants me to leave it and go abroad on some bright chase. Ideas are at a discount. . . . Did I tell you that there isn't a decent restaurant in Boston and that it closes at 8:00 in the evening?

JULY 22. Terribly hot here. It's been 98 in the shade. Last night heard the symphony at the Stadium, Bethoven's Ninth, and enjoyed it much. Fear there is another 'e' in his name.

JULY 25. Sunday. Ronald Elliott of Cleveland is here. I met him yesterday and am just come from eating with him at the Moon. . . . Sam will be in Cleveland next week and occasionally I hear he intends scandalizing GD. Confess I can't get very excited about it. I have little use for anyone who can care about such things. . . . Tomorrow night I go to Stadium with Ronald. There's a new UFA at the Rialto and I think I'll go as soon as I've re-washed my face.

JULY 26. Saw UFA's "A Vienna Waltz"[97] last evening and enjoyed it. The Germans for some reason, perhaps only because they are fresher at it than we, make their cinemas more real. . . . Have promised to go to symphony with Ronald and RK. Guess I'd better quit amusements for rest of week.

---

96. *Variety* (Famous Players–Lasky, 1926), directed by E. A. Dupont; starring Emil Jannings, Lya de Putti, and Warwick Ward.
97. Kirk refers to *A Waltz Dream (Ein Walzertraum)* (UFA, 1926), directed by Ludwig Berger; starring Jacob Tiedtke, Mady Christians, and Carl Beckersachs; adapted from Oscar Straus's operetta.

JULY 27. Am hungry and am going out to eat very soonly. Later. Ate about ten with Ronald at Drake's and ordered a blackberry—gosh, I forgot what to call it—and it was delicious. Made a meal on the free pickles—including pickled cauliflower and onions—and the three kinds of rolls, my favorites being the cinnamon. I considered it quite a triumph when I had the waiter bring in more pickles and more butter for me on a 30¢ order. Went to symphony last eve and it wasn't so good, "Sacre du Printemps" blah and as for "Andante Cantabile" and the "1812 Overture," ugh! Hope to be able to go Friday night even though Sokoloff[98] conducts, as there's a good Brahms program.

JULY 28. Do you think you could ever love me as I deserve to be loved?

JULY 29. Poor Lu—to be turned out from everything she loves! What right had Bill to have scarlet fever? I had it when quite a child and Mother and I were quarantined over Xmas. Al is on vacation. Summer list is coming. Gosh! How should I know whether or not CBS is a paying proposition? I'm no bookkeeper. . . . How much do I want CBS to go? Where? . . . Douglas's *House with Green Shutters*[99] is the book I like, which I think comparable to *Wuthering Heights*.

JULY 30. Elliott is here till the end of the week. I like him in a mild sort of way. . . . Dunno what sort of scandal Sam plans to purvey, nor whether he will, it depends upon his mood. But if you see him and give him, not too openly, a few leaders, I'm sure you'll get an earful. . . . Kalem is sorta, but Belknap is at Thousand Islands and dear Jim's father just died, so he's somewhere in New England because of that.

AUGUST 1. Tonight a gang goes to hear "Iolanthe." . . . Must finish several letters ere boys come.

AUGUST 2. Heard and saw last night the Winthrop Ames production of "Iolanthe," and do proclaim it the best G & S I ever have seen. . . . Just had some delicious fresh peach ice cream, which I shared with Jeanette.

---

98. Nicolai Sokoloff (1886–1965), Ukranian violinist and conductor of the Cleveland Orchestra (1918–33).
99. *The House with Green Shutters* (1901), a novel by George Douglas (pseudonym of George Douglas Brown, 1864–1902).

AUGUST 2. Did I ever copy for you Howard's pretty poem on Oscar? Here it is: ["In Memoriam: Oscar Incoul Verelst of Manhattan, 1920–1926" (see p. 189).]

AUGUST 3. Only 7:30 and I'm a tired boy. Guess I'll go out for a bite or two and a few minutes' walk, then back at work. Gosh, I almost forgot, I must do the *Times* ad ere I go. And I've nothing to put in it. Think I'll have to manage to get someone else in, as I must have some time to get around and see things.

AUGUST 6. Am about to go out with friends to eat and must finish mail within one minute. . . . Haven't had much sleep lately—last night 4:30 to arise before 7:00. But I seem to be bearing up. Jeanette has just put away a whole can of salmon and is extremely fat.

AUGUST 10. Tuesday. Just a week ago you wrote a letter that made me quite peeved. At first I laughed. But when I had thought it over a bit I became angry. . . . Al doesn't room with me, gosh! I was about to prepare to fix my own breakfast, but Al wanted to come in on it, so I didn't. He gets on my nerves.

AUGUST 16. Sam just telephoned to say that he's coming over, arrived this a.m. Belknap was in yesterday; has been with his parents at Thousand Islands. LATER. The rain still is with us. Jeanette also is. She chased out Melinda as well as any other stray cats that venture into the shop.

AUGUST 28. Would that I knew that you'd get this Sunday. But I remember you thought quarantine would be lifted by the time you returned. . . . "Iolanthe" our last eve, the river ride and boat ride at Crystal Lake—I think often of these and other affairs made dear to me by your presence. [Note: Lucile visited George in NYC in mid-August.]

AUGUST 30. Ed is here and we ate at Camellia's Place. The rice was served in a sort of brick—a huge order about 3 × 3 × 6, solid with a dressing on top of tomato and cheese. Very nice it was. In the chicken soup we each got about half of a chicken, so neither of us was able to do full justice to the second dish.

AUGUST 31, Tuesday. Jeanette is lying peacefully on the desk. . . . Kalem here again tomorrow eve. Talked today with Sam and he says he won't come over because of Belknap, upon which I promptly dubbed him a fool.

SEPTEMBER 2, Thursday. Had a pleasant meeting last evening. Old Jim is a prince; I should like you to know him. Read *Dracula* [100] yesterday—did little work after I had started it and had to finish before I went to sleep. RK stayed over with me. After the youngsters—Belknap and Al—had left, Jim and RK and I had a pleasant chat lasting until after two. . . . Mellie (Melinda), I wonder if my mother'd object to having a cat called after her, should be presenting the CBS with about six pussies ere many Thursdays have added their dull toll to the weary days of life.

SEPTEMBER 4. Just gave Al a rather sharp talking to, told him that since he didn't do things I asked him to do I should have to tell him to do things and expect him to do them. If it doesn't work, I shall give him notice next week, as I tire of the way things are going. . . . Sam wants me to go to Phila with him, but am not enchanted at the prospect. I do wish to go to Trenton again after books.

SEPTEMBER 5. Monday. Mimi Aguglia—the actress of whom Arthur Symons thought so highly and of whom he wrote several essays, is to be at the 14th St. Theatre soon—possibly tonight. . . . Shall tell you of her if I see her. This is the theatre Eva Le Gallienne is to have for her Repertoire Theatre. It should be good. Nothing much doing. Writing, cataloging, reading. Took some favorite old folios out of trunk and am looking them over—Tacitus, Thomas Brown, etc. Brown's prose has seldom been equaled.

SEPTEMBER 8. Going to Kalem tonight at Belknap's. Arthur called here today from Chicago while I was out. . . . Intend having some fun tonight. If successful, I may tell you of it, though I half recollect your stating that you are little interested in arguments.

SEPTEMBER 9. Jake and Sam and Arthur have left for theater. I pretended to have some work that would keep me a while. Jake has read to us the few chapters he has finished of his novel, and I think it will take hold big. It is one of the best things of its sort ever written—in the Rabelais, *Tristram Shandy*, *Till Eulenspiegel* [101] class. Sam compares it to *Jurgen*,

---

100. *Dracula* (1897) by Bram Stoker (1847–1912).

101. *The Life and Opinions of Tristram Shandy* (1760–67), a picaresque novel by

but it has more poetry in it than Cabell ever heard of. The last chapter—
he's writing the others to it—is a powerful and poetic bit; hearing it
brought tears to my eyes, and I'm not as emotional about such things as I
once was, and this was without the intervening chapters and in its unfinished state. Doubleday Page is interested in it. I should be glad to see
Jake come into his own. . . . Damned my head. W. Paul Cook isn't coming from Boston. . . . Guess old Galpin isn't coming from Paris either, as
I hear his wife is going back and they're to stay another year. There's bedlam for you. I am really becoming a bit tired of being sober. . . . Understood that HL was married to some brawny westerner. No? . . . Am I
social? A whole one in myself, my dear. Have a new line: the younger de-
generation. Did I give you: "How Odd / Of God / To choose / The
Jews?" I believe I did. Here's Hypothesis: In haste / His taste / Perhaps
/ Could lapse. HPL. . . . I don't mind confessing that I despise more easily than I appreciate—my easiest attitude is one of slightly scornful indifference. I think I am mostly over my youthful superciliousness.

SEPTEMBER 13. Tomorrow I go for a hike with RK, Sam, and Ed
Lazare. RK's coming over to be sure I get up in time and so that he
doesn't have the long ride over from Brooklyn. Three in a bed! . . . An-
other reply of HPL's was "De Gustibus. . . . Why scan / His plan." But
I think the other cleverer and think of sending it to editors of the *Week
End Book*.

SEPTEMBER 14. Monday. Spent yesterday with friends as anticipated,
in the Ramapo Hills, reached via Tuxedo NY, the other side of the
Hudson. Very pleasant it was, too. I've more than half a mind to get an
outfit and go regularly with the Paterson Rambling Club, to which three
of my bfs belong. Loose pants, and ankles covered only by thin socks,
aren't so good. Would you allow me to attend next year? Every Sunday
they go. Not so sure that I should be anxious to be along when it rains,
or in heavy snows. HPL to be here tomorrow—plans to return in eve,
but I'm going to try to persuade him to remain a day or two with me.[102]

Laurence Sterne (1713–1768); *Till Eulenspiegel* (1519), a collection of German
satirical tales.
102. Lovecraft returned to Brooklyn in September 1926, evidently at
Sonia's request. He stayed for about two weeks.

SEPTEMBER 15. Had fun Thursday night, but don't much recollect details. Mostly picking flaws in ideas of Kalemites. . . . Galpin's the chap who was in Cleveland, from West, then Paris, here for a day or two, now instructor in French, Northwestern U. LATER. Am *so* beautifully broke. Received a returned check for three plunks and a request for a postal money order for the amount. And can't buy one because I've only 35¢, or 37¢ counting that in the cash drawer. That's what comes of working only at catalog. And Al wants to sell the Nonesuch Miltons at $15. Think of it! But don't bother to condole for, of course, by the time you can reply I shall have raised some money. Poor little Jeanette is hungry. Last night didn't get to bed until after three. What was the cause? I don't know; perhaps being wet in the cold air, but after I was in bed and perhaps after I was asleep I found myself gasping for air. HPL just called and is at Belknap's so, as Belknap's father is my dentist, I shall see him at 2:00. . . . Curious how Jeanette even though in the rear room can tell when I come in and is always at the door.

SEPTEMBER 16. HPL, Belknap, and I went to Spanish and American Indian Museums yesterday. Spanish interesting. In A. Ind. were some human heads that had been normal size—the Indians had removed the skull and dried them until only a few inches in size, though with long and thick hair. A whole body had also been so treated—all the bones having been removed—and was only about fifteen inches long. Quite horrifying. Meeting is here this evening.

Must answer phone. Thought maybe I wouldn't have to, but it continues ringing and ringing. Most irritatingly. After the phone comes a browser. Oh the trials and tribulations of a bookseller's life! LATER. From one last night to the time Ed had to leave for camp I played checkers with either him or Al while HPL read. Even I had enough of my latest craze. . . . All my boyfriends are visiting the Bronx Zoo to see the newly discovered dragons. Jim thinks they'll die.

SEPTEMBER 17. HPL left this a.m. for Philly without me. Alas. Sunday I hike again. Last Sunday's hike I enjoyed so much, and it made me feel so well for days afterwards, and gave me such zest for whatever was to do, that I shouldn't wonder if I should keep it up quite regularly. RK will stay with me, coming in late, to be sure that I get up at so early an hour.

SEPTEMBER 19. Have just come from the barber's. Am going tomorrow on hike with Paterson Rambling Club, which, for tomorrow, Jim Morton leads.

SEPTEMBER 20, Monday. Had such fun yest. on hike. From Paterson went on long bus ride half way up young mountain, then walked to fire tower at top. Nothing of a walk at all, and most stayed there to hear Jim harangue. He loves to. RK and I from the top of tower had seen lake and decided to walk over—it didn't seem far. We did. Where it had looked as though you had merely to go down and up to be there we found there were six ridges between steep mountain rocks and marshes between them. RK almost stepped on a snake. I saw it curled up and took his stick and poked it. It started to glide away and proved by sight and sound to be a rattler (we had been on rattle-snake trail to tower.) I gave it a crack just back of the head and the head came off and I am very proud to have killed my first rattler and the only one seen by the crowd for some time. I was reproved later for not taking the rattles as a souvenir. Am told they're worth a dollar a rattle. In which case I could have had five or six plunks. But I think I should rather have sent it to you. Shall watch for another. We had a very pretty scramble of it over the rocks and through underbrush where we had to force our way. It made the day for RK and me, as that's what we like.

SEPTEMBER 21. Yes, love, I recall your first visit to NYC very well. Though I confess that I don't know how you remember dates so well. HPL does it—almost any day in his life—at least he makes a good bluff at it, and not infrequently it's been checked up. I can't. I don't know how long I've been in NY, how long the CBS, 365, GD, C, anything, or the lack. . . . Dunno whether you could go on hikes with RK and me. But you could go on regular and ordinary Paterson Ramblers'. Mostly very easy. A number of females go. . . . HPL is still in Philly but due back this eve. LATER. Sam was in. HPL is back and is writing cards.

SEPTEMBER 22. Just had dinner with Bill Rigby and Howard Wolf, Akron boys of whom you have heard. They came in today. . . . I soon go to Sam's to Kalem meeting. But I shan't go too early as a chap's there from upstate whom I dislike.[103] He says little, but his very presence makes me tired. Some tire me by talking too much.

SEPTEMBER 23. Now, on the eve of the great fight.[104] . . . Otherwise I've been at desk writing letters all day and looking forward to Sunday's hike and wondering when I could go to Philly and see, as I never have, the famous Wissichickon Valley—claimed to be one of two or three beauty spots of the world. Though I'm not at all certain as to its spelling. Am afraid it's going to rain and fight will be off and all bets likewise. In which case I won't get the five spot that's coming to me otherwise. For D will win and there'll be no KO, at least that's the belief of this wiseacre, though, alas, he shares it with many.

SEPTEMBER 24. Akronites start back Sunday a.m., and may go a ways, perhaps only to Philly. Back Monday noon. Or may hike as planned.

SEPTEMBER 27. Sunday Eve. Last night I was busy with Akronites, and of course after two or so, if not earlier, it was too late for Sunday letter. Rose at 6:00 this a.m. for hike, which was very good. A copperhead was killed, but not by the redoubtable GD. . . . Shall probably go to sleep even though I am supposed to stay awake until about 1:00 to let in RK. No, I didn't marry him nor set up housekeeping with him. But he leaves his civvies here over Sunday and his hiking outfit here the rest of the week. Tonight we went to Dench's at Hohokus.

SEPTEMBER 28. Mellie, love, is short for Melinda, whom Jeanette supplanted, and is the name of my late Mother. . . . Peeved with Al again today and would have given him notice had he said more about the subject. . . . He does little nowadays but read, but when cat[alog] is underway he works well enough and has helped me in giving the shop a desirable reputation as to promptness. But I become very tired of him

---

103. Possibly a reference to Wilfred B. Talman (1904–1986).

104. The Dempsey–Tunney fight, which the Kalems listened to on the radio that evening. It was also on this occasion that Howard Wolf met Lovecraft; he later wrote about Lovecraft in his column, "Variety," for the *Akron Beacon Journal.* The date of the column has not been ascertained, but a clipping of it survives. See *Lovecraft Remembered,* ed. Peter Cannon (Sauk City, WI: Arkham House, 1998), pp. 403–5.

and his ways. . . . Have a card from HPL who enjoyed his trip through his beloved New England and glad to be again in Providence.

SEPTEMBER 30. As to Davis's catalog, much of it was compiled by Arthur Leeds, onetime of the CBS, now of Chicago, and is quite without rhyme or reason. My catalog, since you ask, is better, though I don't see why you should have to ask.

OCTOBER 2. RK and Ed are staying with me this eve. We meet Sam at ferry and proceed to Paterson where Rambling Club gets on the same train. Then ho! For what have you. . . . Am tired and sleepy and have yet to shave and boys are in bed and I fear this is too late anyway as I'm not going to dress again to take this to PO but shall chance it in the corner box. . . . I need 75 plunks by noon Monday and am damned if I know where it's to come from. Oh well, Monday's another day, and Sunday's between.

OCTOBER 3. Sunday Evening. Am tired after a long and rather strenuous hike. No snakes killed today, but about five of us managed to get lost from the crowd. The size of the crowd, and the fact that some are slow and hold up the rest, keep the hikes from being wholly ideal, but it would be very difficult to find the way through such interesting country without the aid of the leaders, who, between them, seem to have traveled over every trail this section offers. . . . I think next summer I shall spend a week or so in the woods—it's twelve years since I have slept in the woods, and then I did so because I was lost and I was, I admit, much frightened. . . . Have just had a pretty chicken dinner at Papa's, wrote several letters, beat two games of solitaire (since Ed wouldn't let me beat him at checkers).

OCTOBER 4, Monday. I enclose the finest hate poem I know, which please return to me, as I must send it back to HPL. I don't know how it was provoked, but if it had been written to me and author was at hand I do believe I could kill. It was published in Amateur paper.[105]

OCTOBER 6, Noon. Aunt Emma and Meg, cousin Clark's wife, came in on the Majestic this a.m., due at 10:00. . . . The kid is rather cute, and though tired is rather good-natured. . . . Must go back now as I said I

105. Perhaps a reference to Lovecraft's poem "Medusa: A Portrait" (*Tryout*, December 1921).

would wait in mezzanine, and they're tired and hungry. Shall try to make their day pleasant: they leave on NY Central at 5:30. . . . LATER. Wearisome, rather, showing relatives around, though I rather enjoyed seeing them. Tomorrow I shall have to take decisive measure to prevent a catastrophe. Seems strange to be in such a hole because of the lack of a few hundred dollars. So it goes.

OCTOBER 7. Sam pays his bet tonight after 10:00 by dinner at Castle Cave. I'm in training till then. . . . D'I tell you name of printers? The Southworth Press, Portland, ME. They specialize in book cats., and it is pleasant to deal with one who understands the various points of bcs. Pleasant meeting here last eve, though I confess I spent much of the time correcting proof. LATER. Sucha turribl accident just had, sweet. Opened a little parcel from gorgeous LD and as I was unwrapping, it tore through paper and board and hit poor Jeanette on her back, breaking it and killing my poor pussy. From which it hit my foot, totally crushing it and, when I raised my foot, and the thing which was in the form of a bun hit the floor, I thought it was about to make its way through this floor and the next into the cellar. But our floor, after much shaking, withstood the great shock. Justa trifle more seriously, Lucia, it was a ver good muffin I had. At first I felt that it would be a sacrilege to eat it, then I thought I would eat just a bit and save the rest, then, when I tasted it and found it really better than I had expected, I discovered I was hungry and went out of training sufficiently to eat it all. . . . And now, love, accept my hearty congratulations upon the startling success of your early attempt at baking.

OCTOBER 8. The two English boys were here last eve: one from Bath and one from Liverpool. Not so educated but both have been in many ports, have seen interesting things, and are not unintelligent,

OCTOBER 9. Pretty Jeanette is sitting on desk watching me type. Shall we have a cat? Or only at the shop? Must work. The English chappies will be here soon to dine with me.

OCTOBER 11. Hiked yesterday in wet and cold and don't know whether strain or rheum caused by wet feet, etc. is cause of soreness in arms and shoulders. But it is, anyway, slight. Hike was pleasant but too short. A marvelous view, however, from Great Tor, which overhangs Haverstraw and the Hudson.

OCTOBER 14. Have much on my mind tonight to do and may stay up all night after I'm back from Belknap's. And now must get ready some stuff with which to stop in at a shop on the way to B's. LATER. Got back from B's about two. On way there stopped at restaurant and left and lost brief case full of books. Books of slight value, but case good.

OCTOBER 15. Tonight I go to RK's, where Sam is to be, and where we have a poetry reading. Sammy is to bring his recently acquired *Home Book of Verse* and *Modern*, truly marvelous anthologies.[106]

OCTOBER 18. Dr. Long told me not to come to him no more for a while, that he has done all possible at present. Anyway, all the visible work is finished. . . . HPL wrote lately. Is doing work for Houdini.[107] Sent me the MS of a story about my 14th St. house. Sam's coming over tomorrow eve. Kalem's here Wed. . . . Changed much since 1924? Yes, dear, I have. . . . Trying to persuade RK to help me write a novel we've in mind, but he's not easily persuaded. It's imaginative. Was going to have a MS translated from a language until then unknown—as the Malayan is now—with a tale of a civilization of which we have no record. I think it would have taken place in NYC. But much of interest of such works is tying up with modern life, and this would do so only in possible resemblances in civilization and in place, and the latter is slight. So, instead, it will begin in the future. Somehow, civilization as we know it, will have disappeared; machines unknown for thousands of years, and when even simple mechanical affairs are discovered from the earlier ages they are preserved in museum. Manhattan's fate has been: it is believed by many that Manhattan is a ledge of rock and that there is a possibility that the weight of buildings at end may someday break it off. I have ledge larger, and it breaks off both because of weight of buildings, but also because of a huge excavation made where ledge hangs on, probably about 60th St., and made for huge building. I'm too lazy and sleepy and ideas are too vague to make it very clear. You may catch the drift. Fills over with sand. Bays fill in. Land rises. Ahead again. Digging

---

106. Two anthologies of poetry edited by Burton Egbert Stevenson (1872–1962), *The Home Book of Verse* (1912) and *The Home Book of Modern Verse* (1925), both of which went through many editions.

107. *The Cancer of Superstition*, a polemic against superstition on which Lovecraft and C. M. Eddy were at work. The project collapsed upon Houdini's sudden death on October 31.

for some reason, whether to bury, agriculture, or what not, a lone man hits peak of Woolworth Bldg. Curious, he digs further, and finds he can enter. Gets light, works way down, into, through subways, thence into other bldgs, etc. Others come. Conjectures as to habits of life among strange people, uses of things, etc. And now, having given you what I hadn't thought to give now, and being sleepy and tired and with mail still to go over, I beg off to finish work and hit the balmy.

OCTOBER 21. Kalem here last evening. McNeil didn't come, and we wondered if the old boy remained hurt because of the way we, and especially Sam, pitched into him last week on prohibition and later on more personal topics. The oldster writes a very passable boy's book and is coming to be recognized, but he thinks, rightfully, that he is not considered as being a literary man. I, I confess, can't, and don't care to, read him.

OCTOBER 22. Sam telephones he really has his book, *The Hermaphrodite*, and I'm very much pleased. . . . Jeanette's condition becomes interestinger and interestinger. Hope they're cute. LATER. Soon I go out with Sam to the delayed dinner at Castle Cave, which now has the added glory of a H[*ermaphrodite*] celebration. I am certain that it's a great poem and I hope it gets the recognition it deserves. And when I say a great poem I mean that there is nothing to compare with it in the last ninety years. I look forward to seeing Jim when he sees the book. He has, if anything, a higher opinion of the poem than I have, and thinks a great deal of Sam.

OCTOBER 23, Saturday. Once upon a time, many, many years ago, in a kingdom by the sea, (or was it a lake?) I knew the significance of all things. Now I am too busy with tiny, inconsequential things to know much at all. Or to be much at all—I the great I, who once was the GK of all time. Time and man passes and is no more. . . . Meanwhile, Degan, our smut hound, who recently we have been pushing into a more literary line, has come in and is talking with Al. . . . And I hope we hike tomorrow over about thirty miles of NJ woods.

OCTOBER 25. Remainder of catalogs came and most are sent out. Am tired. Saw a strange thing in Paterson yesterday—six planes in the air at one time and all visible, but not together nor all going in the same direction, and without anyone in any one, but all controlled by radio.

LATER. I had the water turned for a more thorough rubdown and lay on the bed and read *Nicholas Nickleby* until it was ready. Or almost until it was ready. And slept until RK woke me with his bell ringing. And then it was midnight, and we slept from 1:00 to 7:30 like a pair of logs.

OCTOBER 26. [Written on subway from Staten Island.] Thursday I appear in court on Knopf case against CBS I don't know who's right, but I hope I win. Amn't having a lawyer. . . . Sam is coming to eat with me. Went to two Salvation Army stores and one junk shop. Bought four books. Inclusive cost, with fares, 80¢. Selling price about $16.00. . . . When I go to Kalem you may read *Quo Vadis*.[108] Pret story about Lygia. Glad you're tired of work. . . . As to finances—gimme time.

OCTOBER 27. Monday. Sunday evening really is my best chance of being alone, and that's not always easy. If I go to NJ I'm expected to stay later with Jim or Ernie Dench. Last Sunday I should have had to go to Jim's new place had I been less wet. . . . Please be gracious—I always remember you as being so. Go to Belknap's for Kalem tonight.

OCTOBER 28. Went to court this a.m., but allowed case to be postponed for a month. . . . Yesterday at about 4:00 p.m. Jeanette presented me with four darling kittens. Belknap wants one and Al wants to take one to his home. J is so proud of them, so careful, and lies and purrs so contentedly, that it really is fun to watch them. . . . Kalem was pleasant, but it really isn't so good with James absent, and I don't care so much for one of our new visitors, one Talman, who is mostly interested in genealogy.

OCTOBER 30. Havva copy 'Erster Stew.' Want? . . . Knopf case postponed. Somehow doubt my chances of winning. . . . Sam's H[ermaphrodite] printed by printer of Belknap's book. Shall send to you soonly. . . . Al stands here like what you can guess, wanting the machine. Poor boy, guess I'll do a line or two in ink. . . . Going Monday Newark, Jersey City too, maybe, as I should like to see exhibit of American Printers' Association. BR. Kelmscott, Doves, etc., and Jenson, Baskerville, Caxton, and other famous presses and printers.

NOVEMBER 6. Thursday. Tomorrow I intend buying some hiking tops and suitable shoes for hiking this winter. I enjoy going too much to care

---

108. *Quo Vadis* (1896), an historical novel about Jesus Christ by Henryk Sienkiewicz (1846–1916).

to be deterred by the weather, but I don't care to be killed by it either. I can easily bring to mind pleasanter methods of committing suicide. NOVEMBER 9. Hope to get off that there letter ere long. Thought to do it last night but was too tired and sleepy even to get to bed. Slept in robe as I came from bath with windows closed and all lights on.

NOVEMBER 10, Monday. Hiked pleasurably yesterday, and am v tired. Little sleep Fri and Sat nights and to bed this a.m. at 3:00 and awakened at 8:30 by the customer who's now looking at art and curiosa. Wore new outfit yesterday and found it pleasant to be in another sort of costume for a day. LATER. Kalem Night here. Boys are due soonly and I've still much to do. Am in part of a curious mix-up regarding a book about which I shall tell you soon. Perhaps tomorrow shall have a denouement.

NOVEMBER 11. "Cabinet of Dr. Caligari"[109] is showing again but I fear I can't get over for it. Tomorrow night shall go to Civic Theatre's "Three Sisters" by Chekhov, with Eva LeGallienne starring,[110] where I am to be taken back stage after the show and meet Eva. . . . Am much enjoying Trollope. Kalem here last night, and lost two games of checkers to McNeil and won one. Playing with bum players has made me careless, but the one I won was the last and I think I can do it again. . . . Thanksgiving, did I tell you? Ernie Dench, Sam, and certain other bachelor ramblers (Dench isn't a bachelor but his wife's leaving him to visit her family in Washington) will hike, and then dine at The Copper Kettle, a pleasant French Inn. I go too. Too bad you aren't. Then we could finish at Ernie's and you could prove your ability by cooking for the gang.

NOVEMBER 12. Up late today. Worked and then read rather late last eve. after going to "Caligari" with Al. Very fine. I saw it first about four years ago in C, and saw it then about five times. It holds up well.

NOVEMBER 13. Rather late Saturday. Saw Chekhov's "Three Sisters" which was Russian in the worst sense, dull, long, depressing, everyone

---

109. *Das Cabinet des Dr. Caligari* (Germany, 1920), directed by Robert Wiene; starring Werner Krauss, Conrad Veidt, and Friedrich Faher.
110. *Three Sisters,* a four-act play by Anton Chekhov, was playing at the Civic Repertory Theatre. British actress Eva Le Gallienne played a minor character.

continually sighing and moaning, "I'm tired, oh how tired I am." So were we all. Went back stage but didn't meet Eva. Went with friend to his apartment but got home fairly early. . . . L, my own, do you smile at the idea of my rising Sundays at 6:30? I do, nevertheless. I look forward to the hike with much anticipation. Would you come with? Shall?

NOVEMBER 14. Plan a nice little campaign that will or should make me or break me or send me to Leavenworth. Little danger of the former and much of the latter. Or vice versa. Shall tell you about it some day.

NOVEMBER 18. Righto, did buy some lemon and sugar and put it in tea this eve for RK, Al, and me. . . . Am still with good old Trollope—now at *Dr. Thorne*,[111] which I think I shall like.

NOVEMBER 19. S and A and I have been having fun watching our three kittens. So cunning! . . . Last night a woman died on the top floor from gas. Clues point both to accident and to suicide. And Charlie, the spaniel, saw her carried out and he cried and said he had been all around the world and that he never saw such a goddam country and went out to get drunk and so quiet his nerves. I hope he doesn't tear down the house when he returns.

NOVEMBER 20 Sam and I plan to go to Providence end of the second week [of next year]. Am giving Al two weeks' notice. Shall be in Cleveland for Christmas and New Year's, but amn't certain of aught other.

NOVEMBER 22. Sunday's hike had promised to be too easy for words, though part of it was very pretty—up a steep hill beside a rapid little stream with many falls. But our leader, Mr. Adam, is very good, and added to it and made it several miles longer and more interesting.

NOVEMBER 24. Just discovered further details about the woman upstairs. She looked about seventy but was only forty-three, used dope, and died not from gas but from the fumes from the little gas stove which she kept going while she was there behind her locked door, and so probably was not a suicide. . . . At Thanksgiving affair will be Mr. and Mrs. Adam of Paterson, Jim, Sam, RK, about six Paterson Ramblers, and G. We made a new trail, which was to have been called The

---

111. *Doctor Thorne* (1858), a novel by Anthony Trollope.

Paterson Ramblers' Trail, but it is to be named after an elderly member who died in the spring but whose name I forget. I expect to enjoy it.

NOVEMBER 27, Saturday. Hike with the Paterson Ramblers. I expect to be made a member at the next meeting. . . . Had a very pleasant day Thanksgiving. We, about twelve in number, had a beau hike from Midvale over a couple of mountains including the Windflower or something similar on which there is a fire tower, which we climbed. Then on to the Copper Kettle, a pleasant little inn, where we had a marvelous meal. I thought the preparation of the vegetables showed especial art: the cauliflower baked whole, the spinach green and tender without being cooked to goo. And all of us so hungry we could have made a meal from bread! . . . Sam is to come over to relieve me so that I can go out to eat. Yesterday, after a day in the shop, I ate a whole sea bass at Pop's. Um-m-m! Am still enjoying *Dr. Thorne*. In some moods I prefer Trollope to Dickens. But there is room for both.

NOVEMBER 30. Usually there are several girls with the gang. We ate only at the Copper Kettle. . . . Al came in from hospital [after a hernia operation] last evening and I finally gave him the gate and paid him off. I'm glad it's done. Finished *Dr. Thorne* and now want another Trollope, *Barchester*. . . . Al just came in: he has, thank goodness, given me the keys. I imagine he wants to see the English boys who promised us some Scotch and some rum. Here's hoping.

DECEMBER 2. Kalem here last evening. And I have a bit of time because I rose at 6:00 with Jim, who stayed with me overnight. But have used up most of it in cleaning up the dump. So popular I'm becoming! Have had the honor of turning down bids for three parties in as many days. Should have accepted one for New Years' Eve as it isn't a b&g affair, but a P[aterson] R[amblers'] C[lub] one. Then gang intends to hike New Year's and dine and dance. . . . But if I amn't dead broke and have someone to keep shop shall be in C with you.

DECEMBER 4, Saturday. Al is looking for another job, hanging around. Ed will work for me when he's out of the army. Thinks he can make it by Christmas. Guess Sam and I won't go to Providence for a bit. I'm too busy. . . . Ed is here and when I have finished this and one other letter and have prepared and mailed mail I shall beat him in a game or two of checkers and then go to bed and read awhile. Although I have not gone in for a very social life here, I have, within the past week, turned down invitations to three parties. Tonight, at Denches, the evening of the 18th at a girl Rambler's in Newark, and New Year's Eve at Elsa's in Paterson. Elsa is the Secretary of the Ramblers, and although, as RK has said, it is hard to imagine any man having a sentimental feeling for her, she is rather fun and I should rather, if I were going to any, go to hers. She takes more kidding than any other member for her fear of insects and snakes and salamanders, etc., and for her not uncommon foot-wettings when we cross water on stones or insecure bridges.

DECEMBER 5, Sunday. And there has been worry, too, and the growing realization that I must have the place elsewhere than at 365, someplace where there will be a transient trade, and the unpleasant not unnatural dislike of confessing to you that CBS is in such condition and that it would be foolhardy to marry when I at least had planned, and we both so much desired. Now that I have told it to you it will bother me less. . . . I have given Ed the money to buy out of the Army, and he thinks he will be free the first of Christmas week. That will give me several days to get him started before I leave. . . . I amn't hiking today. Haven't, in fact, been out of the house. Ed and I rose about ten and have scrubbed the floors and picked up in general and Ed is washing the accumulated dishes while I write. I intend putting on my boots and breeches when I go out for dinner—we plan to go to Batchelder's. . . . Have I told you that three of the kittens have died and that only one remains? She, however, is quite healthy, or rather is shaking off the cold that killed the others, and is quite active and playful.

DECEMBER 11. More disagreeable persons were here today than even Howard ever imagined to be here. Did I tell you about the surprise planned for Belknap? Well, I shall on the 24th or 25th or thereabouts.

[Kirk spent Christmas 1926 in Cleveland with Lucile Dvorak.]

1927

JANUARY 8. Read *Weird Tales* and *L. Mercury*[112] until midnight in smoker and smoked another pipe in birth over *L.M.* Then slept somewhat fitfully for a while, then more soundly. Didn't ask to be wakened as we were due [in New York] at 7:55 and I felt sure porter would awaken in time. . . . Taxied down and have since been hard at work. Place not in such a terrible mess as I had feared. This afternoon looked at stores and found only one at all suitable—58 W. 8th St., South side, for which they ask $200 per month, and for which I am advised to offer $100 and go as high as $125, but no higher. . . . Find, upon getting back, that I must have had a great time in C. Friends tell me I am thinner and I know I am, perhaps, tireder than when I left. Reckon 'twas the excitement of your companionship made me feel wonderful in C.

JANUARY 10, Sunday. Didn't hike today. Instead, slept till noon, bathed and showered and dined at Village Moon with Sam and Ed. Heard some things about Al that so incensed me that I determined to turn him out if ever he comes here.

JANUARY 12, Tuesday Evening. Nothing very exciting. Talked with store agent yesterday, offered $110 as against $200. Now must wait. Daren't acknowledge my hurry for fear he will hold out for full amount, which I shall not pay.

JANUARY 15. Regret to have to report that the storeowner claims he can get $200 for his store. Has a place next door that will be ready March 1 at $125, but it's only eight feet wide, two feet off for shelving on each side leaves only six feet, ant that, I fear, is impossible. Going over ground again this p.m. Another agent is trying to sell me on 4th St., but I think it's not so good. . . . Am coming on a bit with chess, though I don't understand all points in play as yet. One reason for wanting to hike tomorrow is that I want to ask James some questions. . . . Gave Sam his birthday dinner last evening at the Moon and we had cocktails before dinner, but no wine. Then went to 66 Fifth Ave and saw "All for a Woman," and "The Last Laugh."[113] . . . I think I

---

112. The *London Mercury*, a leading British literary magazine of the day.
113. *All for a Woman* (First National, 1921), directed by Dmitri Buchowetzki; starring Emil Jannings, Werner Krauss, and Robert Sholz.

ought to warn you that I am so used to having many things done for me that I may make a poor sort of husband. I told you once about Geo Davies—how he let his mother do everything for him—even to letting out the water after his bath. I can do that for myself, but I fear Ed is carrying on the Spoilation. Perhaps I should take a course in husbandry. Will you get out of bed—close the windows, start a fire and breakfast—before you waken me? I wonder. . . . Am ordering you your cookbook. . . . There's a lovely snow falling. Haven't been out—Eddy says it's very cold.

JANUARY 20. Kalem last eve at Belknap's. Very fine. Jim stayed with me and this a.m. Bill Rigby, now of Akron came in. He's now out but will be in for lunch, after which I go to Brooklyn to see some books. Bill goes to Providence, his hometown, Saturday. Should like to go with, but promised to go to Ramblers' Yearly Banquet Saturday eve, and shall stay overnight with Jim and hike Sunday. . . . Didn't tell you of Sunday hike, did I? About four inches of very soft, light snow covered ice, and the boys say it was the slipperiest day they have hiked. At one time on a slope six persons were down at one time. Near the top of a bluff where the ice sloped over the edge, Van Westrom, a fat Dutchman, fell, fell again trying to rise, then started to crawl away on his hands and knees. Hands bare, too, and bitterly cold—six degrees until one p.m. But we had a jolly good time. . . . James showed us more of checkers last eve, and wiped me quite off the board. If I know sufficient of the game by March 5, I shall try to teach it you. Am also to try to teach Sam and RK, but I fear neither will take sufficient interest to ever make me a decent game. Ed I can beat easily, though not so neatly as Jim did me. I told Jim I shall never hope to beat him, but I do look forward to being able to make him an interesting game. . . . That will have to do for gossip. I shall answer your letters when poss. I may take the 8th St. joint—I can't continue to lose money here, and I don't so much like advertising and sending out cats from here just before I move. I have the choice of only the two stores—the only others are either above three hundred, or are yet to be made over and the rental fixed.

The Last Laugh (UFA, 1925), directed by F. W. Murnau; starring Emil Jannings, Mary Delschaft, and Kurt Hiller.

JANUARY 24. Am at the Paterson Ramblers' Club Banquet and have been much bored. Not so sorry I came; somehow it strikes me it's good for what soul I have. They're having a piano solo upstairs—I am in lobby with very good jazz in the next room. . . . Have just been called a stick because I refused to dance, so there you are. . . . But I am shown further what I have long believed: these are pleasant persons to be with on hikes, but I wasn't cut out for their indoor affairs. . . . Monday morning I meet my agent and property owner and may arrange about lease. Can get for three years at $100 and presume it's as well as I can do on short notice. . . . I stay with Jim tonight and hike tomorrow. . . . Probably shall go to "Pirates"[114] Tuesday evening. Doncha envy me?

JANUARY 26. Had a good time yesterday. It rained, and was cold, so that our jackets were stiff with ice, and my head was caked with it. We didn't, though, hike all day, but stopped at a cabin owned by a fellow Rambler where them as danced, danced, and I read and smoked and played checkers. . . . Saturday night after my note I went upstairs and sat and talked with Miss Everett, a rather masculine maid of about thirty-five, who is a friend of Jim's. Left at 1:30, and went to Jim's apartment, where he showed me his books and minerals and where I lost a game of chess. In the morning I checked my bag with my civvies and my slicker, and when RK and I returned from Denches I jumped off the train and got them, and just managed to get back on. But poor RK didn't see me get on, and he stepped off, and so had to wait an hour for the next. . . . In a few minutes I go over to agent and shall probably sign up, or at least give a deposit, on 58 W. 8th Street.

JANUARY 29, Saturday. Received lease today. Monday I shall confer with lawyer and if it is okay shall sign it. Place to be ready by March 15. Means fast work for them if it is done. . . . Expect to hike tomorrow. Hope the weather will not be unpleasant. . . . Tonight I dine with the English chaps. They brought me some rum which I shall save for us and rum punches. LATER. Amn't going without lunch or Kalem—but am writing while RK and Stanley Huckle are here—only both aren't—since we have just returned from seeing Stanley to his ship, the Minnewaska. Right now RK is talking DeQuincey to me voraciously. Which keeps me

---

114. Gilbert and Sullivan's *The Pirates of Penzance* (1879) was playing at the Plymouth Theatre in December 1926.

from thinking very deeply. . . . Have had a curious chap, an anarchist, around, but guess I have finally gotten rid of him. His wife or woman is coming to NY and is expected to have a child while here. The CC looked at Bill Rigby while saying, "You know, I'm so anxious to have a child." Bill, quite serious, replied, "Mr. Kraemer, I can't bear children."

FEBRUARY 2, Wednesday. Haven't been hearing from Al. And please don't ask me to think of things unpleasant to me. Not now. . . . Shall discuss wearing of hat in C[leveland]. Old Stone OK if we must go to church. Shall think over list for announcements and invitations and let you know soon. You can let them go ahead for March 5, and let them know quantity later. I shall not have a ver large list—only a few friends. . . . Sam would much like a note of appreciation from you— he's asked me ten times whether you liked it [*The Hermaphrodite*]—78 Columbia Heights, Brooklyn. . . . Signed lease, check, etc. today, possession Feb. 15. They certainly show speed and promise of finishing work in time. Upstairs are one and two room apartments—$65 and up—mostly latter. Village rents higher than many decent parts of city. . . . D'I tell you that Sunday I sprained my leg and now must carry a cane. May I bring it to C? The cane, I mean.

FEBRUARY 3. Have been hard at work all day and now it's almost ten o'clock and I haven't looked at mail nor written checks for letters and bills and water is on stove for tea and Eddie's girl called to visit and left and I am ready for bed. . . . Knee is somewhat better—have hopes of being able to hike next Sunday. Like having to carry a stick, but dislike the occasional twinges, and they make me feel weak in tummy. Be good, Lucy mine. And don't forget to bring your hiking togs to NYC.

FEBRUARY 5. Not certain whether I can hike tomorrow, as knee is still swollen and sore and stiff. Shall decide this evening. Too, have much work to do.

FEBRUARY 8. Today have been busy with movers, etc. Sam just came over and he and RK and I are going out to eat as soon as I finish this. Am hungry too. Rose at 8:30 and couldn't have breakfast till noon, and even then was disturbed. Am anxious to get the place underway. . . . Am tired; got to bed late last night. Dined at Ed's girlfriend's apartment and stayed there till after two. The girl is mentally ill—two friends have committed suicide lately, and the husband of her best girlfriend died a few days ago by blood poisoning from a razorblade. She is unable to sleep and wanted company.

FEBRUARY 10. Eight o'clock and am going over to 66th theatre with Ed. Have been busy all day with printers, sign-makers, etc. Getting a place ready certainly means a lot of work. Half believe we will put up shelving ourselves, as the carpenters all want over two-hundred plunks and there is nothing much we can do while it is being done. So I doubt I shall hike Sunday. After the 15th my only address is: 58 West Eighth Street. Telephone: Spring 6866.

FEBRUARY 16. [Cornish Arms Hotel, 311–323 W. 23rd St.] Yesterday finally got moved—58 West 8th Street. No grave mishaps, though various delays. Much work. Luckily have heat and electricity, but not water nor phone. . . . Played 2 games checkers with RK last night and didn't get to bed till 2:30. Up at 8:00, but almost went to sleep in tub. . . . Ed and I are staying at the hotel for the present.

FEBRUARY 20. Went to sleep immediately after calling you last night, and slept till one this p.m. and have fooled around with toilet, etc. until three. Ed just woke up and when he has come down and breakfasted we shall go and work as late as necessary to finish up what can at present be done. . . . I shall not be able to spare much time away from business so soon after opening, dear Lu, and we shall have to be satisfied with Sat. and Sun. there [in Cleveland]. Probably we had best make all preparations Sat. and be married Sunday.

FEBRUARY 23. Hallelujah! Glory be onto the lord god on high! We've a toilet! And it works. Also we have a telephone: Spring 6866. . . . As to whether to leave C Sat. or Sun. . . . it seems to me it should depend upon whether the supper is to be a late or an early affair, and upon whether or not you prefer to be with family or friends for the one day of married life you might spend in C for a time.

FEBRUARY 25. English boys came in today and I took them out to dinner and bought some wine. I, too, drank. Was glad to have some good booze, as I want to bring some to Cleveland and to have some for us. Took them to shop in cab and then came to hotel. And now must go up to bed. I am still trying to catch up on sleep lost last week. Ed figures that we had 21 hours' sleep during the past seven days.

FEBRUARY 26, Saturday Noon. Got in at one last night and beat Ed in a game of chess and then was too tired and sleepy to bathe. Whether I have to be up late tonight depends on whether I decide to hike tomorrow. Shall let you know later.

FEBRUARY 28. English boys have just left. They sail tomorrow. They brought me some beau Scotch which I am saving for us. . . . RK is looking at a paper. He just lost two games of chess and thinks he may get revenge in another. But I doubt he will. . . . Shall go now and play another game.

MARCH 1. Shall want announcements sent to Kalemites and some Ramblers but heat, damn it, is off, and it's too cold here to write or think. . . . Should like to make Boston ere so very long. When we are a bit settled and I can leave Ed with some safety we'll run up for a day. Perhaps HPL will make the town for the day. . . . If I were less cold I should feel more like writing. Ed is off for the evening and RK is here. Think I shall leave him and go across the street for hot coffee.

MARCH 2. Played two games of chess with RK and had so little interest in the first that I lost badly. Then had to play another for revenge. . . . Now shall get me some breakfast and hurry down to the shop. Feel as fit as a fiddle. But hungry! . . . I dreamt this a.m. that I murdered Frank Belknap Long's mother. Rather cleverly done, I think. Shall tell you of it in a few days.

MARCH 3. You're quite right. 'Twould never do to postpone again. Shop will go, even though not with a rush, and we'll soon be quite in shape. In meantime we shall have to be careful. I am happy that you feel about it as I do.

MARCH 4. Thank you for all the pretty things. I'll keep them and give them to my wife. Do you want to stay at Cornish Arms till we get an apartment? If so, I shall leave my trunks there?

[On March 5, 1927, George Kirk and Lucile Dvorak were married at Old Stone Church in Cleveland. No Kalem members attended the ceremony.—M. K. H.]

Writings by the Kalems

George Kirk ♦ Rheinhart Kleiner

George Kirk on His Wedding Day

GEORGE KIRK

(1898–1962)

George Kirk left Cleveland in August 1924 to establish himself as a book-seller in New York. At twenty-five, tall, slim, and with an abundance of dark hair, Kirk was already a relatively sophisticated man. He left high school after his junior year, was orphaned at nineteen, and at twenty-one married Harriet Louise Brooks. They moved to Berkeley, California, where Kirk worked for bookseller Paul Elder and became friends with Clark Ashton Smith.

But by August 1922, when—through their mutual friend Sam Loveman—Lovecraft met Kirk, he lived alone with his cat, Hodge. What happened to the marriage? We do not know. That same fall, Kirk published *Twenty-one Letters of Ambrose Bierce*, a slim, handsome volume of 1000 copies.

In December 1923 George Kirk and Lucile Dvorak became engaged. She set him three criteria before they could marry: erase his debts, prove that he could support them both, and have significant dental work completed.

Kirk, used to living on his own, was resourceful and self-sufficient. The only person he knew in New York was Lovecraft, whom he contacted immediately. Within a few days, Lovecraft introduced him to Rheinhart Kleiner, Arthur Leeds, James Morton, Everett McNeil, and Frank Belknap Long. Soon Kirk entertained them all in his 106th St. rooms, offering coffee and crumb cake, thus beginning his association with "the gang," which—except for Loveman—was to become the Kalem Club.

Kirk was impressed by these men, their erudition, stimulating lively talk, enthusiasms, and artistic sensibilities. He praised Lovecraft and Morton most highly. Kirk and Lovecraft soon began their all-night walks, sometimes joined by others of the gang.

From January until May 1925, Kirk lived directly above Lovecraft at 169 Clinton Street, in Brooklyn. During those months, Kirk, Lovecraft, Kleiner, and Loveman saw each other almost daily. This time marked a special bonding among the four, including Sunday afternoon promenades on Clinton Street.

In a letter dated January 6, 1925, Kirk describes the decision to give "the gang" an official name: "Because all of the last names of the permanent members of our club begin with 'K,' 'L,' or 'M,' we plan to call it the Kalem Klybb." As the months passed, although Kirk wavered between delight and boredom with these male friendships, he never tired of Lovecraft.

Kirk granted many favors to the Kalems. He helped Loveman move, paid them to help with his book catalogues, let friends stay with him whenever they wished, and hired Arthur Leeds for a while. When that didn't work out, Kirk helped Leeds find further employment. Perhaps Kleiner in "After a Decade and the Kalem Club" best describes Kirk at this time:

George's ability and perseverance in brewing coffee, his liberality with buns and sandwiches, left nothing to be desired. Nor need it cause wonder if certain individuals became so attached to proprietor and shop as to appear every evening, often with the expectation—which was never disappointed—of sleeping there. A host, whose bed in the rear room could accommodate five guests, if they did not toss too much, was never at a loss when visitors declined to go home.

After working as a book scout for some months, and helping Martin and Sarah Kamin, Kirk established the Chelsea Book Shop at 617 West 15th Street. Within a few months he moved to 317 West 14th Street (where Lovecraft's "Cool Air" is set), and finally settled at 58 W. 8th Street. At both the 15th and 14th Street locations, Kirk had two rooms, with the shop in front and his living quarters in the rear. When he and Lucile were married, in 1927— incidentally, with none of Kirk's criteria met—they lived above the 8th Street store

These Kalem years were among the happiest of my father's life. Never again would he experience such freedom from cares, such erudite conversation, or have such fascinating male friends. He remained a genial, generous host, a lover of books and cats, and always ready to walk or talk all night.

After the Chelsea Book Shop closed in 1939, George sold books from home and took factory jobs. He received his high school diploma in 1959. Lucile, as an editor at Parents Magazine, supported the family. George, Lucile, and their two daughters moved to Pelham, New York, in 1945. Kirk lived there until his death from colon cancer, at sixty-three. Lucile lived on until 1994.

Although Kirk had the distinction of being the only non-writer among the Kalems, he left two short manuscripts, "Book Collecting" and "An Enchanted Evening," which describes an evening at the Lovecraft's. Unfortunately, only one page of the latter essay is extant. The Kalem Letters are Kirk's most important writing.

Book Collecting: The Prince of Hobbies

So far back as antiquity the collecting of books and manuscripts perpetuated. Along the fertile and living Nile grew the broad leaves of the papyrus. A slight, though probably tedious, operation and the leaves that had swayed to and fro so softly in the mild Egyptian wind became flat sheets. Still earlier, slim, fire-baked bricks or tablets perpetuated the written or spoken word. In after-years whole libraries were amassed. Alexandria, the greatest cradle of learning in the marvelous history of civilization, had such a one. The intellectual world lay at her feet. Slave and satrap and emperor, the sacrifice of a lifetime became the consummation of an epoch. Here were harbored the manuscripts of Aeschylus, Sophocles, Herodotus, lost mimes, lost plays, lost poems, the work of burning Sappho in its entirety—"first the singer of Lesbos and then the others"—a cycle of love, learning and beauty, now hopelessly and irretrievably lost.

In early A.D. came chaos and intellectual darkness. Libraries, so carefully the depositories of their precious scripts, were despoiled, marble fanes and columns ravaged, busts of memorable celebrities hacked and hewed with the malignity of a venom exceeding anything else known. Then fell the night.

Scholars quibbled pretentiously over the unknowable. Art was dead, inspiration unknown. During the Renaissance came the awakening. In the monasteries were collected a few of the remaining manuscripts. Printing became a permanent and co-operative fact. Beautiful handmade paper with the texture of parchment or vellum was manufactured to accommodate the newly-discovered art. The long and glorious era of print had set in. Men collected books for the love of books. It was, indeed, the Prince of Hobbies!

Early in the nineteenth century, with Thomas Frognall Dibdin, the Hobby became curiously associated with the value of a book as a rare book—in other words, a monetary value had been set on the volume or manuscript, which fluctuated as the demand increased or halted. In the forties and sixties began the Bohn and Quaritches. It was observed that certain of the larger collectors were willing, either personally or through their agents, to pay any conceivable price for the object of their acquisition. A certain Boccaccio, for instance, ran up to thousands of pounds. The frenzy for volumes printed in pure vellum increased. In the eighties, the value of many books seemed to advance in rarity with the increasing prestige of their author—Keats, Shelley, or the First Folio of Shakespeare, which was practically priceless. Beauty was worshipped at the shrine of William Blake—and paid for accordingly. Since the day of the tremendous Upcott collection, autograph manuscripts had been mainly associated with books. Here, also, there seemed no limit to the collector's activities.

The eighteen-nineties was a second Renaissance. Presses for the printing of books, lovelier than anything since the inauguration of type, were established. With the passing of a very few years, these items increased in startling rapidity from the set, original price. The Kelmscott Chaucer, to cite only one memorable instance, achieved from a comparatively moderate few pounds at the time of publication, the present value of nearly a thousand dollars. Dickens, Thackeray, Moore, Masefield, Swinburne, Borrow, Symonds, Synge, Dowson, and Wilde were sought for and the highest prices paid. In a certain sense, the industry had become stabilized. There could be no step backward. Hand in hand with the love for art, learning, and literature, proceeded the growing interest in collecting.

More recently, specialization has set in. Some collect Shakespeare, the Elizabethans, Junius, Folklore, Chess, or Erotica. The hoarding of Americana has become tremendous. Over in England and on the Continent, catalogues with such items are regularly priced and issued for the consumption of their American patrons. Extremely early Americana is, as it has always been, a matter of great commercial value. The Virginia pamphleteers and their scarce output still show up, amazingly. Books on pioneering and the Indians are made solely the crux of entire libraries.

Early American poetry, with the exception of Poe, Whitman, or the delectable Thomas Holley Chivers, retains the normal status of fifteen years ago—not much more. It is to their poetic brethren in England that we turn for increased value and rarities. The prose fiction writers here: Bierce, Saltus, Cabell, and Herman Melville, hold their heads high.

To the present writer, it would scarcely be surprising if a definite literary status were not pre-determined by the rising demand for an author's various first editions. Such an assumption would, at least, have as a basis the immortal and world-old law of supply and demand, with the added consistency of genuine literary or artistic worth. And the possibilities have grown infinite. The book or autograph of a few pence to-day transforms itself into as many pounds tomorrow. Discoveries are still everywhere possible. The Prince of Hobbies—yes, by all means!

Silhouette of Rheinhart Kleiner, made at Coney Island.

RHEINHART KLEINER
(1892–1949)

In 1924, Rheinhart Kleiner, at thirty-two, lived alone at 116 Harman Street, in the Bushwick section of Brooklyn—where he had been born and raised—and worked as a shipping clerk at Fairbanks Scales Company, in lower Manhattan. Until his twenty-first birthday Kleiner had taken the name of his stepfather, Kaufmann.

Kleiner and Lovecraft, both active in amateur journalism, first corresponded in 1915. Three years later, then president of the United Amateur Press Association, Kleiner met Lovecraft, thus beginning a long and important friendship. In 1919, Kleiner wrote the first critical article on Lovecraft, which appeared in the *United Amateur.* Two years later, at an amateur press conference in Boston, Kleiner had the dubious honor of introducing Sonia Greene to Lovecraft, an introduction that eventuated in their marriage almost three years later, short-lived and unfortunate as it was.

In New York, prior to 1924, Kleiner sometimes joined James Morton in his weekly visits to Everett McNeil. These men formed the core of the Kalem Club.

Of the Kalems—with the possible exception of George Kirk—Kleiner took himself the least seriously. As an easy, light versifier and a fine calligrapher, he seemed content to write humorous, charming poems and felt no need for wide recognition. Even without driving ambition, Kleiner brought enthusiasm to all he did. He was an avid bibliophile, anxious to learn more; a frequent all-night walker with Kirk and Lovecraft, and a faithful participant in the Paterson Sunday hikes, organized by James Morton. On one such hike in 1925, Kleiner was struck by a car and suffered painful albeit temporary injuries. In 1929 he became editor of the *Rambler,* the official organ of the Paterson Ramblers' Club.

The Kalems were fond of Kleiner, enjoyed his humor and lighthearted spirit, and found him kindly. Kleiner comes across as a generous, cosmopolitan, gracious, somewhat courtly man. We cannot help but like him. When he lost his job at Fairbanks Scales, Kirk employed him briefly and helped him find other employment.

Tall, slim, with dark, curly hair and a wide smile, Kleiner's dress was, in Lovecraft's words, "frankly impossible." Perhaps he could not afford better. Less constrained, more sensuous and experimental in his personal habits than some, Kleiner used snuff liberally. He loved women, wine (especially muscatel), music, and crumb cake.

He also loved Brooklyn and praised it in verse. He most treasured the months Lovecraft, Kirk, and Loveman lived in Brooklyn also, and saw each other almost daily. Kleiner commemorated this time both in his poem, "The Four of Us," and in his essay, "Bards and Bibliophiles" (see Appendix). He wrote fondly about the Kalem Club in the essay, "After a Decade and the Kalem Club" (see Appendix again). Obviously, the Kalem years were a happy and fulfilling time for him.

What became of Rheinhart Kleiner? At fifty-four, in 1946, he married Ruth Pietchman, another amateur journalist. Rheinhart and Ruth moved to Chester, N.J., where they called their property Kleiner's Hollow, and built a garage there meant to house Kleiner's print shop. It seems he later became justice of the peace, probably in Chester. In 1949 Kleiner died prematurely—as did Lovecraft and Kirk—as the result of a stroke, at age fifty-seven.

A Glee
(For a company of smokers)

My pipe is discolored and cracked & strong,
  With nary a friend but me,
And somehow I happen to have it along
  Wherever I chance to be!
But folks will complain when I light it—what's
  wrong?
They look for the exit and flee!
They look for the exit and flee, and flee.
  And that is the end of my song!

At Providence in 1918

I left my own Manhattan, seeking pleasure,
 And having journeyed hence
A hundred miles, I found it in full measure
 In teeming Providence!

I sought her hidden ways and quaint old places
 That nestled ev'rywhere,
And found that Time had left benignant traces
 On alley, street, and square!

I thought of one for whom these ways had beauty
 And splendour all their own:
My friend, whose path of pleasure and of duty
 These scenes had only known.

And over all the cloud of war hung drearly;
 The summons to the strife
Was soon to come; and one whom I held dearly
 Was near the close of life!

But with unclouded brow and heart uplifted,
 All unaware, among
These scenes and sights, by golden summer gifted,
 I mov'd—for I was young.

Epistle to Mr. and Mrs. Lovecraft

(Imitated from Mr. Pope)

My friends, though Phoebus held the lyre,
And play'd with true, celestial fire,
While, close around, the Heav'nly Nine,
Applauded ev'ry strain divine,—
Yet could not he, whom Loves imbue,
Contrive a fitting song for you!

Alone, did each of you possess
More Worth than Bard might well express;

Together, your Desert is such,
That none could sound your Praise too much!
No Panegyric, then, shall be
The Motive of these lines from me!

But I shall hope that wedded years
May strengthen all that now endears;
That Venus, with as kind an air,
May guard your Love from Doubt and Care;
And Hymen ever linger nigh
To trim the Torch still burning high!

May truth and beauty walk beside,
To warn, to counsel, and to guide;
And Faith and Hope, as well, to keep
Your footsteps t'ward the tow'ring steep,
Upon whose Summit rests the Crown
Of endless Honour and Renown!

The Four of Us (Rondeau)

The four of us forsake the street
For this aloof and calm retreat,
And rest us from the cares of day
That fly, while fresher fancies play
Around us where the hours are fleet!

How sad that Time's unwearied feet
Should hurry most when Life is sweet
And we have much to do and say,
            The four of us!

How often, brothers, shall we meet
With hearts that still serenely beat?
How many years are ours to stay
With minds as cloudless and as gay?
May days to come but kindly greet
            The four of us!

Brooklyn, My Brooklyn

For George Kirk, October 8, 1925

Though other scenes may lure me far
From happiness and home,
No peace would they procure me, far
Away across the foam.
To Brooklyn should I turn again
From fairest towns and shires
And all my bosom burn again
To know her streets and spires!

I'd turn from Glory's very house—
And were it sacrilege—
To see the Fulton Ferry house,
Beside the Brooklyn Bridge:
To hear the passing roar above
Of elevated trains,
That thrill me as they soar above
Unnumbered marts and fanes.

I'd miss the books so pleasingly
Displayed on Fulton Street:
The other wares that teasingly
Remind of things to eat.
I'd weary for that restful place
Where benches, warm and wide,
In Montague's most zestful place,
Look down upon the tide.

'Tis there when Spring were flowering
I'd yearn to watch the bay,
And old Manhattan towering
Beyond the river's play;
'Tis there I'd light my pipe at eve
And watch the sun go down,
For random thoughts are ripe at eve,
When dusk is on the town.
Oh, Brooklyn offers graciously

The gifts she has to give:
Her sons who speak veraciously,
Say, "Here's the place to live!"
When Fate, no longer lenient,
Gives cause to sink and sigh,
There's hardly so convenient
A place in which to die!

Columbia Heights, Brooklyn

For George Kirk, October 6, 1925

Old houses nestling quaintly in old streets!
How many years since faded bricks were bright,
Or crumbling brownstone was a stately sight,
Designed for fashion's realms or wealth's retreats!
The tall apartment claims its ancient seats
Today, and hides the hanging stars at night;
The taxi whirls along too fast for sight
Where rattling wheel of coach no more competes.

Only the river and the bay are still
Unchanged and changeless through the drift of years;
Only the sunsets keep an old-time glow!
And like our hearts that once have known the thrill
Of loves within, and mingled hopes and fears,
These houses die with grief for years that go!

[Prisky]

Frisky, darling, little Prisky,
        Snooping 'neath my elbow chair,
Poke your head out while I stroke your
        Sleekly kept and shining hair!

Purring with the rapture stirring
        In your coy and wistful heart,
Shyly bending with a wily
        Care for sounds that make your start.

Surely you are held securely
    As a feline heart could wish!
Love you? See, we hold above you
    Offerings of your favorite fish!

On a Favorite Cat: Killed by an Automobile

Delightful feline! When shall I
such another one espy
of an equal grace—a charm
that the coldest might disarm!
Often have I lingered where
you disported on the stair
viewed the antics of your play
as you tumbled all the way
watchful still and so alert
that you never came to hurt!

Ah, what mortal ever saw
such a deft and cunning paw?
Such a winning look; a sight
like your whiskers, long and white!

Warm, forgiving, was your heart
where no treachery played a part!
Time's winged chariot hurrying near
filled you with no thought of fear
struck you, ere your nimble feet
bore you from the busy street.

The grave's a fine and private place
with not a mouse for you to chase.
While you slumber, worms shall try
your long preserved serenity,
and not so long shall we refrain
from visiting your cold domain.

To George W. Kirk, upon His 26th Birthday

My dearest George, I would that I might hymn you
    A strain of truest friendship and regard,
Or paint, in words, a portrait that should limn you
    In hues that might oblivion retard!
Thus, haply, might your name outlive tomorrow,
    Nor fear the wreckful siege of battering days,
And I, perchance, a fadeless leaf might borrow
    Of laurel, for the mightiest of my lays!

For sure, these gifts with which the Fates endowed you
    When being woke to consciousness and birth,
In generous measure, with the years, allowed you
    Increasing store of talent and of worth!
Nor otherwise may we account for graces
    Of thought and fancy, that in you have part,
For high nobilities that leave their traces,
    Where all may see, in open hand and heart!

And I could wish that future seasons rolling
    Forever seaward with their golden tides,
Might bring so much of tenderest consoling,
    So much of joy that lingers and abides,
That splendid tomes, high-piled from floor to ceiling,
    Will only whisper of the wealth you hold,
And lovely women, for your favor kneeling,
    Will speak of more, perhaps, than should be told!

To His Peculiar Friend, G. Kirk, Esq.,

An Invitation to Snuff

Dear George, this brown box, when 'tis full of good snuff,
From trouble and strife will be solace enough!
One pinch will rout vapors and fogs from the brain,
And clear the dim vision—why therefore abstain?
Two pinches inhaled with true spirit and zest,
Will bring the heart comfort—is snuffing not best?
Our globe lasts a second and moves scarce an inch,
So join me, my friend, in a jovial pinch!

Your Street

Your street is always tranquil and serene,
With something of the light that in your eyes
And on your brow reflects more peaceful skies,
And gentler days than we have ever seen;
A subtle grace ensnares us in its mien
As in your own, that lends a new surprise
To loveliness and makes the heart more wise,
More apt in fairer meads of truth to glean!

And like the memory of beauty held
Within a heart that falters and is old,
Your little house adorns the dreaming street,
Or so it seems to me, who feels impelled
I know not why, to view the scenes that hold
A thought at once so gracious and so sweet.

Blue Pencil Anniversary Song

(Sung to tune of "Aunt Dinah's Quilting Party")

Once again we meet together
    Once again the brief hours fly;
Who will care for wind and weather,
    Or that Summer days must die?
There's a light forever showing,
    There's a warmth that yet will cheer
In the kindly glances around us glowing,
    In each kindred heart that's near!

Chorus
For we hail the old Blue Pencil Club
    And the fame its annals know;
It began the story of its glory
    Fifteen happy years ago!

We have loved afar to wander,
    On the winding Gipsy trail,
While the long miles lured us yonder,
    Where all cark and care must fail;

We have shared each pain and pleasure
    That the hand of Time has brought;
And the passing seasons held full measure,
    Of rewards that came unsought!

Let us hope the years may find us
    Ever linked in heart and hand;
Ever true to loves behind us
    That no more with us shall stand;
Ever true to those we cherish
    Here beside us while we sing,
For we know that Time when these shall perish,
    Nevermore their life will bring!

What My Ancestors Were Like

The interesting Simians who antedate the race
In each authentic family tree, find an honored place.
Outlandish tribes and races in man's ascending scale
Bequeathed some wants and habits to their sons that still prevail.
The hate that drove the battle-axe of predatory Huns
Survives today in Europe's turmoil and the thunder of her guns.
But as for me, I cannot think that slaughter filled the mind
Of any ancient Kleiner, for they were more inclined
To dance and game and cheerful mirth, and talk beside the fire
While one amongst them raised a song and strummed a tuneful lyre.
I really think they spent more time in wooing gentle maids
Than hunting in the good greenwood, or delving with their spades.
I know it when I feel the glow that loveliness inspires,
I know it when I feel the pangs of love's deferred desires.

The Great Adventure

A pilgrim, with my pack behind me,
    My stout and trusty staff in hand,
With rain to chill and sun to blind me,
    I wander up and down the land—
A land whose sunrise meant but waking
    To me, who knew no time before;

Whose dusk will mean an overtaking
    By sleep, and darkness evermore.
The dawn and dusk are birth and dying:
Life's great adventure 'twixt them lying.

I filled my pack ere pain or sorrow
    Had told of wants that were to come;
Nor thought from this poor staff to borrow
    A comfort, when my feet were numb.
But wind and storm and cold that found me,
    And heat and rain, have followed on;
And doubt, and black despair around me,
    Perplexed a moment—and were gone.
What were the cares that pressed so meanly?
Adventure, to be born serenely.

And joy has met me, too, as only
    The warmth of friendship may reveal;
And not for long have I been lonely
    Where shadows down the mountain steal;
While gentler hands and fairer faces
    Have brought a sweeter balm than all
And they have led my steps to places
    Where it were churlish not to fall.
I may have slipped—been wounded gravely;
Adventure must be challenged bravely.

Let others say their hearts are breaking,
    That all is gone of light and hope;
I think them most unwise in taking,
    For comfort, to the knife and rope.
What matter if the day be gloomy?
    What matter if the way be rough?
The grave is not so very roomy,
    And I shall lie there soon enough.
Though life be gay and sad, 'tis thrilling;
That great adventure finds me willing.

If I Had Lived a Hundred Years Ago

A hundred years ago, had I
Beheld the changeful April sky,
And lived and moved in other vanished days—
Would I have found enough to praise?
Would I have found myself inclined
To streets that were not undermined
By subways shuttling to and fro
And battling mobs that come and go?
Would I enjoy a vista yet
Quite free of lofty parapet
Of pinnacle that scrapes the stars
And shuts me in with iron bars?
Ah, who can say? And who will groan
For joys undreamed and bliss unknown?
And yet, again, I think my heart
Would pine, and vague desires might start
For something gracious vaguely guessed,
For loveliness still unpossessed!
Some wraiths from distant years to be
Might float across the gulf to me;
Of Katharine or of Isobel
My secret cherished dream might tell;
Of Winifred or Grace, my thought
Might all unknowingly be wrought.
Felicitas, Elizabeth,
Might float to me on summer's breath,
And Eleanor or Ruth might fill
My lonely heart with quite a thrill.
Esther or Iva could entrance
Across the years with one sweet glance.
And Alma's shade might serve to keep
My drowsy eyes from restful sleep.
So let me cease! My spirit faints
At raptures that my pencil paints!
But life for me indeed were slow
If lived one hundred years ago!

H. P. L.

You sit among us when we pour the wine
And read the lyric or intone the song,
When melody and mirth the hours prolong
And talk is fervent and our faces shine;
Shedding a glory or a spell benign
Among the fancies that about us throng,
Your presence seems as certain and as strong
As if your voice had called, or you had made a sign!
We speak of you and what you felt or thought;
We quote you as we might some friend away,
And chuckle at some foible all your own;
So vividly and variously you wrought
Your magic in our pliant hearts, that they
Hold warm a name now chiseled on a stone!

ARTHUR LEEDS ♦ FRANK BELKNAP LONG
H. P. LOVECRAFT ♦ SAM LOVEMAN

THE RETURN OF THE UNDEAD
by Arthur Leeds

"That the ghastly extremes of agony are shared by man the unit, and never by man the mass—for this let us thank a merciful God."—Edgar Allan Poe, *The Premature Burial.*

TO HAVE died—and yet to be undead! What a horrible thought! And yet, what a fascinating story, albeit one that fairly set every nerve in my pain-racked body trembling with the frightful suggestion contained in it! And to think that this book that I had just finished reading told, in the form of fiction, what the poor devil of a German also had told me as he lay there beside me in shell-scarred "No Man's Land," waiting for his ticket to "go West," only a few months before.

"Yes, there are wehr-wolves," he assured me, solemnly, his face contorted with pain the while he talked—in his own language, which I spoke almost as well as himself; "they are the slaves of the vampires—*the undead*—those beings who claim their victims after death, and who carry on their terrible act of mutilation and generation"—he paused to cross himself and murmur a word of prayer—"forever and forever! Doubt it not, Kamerad. My brother, now, knew a man, an Austrian, who had met a wehr-wolf at midnight, in the forest district of his own homeland. Shortly after that, in our own Black Forest, my brother himself encountered a wehr-wolf. In the following year, my brother died; and as he lay on his death-bed, he called me to his side.

" 'Karl,' he declared, laying his hand on my arm, 'remember what I have told you in the past. The undead are as swift in their movements and as immune to harm from human hands as were the valkyries of old. I am marked by a being, a vampire—one of the undead host; an overlord of wehr-wolves—and he—*it*—has given me the sign. Therefore, brother of mine, heed what I say; and, as you love me, carry out this, my last request, even as you hope for the death of a Christian and for salvation after death. After they have buried me, you must take my body out of the ground—on the day of my burial, remember, and before sunset. Do not forget that—*before sunset.* You must have help; Heinrich Arndt will assist you; I have spoken to him as I am now speaking to you. Take me from the coffin, and plunge the old sword of our great-great-grandfather straight through my heart. Leave the sword in my body; bind it there with wire. Then, bind the crucifix in the clasp of both my dead hands. Return
589

ARTHUR LEEDS
(1882–1952)

In 1924, at forty-two, Arthur Leeds lived in a hotel room on West 49th Street, in the area of Manhattan known as "Hell's Kitchen." The only father among the Kalems, he had come from Chicago, leaving his wife and children there, in order to earn money.

It didn't work well for him. Oh yes, he had jobs: a columnist for *Writer's Digest*, and for *Reader's Digest*, occasional freelance work, and he sold a few stories to *Adventure* and *Weird Tales*, but, despite his frugality hardly enough to sustain him, let alone to pay off debts, as he had envisioned.

Leeds had the most colorful background of the Kalems. Born in Canada of English heritage, he had been a carnival man, had traveled in stock theatre, and had worked in the movies. We want to know more. Although we can assume Leeds had little formal education, by all accounts, he was well-read and cultivated.

For some months, George Kirk hired Leeds to help in the book shop. According to Kirk, although Leeds was very capable and likeable, he liked to read too much and to talk too much. After letting him go, Kirk helped Leeds find other work.

In all likelihood, Leeds was a friend of McNeil's, who lived in Hell's Kitchen also, and met other amateur journalists through him. All the Kalems liked Leeds. Leeds—who moved from dismal room to dismal room at the Cort, the Ray, for non-payment of rent—was generous towards his friends. He was instrumental in getting Lovecraft several small jobs.

Unfortunately, we have no photograph of Leeds, and know only that he wore a mustache. Leeds's dress was, in Lovecraft's eyes, like Kleiner's— "frankly impossible," with his jacket bursting at the seams; but despite his poverty, Leeds was immaculate about his person: clean-shaven, even wearing pressed trousers. After Lovecraft was robbed, Leeds took him around, trying to duplicate his $5.00 suit purchase, and in this attempt he introduced Lovecraft to the bargain districts of Manhattan.

Accustomed as he was to an itinerant life, Leeds weathered his time in New York well. Comradeship, mutual support, and small comfort found in the Kalem Club helped sustain him. Leeds returned to Chicago in September 1926, but maintained a correspondence with his Kalem friends. By June 1932, long after the Kalems had ceased to meet regularly, Leeds was back in New York, this time living in Brooklyn.

Fortunately, in later life, Leeds achieved some success writing for the Federal Writers Project and its American Guidebook Series. Leeds died in 1952 at seventy.

He Had to Pay the Nine-Tailed Cat

C an hate last beyond the grave? Can an avenging haunt of the dark
past return to destroy its own destroyer?

As a fictional narrative, the story of Captain Guilford Walton
would prove fascinating; but the truth of the tale was attested by actual
eye-witnesses, and as a record of actual fact it holds its own with the
wildest imaginings of Poe or any other writer of bizarre and terrible
tales. Surely truth is stranger than fiction.

The old Walton house of old New York was built by William
Walton, a merchant prince, in 1752, according to the *History of the
Chamber of Commerce*. He died, childless, in 1768, leaving his estate to his
grand-nephew, William Walton. The latter joined the British during the
Revolution, and his estates were in part confiscated. His children went
to England, and one of them entered the British navy.

The house was erected in the fashionable suburbs of the city, in the
locality now known as Franklin Square. The mansion was surrounded
by spacious grounds which sloped down to the East River, affording a
fine view of the fields of "Broekellyn," as the place opposite was called
by the Dutch settlers of a former day. At the time when the eighteenth
century was drawing to a close, it was believed that the Walton family
had become extinct; but suddenly a member of the ancient house appeared. He was a British sea-captain, and his coming made a sensation
in the society of New York, which at that time was limited to Wall
Street and the lower part of Broadway.

Captain Guilford Walton proved to be an intelligent and agreeable
gentleman, who might have been called good-looking had it not been
for a peculiarly sinister expression which marked his face when it was in
repose, but which passed away as soon as he began to speak. The prestige of his name and rank—not in the Royal Navy, but in the merchant
service—rather than any reputation of wealth that he brought with him,
at once commanded access to the best society of the city. Captain
Walton was received among the Hamiltons, the Crugers, the Gracies,
and the other aristocratic families whose mansions fronted the Battery,
or were to be found nearby in Broadway or Greenwich Street.

His own residence, the old Walton House, was no longer in a fashionable neighborhood, but was occupied by a well-to-do family, who

were glad to let a suite of furnished rooms to a gentleman whose name was identified with the house.

Unlike many sea-faring men, he led a quiet, orderly life, and it was noticed that he gradually cultivated a recluse habit. When he did mix with gay society he seemed to show that it was the opportunity for sharing its excitement, rather than ordinary social intercourse, which he craved.

Suddenly his engagement to Miss Anna Barrington of Spring Street was announced.

Captain Walton became a constant visitor at Kirtle Grove, as Miss Barrington's home was called. It was about a mile from the captain's rooms in the old Walton mansion, to the home of his fiancée. It was his custom to take a short cut through several new streets, then half built up with small wooden houses. This path ran from Kirtle Grove to Broadway, and thence across to Mulberry Street, which was hardly more than a crooked highway, skirting the Collect, or pond, which covered what is now the site of Centre Street. One night, shortly after the engagement was announced, he remained unusually late in company with his fiancée and a woman friend. The conversation had taken a religious turn, and Captain Walton had rather shocked Miss Barrington by his flat denial of the evidences of revelation, as well as by ridiculing her interest and belief in the supernatural and the marvelous.

It was one o'clock before the captain bade the ladies goodnight and commenced his lonely walk homeward. As he walked on Mulberry Street, passing some unfinished houses surrounded by heaps of brick and mortar, his steps, in the almost oppressive silence of the moonlit night, seemed peculiarly loud and distinct.

Suddenly it occurred to him that he was not alone. He seemed to hear other footsteps regularly falling, and nearby, too—not more than a hundred feet behind him. It could not be the city watch, for this was off his regular beat, which did not extend so far from the Park. Someone, he felt certain, must be "dogging him." This suspicion aroused, he turned to confront his pursuer.

Instantly the other footsteps ceased. The moon shone brightly—and not a soul was in sight. Walton concluded that the footsteps he had heard must have been the echo of his own, but when he stamped violently on the ground, and then walked rapidly to and fro, he failed utterly to awaken any echo.

Concluding at last that the whole affair was an illusion he resumed his journey. Before he had preceded a dozen paces the mysterious footfalls were heard again in the rear.

There seemed to be a fixed purpose to prove that they were not an echo, for the steps varied in a very peculiar manner. They slackened almost to a halt; then there would be a series of eight or ten rapid strides, followed by a slow walk. Once, as Walton suddenly increased his pace, he distinctly heard his mysterious "shadow" stumble. Such a sound, he reflected, was thoroughly and convincingly material.

A bold, practical man, he again and again faced suddenly about, hoping to surprise the shadow, but on each occasion he was disappointed. He retraced his steps and made a careful search of the neighborhood; but nothing resulted. As he resumed his walk toward Chatham Street, it flashed across his mind that some of Miss Barrington's beliefs were taking hold of his imagination. In fact, for the first time in his adventurous life, a genuinely superstitious feeling began to creep upon him. He was forced to admit to himself his disturbance of spirit.

His nervous tension at last caused him to turn suddenly and cry out:

"Who goes there?"

There was no answer; and then, more from a determination to shake off his pursuer than from actual fear, he broke into a run. At once he heard the clatter of someone of equal speed maintaining the usual proximity.

He resumed his walk—and so did his pursuer. At last he reached his dwelling. The footsteps ceased as he crossed the threshold of his door.

He sat before the cozy fire in his room until three in the morning. His skepticism had not vanished, but it was considerably shaken. He began to feel at least the suggestion of the presence of the unseen world.

He was a long while falling to sleep, and rose the next day at a late hour, in a distressed and nervous frame of mind. He was doing his best to reason the matter out on natural lines, when Fensford, his servant, handed in an ordinary-looking letter, addressed to him at Walton House, which read thus:

> You appear not to recognize me, but perhaps you may when we see more of each other. Meanwhile it is hardly worth while for you to be so

shy. However, I will advise you to keep clear of Mulberry Street, unless you wish to meet

THE DETECTIVE.

Walton read the curious message several times. The handwriting was strange to him—the rude, coarse hand of an illiterate person; yet the wording showed a certain amount of education. Was the writer a friend or a foe? If the missive came from an enemy, why should the unknown send a warning? If from a friend, why should he indicate that Walton had reason to fear him?

Again, what could the term "detective" mean? Could it mean a shadower—a following Nemesis? Walton felt that the whole affair was a complete mystery—and one which he decided to keep from his sweetheart's knowledge, in spite of the fact that, as evidence of possible supernatural manifestation, it undoubtedly would interest her.

At any rate, on returning from his next visit to Kirtle Grove, he carefully avoided Mulberry Street. In order to do this, he took the broad highway (now Hudson Street) on the North River side of the city.

On this occasion, he neither saw nor heard anything to disturb him. His nervousness and apprehension were wearing off, when—

About ten days later, he went to the old Park Theatre—then the only playhouse in New York—with Miss Barrington and her father, and after seeing them start for home in their carriage, Walton turned down Beekman Street.

It was one o'clock as he started home along the almost deserted street.

Suddenly, as on that other memorable night, he became aware of the sound of steps following him. The street was quiet and deserted; no form was visible.

As he reached St. George's Chapel, he noticed that the steps were keeping perfect time with his own. Shortly afterward they changed, and, as on the previous occasion, seemed sometimes slow, sometimes lagging, then hurrying in a run until the usual apparent distance lay between them.

The captain, by this time, was thoroughly a victim of nerves. He hurried on, the relentless tread always behind him, until once more he had reached his home. He was in such a disturbed mental condition that he did not even attempt to lie down, until after daylight had come. He was awakened by his servant bringing the morning mail.

Among several letters his eye instantly picked out one which at once increased the feeling of dread which had gripped him throughout the long night. It read:

> Do you think, Captain Walton, to escape me? You may as well escape your own shadow. I will be with you when I will, and you shall not only hear me, but meet me also; for I am not disposed to conceal myself, though you may think so. Still, why should this trouble you or break your rest? For, if you have a clear conscience, you surely need fear nothing from
>
> THE DETECTIVE.

For days afterward Walton's friends observed that he was moody and absent-minded, but none of them could guess the reason. As for the captain, he felt that however he might try to convince himself that the mysterious footsteps were a mere illusion, there could be no doubt about the genuineness of the equally mysterious letters. Gradually, much against his will, he began to connect the affair with certain happenings in his own life which he had earnestly hoped to forget, but which now came back to his memory with terrible distinctness.

For there was a dark chapter in the past life of Guilford Walton, ex-captain of the high seas. There was a shadow of death—death by cruelty—which sometimes came between him and the fair form of his fiancée. It was a chapter Captain Walton had thought forever closed, but—

Ten years before coming to New York, Captain Walton, while lying in an English port—the town in which his boatswain kept his family— formed a secret attachment to the boatswain's daughter. Learning of her disgrace, the father turned the girl out of his home with reproaches and curses, and within a few months she died of a broken heart.

On the voyage following the girl's dismissal from home, her father, presuming upon Walton's implication in her guilt, behaved insolently toward his captain. Walton degraded him from office. He retaliated on the father for his cruelty to the girl, and subjected him to the terrible severities which were, in those days, within the power of a sea-captain.

The unfortunate wretch made his escape at the West Indies, and died soon afterwards of wounds received from the cat-o'-nine-tails on board ship. Walton, it was learned later, had seen the man die; on a later voyage he had seen the lonely grave beneath the palm trees. And he had turned away, proud, implacable, with that strange, sinister expression on his face.

And now—could a ghost be following him?

In an effort to throw off the gloomy thoughts which filled his mind both day and night, he interested himself in trying to recover, largely through the influence of Aaron Burr, the land which really belonged to Anna Barrington's mother. It had been confiscated and sold at the time of the Revolution. Anna Barrington was now her mother's sole heir.

The excitement growing out of this claim really did bring about a very decided temporary change in Captain Walton's mind and actions. Miss Barrington, especially, noticed and rejoiced over his altered appearance.

It was not long, however, before Walton again was thrown into a state of consternation by renewals of the old annoyance—which by this time he had come to look upon as a pursuing horror from which, apparently, there was no escape.

With some friends, including a boy of sixteen, who later wrote a record of most of these events, Walton had attended a public meeting held in Martling's Tavern, which afterward became old Tammany Hall. Leaving this building, they walked down Frankfort Street to Pearl. Walton, it is recorded, "seemed taciturn and absent-minded, and so different from his usual conversational mood that one might imagine that some deep anxiety was preying on his heart."

Yes, Walton was silent, strange, for he had heard the now familiar footsteps "dogging" him all the way home.

They had reached Franklin Square, and the captain was about to cross the street to reach Walton House, when a stranger appeared before them. He was short and of surly appearance; he was wearing a cap, and had the look of a sea-faring man.

They had seen him coming when he was perhaps forty feet away. He was a strange looking creature; he did not seem quite human as he came along. He was walking rapidly and muttering to himself; he glared savagely from beneath frowning eyebrows. He marched straight on until he was directly in front of the captain; then, halting abruptly, he gazed up into his face for a moment "with a look that seemed almost diabolical with fury and revenge," according to the recorder. He then turned sharply away and disappeared into an alley.

Walton's companions all felt that they had seldom seen so fierce and menacing a countenance, but they hardly felt that it was sufficient to carry terror to the heart of a brave man. Well knowing the captain's reputation for courage, they were astounded to see him reel backward and hear him give a cry of horror. Then he seemed to recover himself quickly, and started off in pursuit of the strange man. In a moment or two he returned, in evident confusion, and sat down upon a doorstep, his face ghastly and haggard.

Believing that the stranger might have struck the captain, his friends made inquiry. He merely shook his head confusedly and asked: "What did he say? I did not hear it clearly. Did you make it out? I know he said something."

The others had caught nothing, and were inclined to believe that Walton was mistaken about the man's having spoken at all. The captain made some excuse about hard work in connection with the Barrington claim, late hours at political meetings, and so on, and presently parted from his friends and entered his house.

A day or two later, Walton, distracted, miserable, had called in Doctor Hosack, who was then considered New York's cleverest physician. He refused absolutely to listen to his patient's explanations of overwork and ordinary nerve-strain. He declared that there was something on his patient's mind, and Walton presently indicated that he had guessed aright. Then he somewhat astonished the doctor by asking him if a dead person might, by any means then known to medicine, be restored to life.

Upon being assured by the physician that the signs of death were usually unmistakable, Walton seemed satisfied on that score. But he asked if it were not possible to procure a warrant for the apprehension of one who might be proved to be a lunatic.

The Doctor, answering that this might be done, but that it was a matter for the law rather than for medicine to take care of, at once realized that it was the mind, rather than the body of his patient, which was suffering. Only a day or two later Doctor Hosack noticed this advertisement in the *Commercial Advertiser*, and at once connected it with his strange interview with Walton:

> If Godfrey Burton, formerly boatswain on board the ship *Petrel*, will apply to Edward King, 14 Wall Street, he will hear something to his advantage. Should he prefer to come after dark, he may call up-stairs on the family at any time up to 11 o'clock.

The physician felt that his patient's distress must in some way be connected with the person named in the advertisement, since the *Petrel* was the vessel Captain Walton had sailed; but no information as to the real purpose of the advertisement was ever divulged by the attorney.

Walton had always been a notably temperate man; but at a grand supper of the Masonic fraternity, held shortly after the events just recorded, he drank heavily. Apparently heartened by the liquor he had consumed, he afterward visited the Barrington house, passed a pleasant evening, and was returning home by way of Duane Street. Suddenly the report of a musket rang out behind him and a bullet whistled past his head. His first impulse was to turn and start in pursuit of the would-be assassin. As quickly, however, he decided to go on; and he had just reached Broadway when suddenly he caught sight of the man in the cap ahead of him. The man walked rapidly toward the captain, who made no effort to hinder his progress. As the strange figure passed him, he distinctly heard deep-muttered threats of vengeance.

It was the Reverend John M. Mason, of the Cedar Street Church, who, a few days after this event, prevailed upon Walton to seek a change of air and a complete rest. Walton, taking Doctor Mason into his confidence, except for the secret which he had so long guarded—assured the clergyman that he was pursued by a demon, that not even God could help him, and that he had, in fact, lost even his ability to pray for divine aid.

Within another month Walton was declaring that he heard accusing voices at all hours of the day and night. He frequently encountered the mysterious stranger, whom he never seemed willing to molest. He was induced by his prospective father-in-law to go on a sea voyage to Halifax, his departure being kept a secret from all but Miss Barrington.

Ten days later they landed in Halifax, and were walking up the street leading from the quay. Mr. Barrington was a few paces in advance. Suddenly Walton ran ahead, his sinister face looking over his shoulder, his eyes strained and wild. Barrington saw no one behind Walton, but—he heard footfalls, the sound of running feet. It was evident that Walton could see what Barrington could not. His voice was raised in a piercing, terrified cry.

"I see him! I see him! He touched my arm—spoke to me—pointed to me. God be merciful to me! There is no escape! He is after me now!"

They returned to New York by the next packet, Walton quite convinced that it was useless longer to try to cheat the fate to which he felt himself doomed. It was plain to Miss Barrington and her father that the girl's marriage to Captain Walton was out of the question; but this did not prevent Anna Barrington from doing all in her power to aid and comfort her lover in his hour of complete physical and mental collapse. Walton had declared that one of the first faces he saw, upon returning to New York, was that of his implacable enemy. Whether this were true or not, it occurred to Mr. Barrington that Walton would be far better off if he were kept in perfect quiet in some rural neighborhood—a secret retreat where his presence would not be known even to his friends. Mr. Barrington picked out a large country house near Kip's Bay, where a family and a special medical attendant should have charge of him.

To guard against actual invasion, Walton was persuaded to confine himself strictly to the house and garden, which had a high fence whose gates were kept locked.

Both Mr. Barrington and his daughter took up their residence in the house. A few cheerful and carefully chosen friends were invited to visit it and help to brighten the captain's confinement.

And then—a kitchen maid, who knew absolutely nothing of the reason for Captain Walton's being in the house, nor even that he was not supposed to view anything happening beyond its walls, was sent to the garden to gather some herbs. She ran back in a state of great alarm, her task but half finished. She said that while gathering some thyme and rosemary in the farthest corner of the garden, singing while she worked, she had been interrupted by a coarse laugh. Looking up, she had found herself face to face with a strange and fierce-looking man, small of stature, wearing a cap. She declared that she had been utterly unable to move so long as the man had kept his eyes fixed upon her. He ordered her to carry a message to Captain Walton, to the effect that he must come abroad as usual, or else expect a visit in his own room.

Having delivered this message to the frightened maid, the stranger immediately disappeared. Mrs. Anderson, the housekeeper, upon hearing the girl's story, commanded her very strictly to say nothing to Captain Walton of what she had seen or heard. At the same time she ordered some workmen, who were repairing the front of the house, to search through the neighboring fields. They returned at last without having seen anyone; and with many misgivings the housekeeper communicated the fact to the Barringtons, who united in the plan of keeping it a secret.

But a few days later, Walton, who had sufficiently recovered in health and spirits to enjoy rambling about the grounds, was strolling by himself at the lower end of the yard when suddenly he found himself face to face with his mysterious tormenter.

For a moment or two he stood rooted to the spot, his blood seeming to turn to ice in his veins. Then he fell to the ground, insensible. There he was found a few minutes afterward, and was carried to his room—the room which he was never afterward to leave alive.

From this time a marked change was observed in his mental condition. He was no longer the excited, terror-haunted man he had been for so long, no longer oppressed with extreme despair. In a talk with Mr. Barrington, he quietly asserted that he was assured his sufferings would soon be over.

"Nonsense, my dear fellow," answered the old gentleman. "Peace and cheerfulness are all that you need to make you what you formerly were."

"No, no! I can never be that," replied Walton, mournfully. "I am no longer fit to live. I am soon to die; but I do not shrink from death as once I did. I am to see him but once again, and then all will be ended."

"He said so, then?" Mr. Barrington asked in astonishment.

"He? No, no! Good news like this would never come from him. I have—other sources of knowledge, and of comfort!"

"But cannot you see that this whole affair is, as the doctor suggests, partly a series of dreams, or of waking fancies, coupled with the appearance, every so often, of some cunning rascal who, for some reason, owes you a grudge?"

"A grudge, indeed, he does owe me," answered Walton. "When the justice of Heaven permits the Evil One to carry out a scheme of vengeance—when its execution is committed to the lost victim of sin who owes his ruin to the very man he is commissioned to pursue—then, indeed, the torments of hell are let loose on earth. But, though death now is welcome, I shrink, with an agony you cannot understand, from the last encounter with this demon. I am to see him once more, but under circumstances unutterably more terrible than ever!" Then he muttered something Barrington did not understand—something about a nine-tailed cat.

Walton now insisted that the window blinds be kept closed. His body-servant slept in the same chamber, and was not out of it day or night. The physician was dismissed, since his services seemed to help the unhappy man not at all. The servant was considered perfectly capable of waiting upon the captain and keeping an eye on that part of the house. Walton insisted upon the presence of this young man—when others were not with him—at all times. Total solitude was the one thing which he seemed to fear above everything else. Thus, a self-made prisoner in this one apartment, he awaited the end, which he declared was not far distant.

The climax of this remarkable drama came about two o'clock on a winter's night. Walton was in bed, as he had been for most of the day. A lamp burned constantly; his servant slept on a couch in the corner of the room. The man was roused from his slumber by Walton's voice calling to him:

"Get up, Wilson, and look about. I can't get it out of my head that there is something strange in the room or the passageway. Make a thorough search. Such hateful dreams!"

The servant arose and, lighting a candle, peered into every corner of the room. Finding nothing at all unusual, he opened the door and started to walk down the passage. He had advanced only a few steps when the door of the room, as if moved by a current of air, swung to behind him. The man was not in the least disturbed by this brief separation from his master, as the ventilator over the door was open, and he knew he could hear distinctly any call from within the room.

He continued to look about the passage, when suddenly he heard Walton's voice calling to him. He did not call loudly in reply, as would have been necessary at that distance, for fear of disturbing the household. He walked quickly back, however, and seemed stricken with a terror that held him paralyzed, just outside the door, as he heard a strange voice in the room, responding to his master's tones.

Still rooted to the spot, the servant presently heard Walton cry out: "Oh, God! Oh, my God!"

There came a momentary silence, which was broken by a scream of agony, appalling and hideous. Driven by ungovernable horror, the servant tried to open the door, but he was too paralyzed with fear to turn the knob.

As he stood there, cold with dread, yell after yell came from the room beyond, and then rang with terrible echoes through the otherwise silent country house. What was happening in that guarded room? Suddenly released from his thralldom of fear, the man turned and ran aimlessly up and down the passage, until a minute or two later, he encountered Mr. Barrington.

"What is it? Who—where is your master, Wilson?" he asked wildly. "For God's sake, is there anything wrong?"

Then, without waiting for the terrified servant's reply, the old gentleman burst open the door and entered the room, with Wilson at his heels.

"The lamp has been moved from the table," said Wilson. "See! They have put it by the bed."

Ordered by Mr. Barrington to draw the curtains which draped the bed, Wilson drew back in alarm. Mr. Barrington took the candle from his shaking hand and, advancing to the bed, himself drew the curtains apart.

The light fell upon a horrible figure, huddled together and half upright at the head of the bed. It appeared to have slunk back as far as the solid paneling would permit, and the hands were still clutching the bedclothes.

Calling the captain's name, Mr. Barrington leaned forward and held the candle nearer to the white, drawn face, the eyes of which held a look of unutterable horror. The jaw was fallen; the terror-filled eyes gazed with frightful penetration toward the side of the bed where, a moment before, had hung the drawn curtains.

"Great God, he is dead!" cried Mr. Barrington, as he gazed upon this fearful spectacle.

"Cold, too!" added the servant, touching the dead man's shoulder. "And see, Sir, there was something else on the bed with him! Look there—see that!"

As the man spoke he pointed to a deep impression at the foot of the bed which plainly had been caused by the pressure of something or someone upon which—or whom—the dead man had lately bent his now sightless eyes. He had met his Nemesis: the strange follower who had dogged him for so long, at last had been avenged for a wrong committed years before. So ends the strange story of Captain Walton. If only he could have realized the full consequences of his cruelty before it was too late!

Frank Belknap Long

FRANK BELKNAP LONG
(1901–1994)

In 1924, Frank Belknap Long at twenty-three still seemed like a boy. (Long habitually lied about his age, claiming that he was born either in 1902 or 1903; but research by Peter Cannon has established that he was born in 1901.) Perhaps this was because, as an only child of a successful orthodontist, he had been pampered. Long, who lived with his parents in Manhattan's upper west side, was the only Kalem member who had much physical comfort. Despite his upper-class upbringing, Long railed against the economic disparities caused by the capitalistic system.

Long's parents were kind and generous to the Kalems, inviting them to holiday meals and graciously holding occasional Kalem meetings there. Of course the Kalems were delighted to go to the Longs', knowing they would be offered well-served, substantial meals. The Longs invited Lovecraft on many of their car travels, and hosted him frequently after his return to Providence.

Small-boned, dark-haired, spectacled, smoking a pipe, Long tried to grow a mustache to emulate his idol, Poe. Lovecraft called him an "exquisite boy" with a "delicate, beautiful face." Long dressed well, sporting spats and a fedora.

When, still a teenager, Long published "The Eye Above the Mantel" in the *United Amateur*. Lovecraft praised this story, thus beginning a long and close friendship, which lasted until Lovecraft's death. They met in April 1922, when Lovecraft visited New York. Already, Long so admired Lovecraft that he carried his picture in his wallet. Lovecraft also took to Long, in whom he saw great promise, and he became, for the next fifteen years, Long's mentor and closest friend.

Although in November 1924 *Weird Tales* published his story, "The Desert Lich," Long considered himself mainly a poet. Of his first book, *The Man from Genoa and Other Poems*, printed by W. Paul Cook in 1926, Samuel Loveman wrote: "At twenty-three we find him writing poems for his first, glorious volume—poems that might have been penned by the greatest of the lesser Elizabethans, with at least one, 'The Marriage of Sir John de Mandeville,' worthy of Christopher Marlowe." High praise, indeed for a young poet!

Was Long prepared for adult life? How did he make a living? For several years in the late 1920s, Long and Lovecraft partnered in "ghosting." They advertised in the *New York Times* and in *Weird Tales*. Probably Long received an inheritance from his parents, and supplemented it with money earned as a writer and editor. He published hundreds of stories, poems, and articles, and worked during his middle years as a magazine editor. At sixty, Long married

Lyda Arco, a former singer and actress of Russian descent, and wrote romances under her name. They had no children.

Long was destined to become well-known for his weird tales and science fiction, not his poetry. By his death in 1994, he had received both the Bram Stoker Award and the Lifetime Achievement from the World Fantasy Convention. Among his best-known books are *The Hounds of Tindalos*, *The Horror from the Hills*, and *The Rim of the Unknown*. Little financial gain accompanied this literary success, and Long, sick, and old, died in poverty, in their Chelsea apartment January 1994. Lyda survived him briefly.

A Man from Genoa

I saw a man from Genoa
　　Who turned and smiled at me,
And something in his wistful gaze
　　Was like a blasted tree.

He told me then that he had come
　　With flaming plumes and vair,
And cloths of saffron and of gold,
　　And vests of camel's hair.

And he had beads from Carthage
　　And silks from windy Tyres,
And tiny chests of spikenard
　　Preserved from Ilium's fires.

And once in gracious Babylon
　　Where virtue is unknown,
He bought a girl from distant Ind
　　With bits of colored stone.

The man who came from Genoa
　　Had sorrow in his eyes,
And yet he turned and smiled at me
　　And made a stout surmise.

"My silks, they say, are waterlogged,
　　My spears and helmets worn;
And yet I came from Genoa
　　Around the southern horn.

"The Lords of War have laughed at me
　　And will not take my vests!
They are too small and fiberless
　　To span their thunderous chests."

And then I somehow pitied him
    And bought the worthless things,
The silks and grails and parakeets
    And gold and copper rings.

I have them yet and know quite well
    Their uselessness to me;
And yet the man from Genoa—
    His eyes were like the sea!

I saw him go upon the quay
    And whistle through his hands;
I saw his galley swing to port
    Above the yellow sands.

The ship that veered before the wind
    Had green and scarlet sails;
And turbaned prophets paced the poop
    And Nubians thronged the rails.

He waved his hand, and jumped aboard
    And danced upon the deck;
And then I saw him take command
    And clear the harbor wreck.

They passed a town with marble streets
    And spires of malachite;
Where centaurs worshipped headless gods
    Whose limbs were zoned with light.

I saw them sail into the East—
    And now in far Cathay
I seek the man from Genoa
    Who bore my gold away.

Come, Let Us Make

Come, let us make a peacock tune
    And stroll about the garden,
And take our magic from the moon
    And never beg its pardon.

There are so very many things
    We do not know at all:
Did Rachel wear her hair in rings?
    Was Heliogabalus tall?

Had David fifty hundred sheep?
    Was Simon Magus right?
Was Sheba's Queen a negress?
    Are Virgil's stanzas trite?

A man may go on living
    And never even ask
If Shelley work pajamas,
    If Dante wore a mask.

But we'll get answers from the moon
    And never beg its pardon,
And when we know we'll make a song
    And stroll about the garden.

The Man Who Died Twice

When Hazlitt saw the stranger at his desk his emotions were distinctly unpleasant. "Upcher might have given me notice," he thought. "He wouldn't have been so high-handed a few months ago!"

He gazed angrily about the office. No one seemed aware of his presence. The man who had taken his desk was dictating a letter, and the stenographer did not even raise her eyes. "It's damnable!" said Hazlitt, and he spoke loud enough for the usurper to hear; but the latter continued to dictate: "The premium on policy 6284 has been so long overdue—"

Hazlitt stalked furiously across the office and stepped into a room blazing with light and clamorous with conversation. Upcher, the President, was in conference, but Hazlitt ignored the three directors who sat puffing contentedly on fat cigars, and addressed himself directly to the man at the head of the table.

"I've worked for you for twenty years," he shouted furiously, "and you needn't think you can dish me now. I've helped make this company. If necessary, I shall take legal steps—"

Mr. Upcher was stout and stern. His narrow skull and small eyes under heavy eyebrows, suggested a very primitive type. He had stopped talking and was staring directly at Hazlitt. His gaze was icily indifferent—stony, remote. His calm was so unexpected that it frightened Hazlitt.

The directors seemed perplexed. Two of them had stopped smoking, and the third was passing his hand rapidly back and forth across his forehead. "I've frightened them," thought Hazlitt. "They know the old man owes everything to me. I mustn't appear too submissive."

"You can't dispose of me like this," he continued dogmatically. "I've never complained of the miserable salary you gave me, but you can't throw me into the street without notice."

The President colored slightly. "Our business is very important—" he began.

Hazlitt cut him short with a wave of his hand. "My business is the only thing that matters now. . . . I want you to know that I won't stand for your ruthless tactics. When a man has slaved as I have for twenty years he deserves some consideration. I am merely asking for justice. In heaven's name, why don't you say something? Do you want me to do all of the talking?"

Mr. Upcher wiped away with his coat sleeve the small beads of sweat that had accumulated above his collar. His gaze remained curiously impersonal, and when Hazlitt swore at him he wet his lips and began: "Our business is very important—"

Hazlitt trembled at the repetition of the man's unctuous remark. He found himself reluctant to say more, but his anger continued to mount. He advanced threateningly to the head of the table and glared into the impassive eyes of his former employer. Finally he broke out: "You're a damn scoundrel!"

One of the directors coughed. A sickly grin spread itself across Mr. Upcher's stolid countenance. "Our business, as I was saying—"

Hazlitt raised his fist and struck the president of the Richbank Life Insurance Company squarely upon the jaw. It was an intolerably ridiculous thing to do, but Hazlitt was no longer capable of verbal persuasion. And he had decided that nothing less than a blow would be adequate.

The grin disappeared from Mr. Upcher's face. He raised his right hand and passed it rapidly over his chin. A flash of anger appeared for a moment in his small, deep-set eyes. "Something I don't understand," he murmured. "It hurt like the devil. I don't know precisely what it means!"

"Don't you?" shouted Hazlitt. "You're lucky to get off with that. I've a good mind to hit you again." But he was frightened at his own violence, and he was unable to understand why the directors had not seized him. They seemed utterly unaware of anything out of the ordinary: and even Mr. Upcher did not seem greatly upset. He continued to rub his chin, but the old indifference had crept back into his eyes.

"Our business is very important—" he began.

Hazlitt broke down and wept. He leaned against the wall while great sobs convulsed his body. Anger and abuse he could have faced, but Mr. Upcher's stony indifference robbed him of manhood. It was impossible to argue with a man who refused to be insulted. Hazlitt had reached the end of his rope; he was decisively beaten. But even his acknowledgment of defeat passed unnoticed. The directors were discussing policies and premiums and first mortgages, and Mr. Upcher advanced a few commonplace opinions while his right hand continued to caress his chin.

"Policies that have been carried for more than fifty years," he was saying, "are not subject to the new law. It is possible by the contemplated—"

Hazlitt did not even wait for him to finish. Sobbing hysterically he passed into the outer office, and several minutes later he was descending into the elevator to the street. All moral courage had left him; he felt like a man who has returned from the grave. He was white to the lips, and when he stopped for a moment in the vestibule he was horrified at the way an old woman poked at him with her umbrella and actually pushed him aside.

The glitter and chaos of Broadway at dusk did not soothe him. He walked despondently, with his hands in his pockets and his eyes upon the ground. "I'll never get another job," he thought. "I'm a nervous wreck and old Upcher will never recommend me. I don't know how to break the news to Helen."

The thought of his wife appalled him. He knew that she would despise him. "She'll think I'm a jellyfish," he groaned. "But I did all a man could. You can't buck up against a stone wall. I can see that old Upcher had it in for me from the start. I hope he chokes!"

He crossed the street at 73rd Street and started leisurely westward. It was growing dark and he stopped for a moment to look at his watch. His hands trembled and the timepiece almost fell to the sidewalk. With an oath he replaced it in his vest. "Dinner will be cold," he muttered. "And Helen won't be in a pleasant mood. How on earth am I going to break the news to her?"

When he reached his apartment he was shivering. He sustained himself by tugging at the ends of his mustache and whistling apologetically. He was overcome with shame and fear but something urged him not to put off ringing the bell.

He pressed the buzzer firmly, but no reassuring click answered him. Yet—suddenly he found himself in his own apartment. "I certainly got in," he mumbled in an immeasurably frightened voice, "but I apparently didn't come through the door. . . . Or did I? I don't think I'm quite well."

He hung up his hat and umbrella, and walked into the sitting room. His wife was perched on the arm of his Morris chair, and her back was turned towards him. She was in dressing gown and slippers, and her hair was down. She was whispering in a very low voice: "My dear; my darling! I hope you haven't worked too hard today. You must take care of your health for my sake. Poor Richard went off in three days with double pneumonia."

Hazlitt stared. The woman on the chair was obviously not addressing him, and he thought for an instant that he had strayed into the wrong apartment and mistaken a stranger for his wife. But the familiar lines of her profile soon undeceived him, and he gasped. Then in a blinding flash he saw it all. His wife had betrayed him, and she was speaking to another man.

Hazlitt quickly made up his mind that he would kill his wife. He advanced ominously to where she sat, and stared at her with furious, bloodshot eyes. She shivered and glanced about her nervously. The stranger in the chair rose and stood with his back to the fireplace. Hazlitt saw that he was tall and lean, and handsome. He seemed happy, and was smiling.

Hazlitt clenched his fist and glared fiercely at this intruder into his private home.

"Something has come between us," said Hazlitt's wife in a curiously distant voice. "I feel it like a physical presence. You will perhaps think me very silly."

The stranger shook his head. "I feel it too," he said. "It's as if the ghost of an old love had come back to you. While you were sitting on the chair I saw a change come over your face. I think you fear something."

"I'll make you both fear something!" shouted Hazlitt. He struck his wife on the face with his open hand. She colored slightly and continued to address the stranger. "It's as if *he* had come back. It is six months tonight since we buried him. He was a good husband and I am not sure that I have reverenced his memory. Perhaps we were too hasty, Jack!"

Hazlitt suppressed an absurd desire to scream. The blood was pounding in his ears, and he gazed from his wife to the stranger with stark horror. His wife's voice sent a flood of dreadful memories welling through his consciousness.

He saw again the hospital ward where he had spent three days of terrible agony, gasping for breath and shrieking for water. A tall doctor with sallow bloodless cheeks bent wearily above him and injected something into his arm. Then unconsciousness, a blessed oblivion wiping out the world and all its disturbing sights and sounds.

Later he opened his eyes and caught his wife in the act of poisoning him. He saw her standing above him with a spoon, and a bottle in her hand, on which was a skull and crossbones. He endeavored to rise up, to cry out, but his voice failed him and he could not move his limbs. He saw that his wife was possessed of a devil and primitive horror fastened on his tired brain.

He made dreadful grimaces and squirmed about under the sheets, but his wife was relentless. She bent and forced the spoon between his teeth. "I don't love you," she laughed shrilly. "And you're better dead. I only hope you won't return to haunt me!"

Hazlitt choked and fainted. He did not regain consciousness but later he watched his body being prepared for burial, and amused himself by thinking that his wife would soon regret her vileness. "I shall show her what a ghost can do!" he reflected grimly. "I shall pay her for this! She won't love me when I'm through with her!"

There had followed days of confusion. Hazlitt forgot that he was only a ghost, and he had walked into his old office and deliberately insulted Mr. Upcher. But now that his wife stood before him memories came rushing back.

He was a thin, emaciated ghost, but he could make himself felt. Nothing but vengeance remained to him, and he did not intend to forgive his wife. It was not in his nature to forgive. He would force a confession from her, and if necessary he would choke the breath from her abominable body. He advanced and seized her by the throat.

He was pressing with all his might upon the delicate white throat of his wife. He was pressing with lean, bony fingers; his victim seemed sunk into a kind of stupor. Her eyes were half-shut and she was leaning against the wall.

The stranger watched her with growing horror. When she began to cough he ran into the kitchen and returned with a glass of water. When he handed it to her she drained it at a gulp. It seemed to restore her slightly. "But I feel as if a band were encircling my throat. It is hot in here. Please open the windows!"

The stranger obeyed. It occurred to Hazlitt that the man really loved his wife. "Worse luck to him!" he growled, and his ghostly voice cracked with emotion. The woman was choking and gasping now and gradually he forced her to her knees.

"Confess," he commanded. "Tell this fool how you get rid of your husbands. Warn him in advance, and he will thank you and clear out. If you love him you won't want him to suffer."

Hazlitt's wife made no sign that she had heard him. "You're doing no good at all by acting like this!" he shouted. "If you don't tell him everything now I'll kill you! I'll make you a ghost!"

The tall stranger turned pale. He could not see or hear Hazlitt but it was obvious that he suspected the presence of more than two people in the room. He took Hazlitt's wife firmly by the wrists and endeavored to raise her.

"In heaven's name what ails you?" he asked fearfully. "You act as if someone were hurting you. Is there nothing that I can do?"

There was something infinitely pathetic in the woman's helplessness. She was no longer able to speak, but her eyes cried out in pain. . . . The stranger at length succeeded in aiding her. He got her to her feet, but Hazlitt refused to be discouraged. The stranger's opposition exasperated him and he redoubled his efforts. But soon he realized that he could not choke her. He had expended all his strength and still the woman breathed. A convulsion of baffled rage distorted his angular frame. he knew that he would be obliged to go away and leave the woman to her lover. A ghost is a futile thing at best and cannot work vengeance. Hazlitt groaned.

The woman beneath his hands took courage. Her eyes sought those of the tall stranger. "It is going away; it is leaving me," she whimpered. "I can breathe more easily now. It is you who have given me courage, my darling."

The stranger was bewildered and horrified. "I can't understand what's got into you," he murmured. "I don't see anything. You are becoming hysterical. Your nerves are all shattered to pieces."

Hazlitt's wife shook her head and color returned to her cheeks. "It was awful, dearest. You cannot know how I suffered. You will perhaps think me insane, but I know *he* was back at it. Kiss me darling; help me to forget." She threw her arms about the stranger's neck and kissed him passionately upon the lips.

Hazlitt covered his eyes with his hand and turned away with horror. Despair clutched at his heart. "A futile ghost," he groaned. "A futile, weak ghost! I couldn't punish a fly. Why in heaven's name am I earthbound?"

He was near the window now, and suddenly he looked out. A night of stars attracted him. "I shall climb to heaven," he thought. "I shall go floating through the air, and wander among the stars. I am decidedly out of place here."

It was a tired ghost that climbed out of the window, and started to propel itself through the air. But unfortunately a man must overcome gravitation to climb to the stars, and Hazlitt did not ascend. He was still earthbound.

He picked himself up and looked about him. Men and women were passing rapidly up and down the street but no one had apparently seen him fall.

"I'm invisible, that's sure," he reflected. "Neither Upcher, nor the directors nor my wife saw me. But my wife felt me. And yet I'm not satisfied. I didn't accomplish what I set out to do. My wife is laughing up her sleeve at me now. My wife? She has probably married that ninny, and I hope she lives to regret it. She didn't even wait for the grass to cover my grave. I won't trust a woman again if I can help it."

A woman walking on the street passed through him. "Horrible!" he groaned. "There isn't any thing to me at all! I'm worse than a jellyfish!"

An entire procession of men and women were now passing through his invisible body. He scarcely felt them, but a few succeeded in tickling him. One or two of the pedestrians apparently felt him; they shivered as if they had suddenly stepped into a cold shower.

"The streets are ghostly at night," someone said at his left elbow, "I think it's safer to ride."

Hazlitt determined to walk. He was miserable, but he had no desire to stand and mope. He started down the street. He was hatless and his hair streamed in the wind. He was a defiant ghost, but a miserable sense of futility gripped him. He was an outcast. He did not know where he would spend the night. He had no plans and no one to confide in. He couldn't go to a hotel because he hadn't even the ghost of money in his pockets, and of course no one could see him anyway.

Suddenly he saw a child standing in the very center of the street, and apparently unaware of the screaming traffic about him. An automobile driven by a young woman was almost on top of the boy before Hazlitt made up his mind to act.

He left the sidewalk in a bound and ran directly towards the automobile. He reached it a second before it touched the child, and with a great shove he sent the near-victim sprawling into a zone of safety. But he could not save himself. The fender of the car struck him violently in the chest; he was thrown forward, and the rear wheels passed over his body.

For a moment he suffered exquisite pain; a great weight pressed the breath from his thin body. He clenched his hands, and closed his eyes. The pain of this second death astonished him; it seemed interminable. But at length consciousness left him; his pain dissolved in a healing oblivion.

The child picked himself up and began to cry. "Someone pushed me," he moaned. "I was looking at the lights and someone pushed me from behind."

The woman in the car was very pale. "I think I ran over someone," she said weakly. "I saw him for a moment when I tried to turn to the left. He was very thin and worn." She turned to those who had gathered near. "Where did you carry him to?" she asked.

They shook their heads. "We didn't see anyone, madam! You nearly got the kid though. Drivers like you should be hanged!"

A policeman roughly elbowed his way through the crowd that was fast gathering. "What's all this about?" he asked. "Is anyone run over?" The woman shook her head. "I don't know. I think I ran over a tramp . . . a poor, thin man he was . . . the look in his eyes was terrible . . . and very beautiful. I . . . I saw him for a moment just before the car struck him. I think he wanted to die."

She turned again to the crowd. "Which of you carried him away?" she asked tremulously.

"She's batty," said the policeman. "Get out of here you!" He advanced on the crowd and began dispersing them with his club.

The woman in the car leaned over and looked at the sidewalk, a puzzled, mystified expression on her pale features.

"No blood or anything," she moaned. "I can't understand it!"

Silhouette of H. P. Lovecraft, made at Coney Island.

H. P. LOVECRAFT
(1890–1937)

In August 1924, when George Kirk and Samuel Loveman arrived in New York from Cleveland, Howard Phillips Lovecraft was a newly married man, living at 259 Parkside Avenue, Brooklyn. He was thirty-four years old, away from his beloved Providence for the first time. At first Lovecraft was enthusiastic about New York, and probably also about his bride, Sonia Greene, another amateur journalist. But, as the months dragged on and he achieved little success in marriage or in gainful employment, enthusiasm turned to regret and depression, and he longed for the beauty, comfort, and safety of Providence. Indeed, in retrospect, Lovecraft detested New York, but not the friends he made there, "the gang." This group of men sustained him and made life bearable. They helped him to find publication venues, small jobs, and to replace his stolen clothing.

Lovecraft had, after all, been pampered, as an only child, surrounded by loving women and grandparents, despite his father's illness and untimely death. Sonia pampered him too during their brief and intermittent married life. She was, by all accounts, an excellent cook, a generous-spirited and indulgent woman, who saw that her husband was well-housed, well-fed, and well-clothed. She also saw that he had ample time for writing, for leisure, and for friendship. Did this indulgence smother Lovecraft? Did Lovecraft abuse this indulgence? Who's to say? Certainly he took full advantage of his freedom.

Unfortunately, financial difficulties arose, and by December 1924, nine months after marriage, Sonia's millinery business—which had supported them both—failed, and she accepted a job in Cleveland. What to do? Lovecraft, who detested the possibility of living in the Midwest—New York was bad enough—moved to rooms at 169 Clinton Street, Brooklyn. Who paid the $40/month rent? Sonia. Lovecraft earned money for food and other necessities by editing, ghostwriting, and selling a few stories, and he helped George Kirk and Samuel Loveman in their respective bookstores. Still, loving relatives in Providence supplemented his income. Alone, Lovecraft lived frugally indeed, subsisting mainly on canned spaghetti, canned beans, cheese, and coffee.

From January to May 1925, Kirk lived directly above Lovecraft at 169 Clinton Street. For these brief months, Lovecraft, Kirk, Loveman, and Kleiner—all Brooklynites—formed a special bond. They shared meals, long conversations, rambling walks, and Sunday afternoon promenades.

In New York, as an eighteenth-century gentleman, one of Lovecraft's chief delights was the exploration of and discovery of Colonial architecture. In this, he had willing companions in Kirk, Kleiner, and Loveman.

As these letters will show, Lovecraft was the glue that kept the Kalems together, and his return to Providence in April 1926 dealt a great blow to the Club. Lovecraft brought to the group his generosity of spirit, kindness, humor, sharpness of wit, and his wide and varied learning. Without exception, the Kalems admired him and felt stimulated in his presence. By all accounts, Lovecraft fulfilled his role as a true eighteenth-century gentleman, in his unstinting generosity toward his friends.

The years in New York tested the waters for Lovecraft: could he sustain almost daily sociability with friends? Yes. Could he make a living in the literary/commercial world? Could he have a successful marriage? No, no, to both these questions, and thus he withdrew himself from the Pest Zone to his comfort zone of Providence. Certainly, Lovecraft was a misfit in New York.

It was easy for Lovecraft, once he was re-established in Providence, to travel freely, and he made frequent trips back to stay with "the gang" in New York. In addition, they visited him in Providence. He took many trips with the Long family, and traveled rather extensively in the U.S., and even to Quebec. In 1929 Sonia and Howard officially divorced.

In retrospect, although Lovecraft referred to these years as his "New York Exile," his admirer W. Paul Cook considered them necessary for his personal growth:

> Lovecraft never became thoroughly humanized; he never became the man we love to recall, until his New York experience. To the very end of his days, he hated New York with a consuming passion. I mean the city itself, not the many good friends he had there. But it took the privations, trials, and testing fires of New York to bring his best to the surface. And it took personal contact with those cultured, clever, sophisticated New York amateurs and semi-amateurs to make him look out and not in, to broaden him so that he could cultivate an artistic tolerance, if not entirely altering his viewpoint.*

Lovecraft died in 1937 at age forty-six of intestinal cancer. He is buried in the family plot of Swan Point Cemetery, Providence. It is startling to realize that during his lifetime Lovecraft only published in amateur journals or pulp magazines. To our great good fortune, and to their everlasting credit, August Derleth and Donald Wandrei formed Arkham House, which has kept Lovecraft's writings alive and made him perhaps the premier writer of weird fiction of the 20th century.

---

*W. Paul Cook, *In Memoriam: Howard Phillips Lovecraft: Recollections, Appreciations, Estimates* (1941), in *Lovecraft Remembered*, ed. Peter Cannon (Sauk City, WI: Arkham House, 1998), p. 115.

Plaster-All

(Apologies to "Pastorale" of Mr. Crane in the Dial.*)*

1

I, who live,
In the fourth dimension
On the third story
Of a not-unfashionable house
In a fashionable neighborhood,
With pictures of Bill Sommer hung on the wall,
And an occasional one by myself—
That one, the woman's uplifted face, for instance—
My best, I think,
A miraculous stroke,
Unthinkingly executed;
But Willy Lescaze liked it . . .
Lescaze . . . smearing the butter on one's bread
With the supreme unction
Of a third-rate director,
Of a fourth-rate playhouse,
Discoursing the pros and cons of art,
Somewhere in a bookshop in the Taylor Arcade,
Smiling to the ladies with bobbed hair
And occasionally to the gentlemen—
How I hate that type!
Hate it—hate it,
With the consistence of a hard substance,
Despising a piece of fluidity.

2

Yes, I know
Most of the "Spittle Review" crowd,
But something,
Money, no doubt,
Draws me to Cleveland,
To the home of Crane's Candies,
Mary Garden Chocolates,

And Laukhuff's Bookshop.
Here it was
That in the light of an interpreter,
Soon I met and succeeded
In surrounding myself,
With a few of the Intelligentia
That Cleveland affords,
Loveman, Sommer, Lescaze, Hatfield, Guenther . . .
But Loveman
Left the fold early—pity, yes!
I might have made much of him,
In spite of his Hebraism,
Which (sibilantly whispered)
I did not recognize,
Even on my mother's hearsay—
But there was much of the rebel,
Inborn and instinctive,
(As in all Jews)
In Loveman,
And so, after a perfectly wild argument,
With him one lovely night, late July,
With the syringas in full blossom
On 115th Street,
We parted
To meet no more—at least as friends.

3

And so,
Realizing, after all,
As I did, and so many before me,
Maxwell Bodenheim, T. S. Eliot, Margaret Anderson, Sherwood Anderson
    (No relations!), James Joyce, Ezra Pound,
And how many others,
Even less than myself,
That what it all amounts to,
In life, as in literature—
Is form.
Not emotion, not poetry, not beauty,
But the hard, visible outline.

Dave Gordon
(I can hardly control myself when I think of him!)
Asserted to Loveman,
Which in a fit of epilepsy, apoplexy or delirium,
Loveman seconded;
That my own work—my own—my own,
Was a shade of T. S. Eliot's, who was a shade
Of Jules Laforgue!
Ridiculous! Stupid! Ridiculous!
Men of genius
Are all derivative.
Shakespeare, for instance,
Has even as much influenced
Internally and externally,
T. S. Eliot.

4

The wind wails
Around the corner of Euclid and 115th St.,
The trees shiver
Like brass, or cymbals of some such metal,
It rains and then it ceases,
But I, seated on my Aztec carpets,
And playing Debussy
On the wheezy Victrola,
(What Rhythms! What Rhythms!)
Conjure for myself
An entire world,
Made of myself, by myself, for myself!
Knowing myself,
To be myself.

To Endymion

(Frank Belknap Long, Jr.)
Upon his Coming of Age, April 27, 1923

Rise, friendly moon, thy beams to cast
On tender genius, grown at last;

And glorify with argent ray
ENDYMION, twenty-one today!
Ethereal child! How brief a span
Hath serv'd to change thee to a man!
But yesterday thine infant mind
Caught dreams of wonder from the wind;
Soar'd with the clouds of roseal skies
Where the lone white flamingo flies,
And sail'd the perfum'd austral sea
That laps the strand of Arcady.
Such dreams the youthful poet light
With flames irradiately bright,
And such—by kind Selene's will—
Immortal boy, possess thee still!
Mine, then, the task to hail this hour
With praise of no new-coming pow'r;
But joying that the hosts divine
Should leave what was already thine.
ENDYMION! Kept by favours rare
For ever young, for ever fair;
Fann'd by the breeze on Latmos' crest
In ceaseless innocence and rest!
Thy world a thousand spells can boast
Which to our duller realms are lost;
A thousand colours delicate,
And songs that unknown birds create;
A thousand vistas, rang'd serene
In many a mystic moonlit scene;
Prospects and peaks that are not giv'n
The light of sun or moon or heav'n—
Great ships of gold, wing'd monsters dire,
And strange sea-caves of liquid fire.
Keep then thy youth—be ever young
As when thy first sweet notes were sung,
Nor let the years corrode the gleam
Of each fresh amestystine dream.
For thee no common view expands
O'er the grey waste of earthly lands;
No common passions seethe along

The crystal aether of thy song:
'Tis thine to paint with brush of flame
Spheres hyaline and void of name.
Blest child, may all thy thoughts of youth
Incline thee still to ways of truth;
To stainless fancy, rich and kind,
Simplicity that calms the mind,
Virtue unstudy'd, reason bold,
Courage thine own proud place to hold,
Ripe scholarship the Muse to wake,
And beauty for its own pure sake.
Best-lov'd of Phoebe! As I scan
The future days that call thee man,
A path of silver light I see,
Unbroken toward eternity.
On that bright path thine elfin feet
Can never falter nor retreat,
But must trip on till Time shall bring
The Aidenns of thy visioning!

Providence

Where bay and river tranquil blend,
    And leafy hillsides rise,
The spires of Providence ascend
    Against the ancient skies.

Here centuried domes of shining gold
    Salute the morning's glare,
While slanting gables, odd and old,
    Are scatter'd here and there.

And in the narrow winding ways
    That climb o'er slope and crest,
The magic of forgotten days
    May still be found to rest.

A fanlight's gleam, a knocker's blow,
    A glimpse of Georgian brick—
The sights and sounds of long ago
    Where fancies cluster thick.

A flight of steps with iron rail,
    A belfry looming tall,
A slender steeple, carv'd and pale,
    A moss-grown garden wall.

A hidden churchyard's crumbling proofs
    Of man's mortality,
A rotting wharf where gambrel roofs
    Keep watch above the sea.

Square and parade, whose walls have tower'd
    Full fifteen decades long
By cobbled ways 'mid trees embower'd,
    And slighted by the throng.

Stone bridges spanning languid streams,
    Houses perch'd on the hill,
And courts where mysteries and dreams
    The brooding spirit fill.

Steep alley steps by vines conceal'd,
    Where small-pan'd windows glow
At twilight on the bit of field
    That chance has left below.

My Providence! What airy hosts
    Turn still thy gilded vanes;
What winds of elf that with grey ghosts
    People thine ancient lanes!

The chimes of evening as of old
    Above thy valleys sound,
While thy stern fathers 'neath the mould
    Make blest thy sacred ground.

Thou dream'st beside the waters there,
    Unchang'd by cruel years;
A spirit from an age more fair
    That shines behind our tears.

Thy twinkling lights each night I see,
    Tho' time and space divide;
For thou art of the soul of me,
    And always at my side!

Waste Paper

A Poem of Profound Insignificance
By Humphrey Littlewit, Gent.

Πάντα γέλως καὶ πάντα κόνις καὶ πάντα τὸ μηδέν.

Out of the reaches of illimitable night
The blazing planet grew, and forc'd to life
Unending cycles of progressive strife
And strange mutations of undying light
And boresome books, than hell's own self more trite
And thoughts repeated and become a blight,
And cheap rum-hounds with moonshine hooch made tight,
And quite contrite to see the flight of fright so bright
I used to ride my bicycle in the night
With a dandy acetylene lantern that cost $3.00
In the evening, by the moonlight, you can hear those darkies singing
Meet me tonight in dreamland. . . . BAH
I used to sit on the stairs of the house where I was born
After we left it but before it was sold
And play on a zobo with two other boys.
We call'd ourselves the Blackstone Military Band.
Won't you come home, Bill Bailey, won't you come home?
In the spring of the year, in the silver rain
Then petal by petal the blossoms fall
And the mocking birds call
And the whippoorwill sings, Marguerite.
The first cinema show in our town opened in 1906
At the old Olympic, which was then call'd Park,
And moving beams shot weirdly thro' the dark
And spit tobacco seldom hit the mark.
Have you read Dickens' *American Notes?*
My great-great-grandfather was born in a white house
Under green trees in the country
And he used to believe in religion and the weather
"Shantih, Shantih, Shantih" . . . *Shanty House*
Was the name of a novel by I forget whom
Published serially in the *All Story Weekly*
Before it was a weekly. Advt.

Disillusion is wonderful, I've been told,
And I take quinine to stop a cold
But it makes my ears ring . . . always ring . . .
Always ringing in my ears. . . .
It is the ghost of the Jew I murdered that Christmas day
Because he played "Three O'Clock in the Morning" in the flat above me
Three O'Clock in the morning, I've danced the whole night through,
Dancing on the graves in the graveyard
Where life is buried; life and beauty
Life and art and love and duty
Ah, there, sweet cutie.
Stung!
Out of the night that covers me
Black as the pit from pole to pole
I never quote things straight except by accident.
Sophistication! Sophistication!
You are the idol of our nation
Each fellow has
Fallen for jazz
And we'll give the past a merry razz
Thro' the ghoul-guarded gateways of slumber
And fellow-guestship was the glutless worm.
Next stop is 57th St.—57th St. the next stop.
Achilles' wrath, to Greece the direful spring,
And the governor-general of Canada in Lord Byng
Whose ancestor was shot or hung,
I forget which, the good die young.
Here's to your ripe old age,
Copyright, 1847, by Joseph Miller,
Entered according to act of Congress
In the office of the librarian of Congress
America was discovered in 1492
This way out.
No, lady, you gotta change at Washington St. to the Everett train.
Out in the rain on the elevated
Crated, sated, all mismated.
Twelve seats on this bench,
Now quaint.
In a shady nook, beside a brook, two lovers stroll along.

Express to Park Ave., Car Following.
No, we had it cleaned with a sand blast.
I know it ought to be torn down.
Before the bar of a saloon there stood a reckless crew,
When one said to another, "Jack, this message came for you."
"It may be from a sweetheart, boys," said someone in the crowd,
And here the words are missing—but Jack cried out aloud:
    "It's only a message from home, sweet home,
        From loved ones down on the farm
      Fond wife and mother, sister and brother. . . ."
    Bootleggers all and you're another
In the shade of the old apple tree
'Neath the old cherry tree sweet marie
The Conchologist's First Book
By Edgar Allan Poe
Stubbed his toe
On a broken brick that didn't show
Or a banana peel
In the fifth reel
By George Creel
It is to laugh
And quaff
It makes you stout and hale,
And all my days I'll sing the praise
Of Ivory Soap
Have you a little T. S. Eliot in your home?
The stag at eve had drunk his fill
The thirsty hart look'd up the hill
And craned his neck just as a feeler
To advertise the Double-Dealer.
William Congreve was a gentleman
O art what sins are committed in thy name
For tawdry fame and fleeting flame
And everything, ain't dat a shame?
Mah Creole Belle, ah lubs yo' well;
Aroun' muh heart you hab cast a spell
But I can't learn to spell pseudocracy
Because there ain't no such word.
And I says to Lizzie, if Joe was my feller

I'd teach him to go to dances with that
Rat, bat, cat, hat, flat, plat, fat
Fry the fat, fat the fry
You'll be a drug-store by and by.
Get the hook!
Above the lines of brooding hills,
Rose spires that reeked of nameless ills
And ghastly shone upon the sight
In ev'ry flash of lurid light
To be continued.
No smoking.
Smoking on four rear seats.
Fare will return to 5¢ after August 1
Except outside the Cleveland city limits.
In the ghoul-haunted woodland of Weir
Stranger pause to shed a tear;
Henry Fielding wrote *Tom Jones*.
And curs'd be he that moves my bones.
Good night, good night, the stars are bright
I saw the Leonard-Tendler fight
Farewell, farewell, O go to hell.
Nobody home
In the shantih.

Primavera

There is wonder on land and billow,
    And a strangeness in bough and vein,
For the brook or the budded willow
    Feel the Presence walking again.
It has come in the olden fashion,
    As the tritest of lutes have sung,
But it carries the olden passion
    That can never be aught but young.

There are whispers from groves auroral
    To blood half-afraid to hear,
While the evening star's faint choral
    Is an ecstacy touch'd with fear.

And at night where the hill-wraiths rally
    Glows the far Walpurgis flame,
Which the lonely swain in the valley
    Beholds, tho' he dare not name.

And in every wild breeze falling
    Out of spaces beyond the sky,
There are ancient voices calling
    To regions remote and high;
To the gardens of elfin glory
    That lie o'er the purple seas,
And mansions of dream and story
    From childhood memories.

I am call'd where the still dawns glitter
    On pastures and furrow'd crests,
And the thrush and the wood-lark twitter
    Low over their brookside nests;
Where the smoke of the cottage hovers,
    And the elm-buds promise their shade,
And a carpet of new green covers
    The floor of the forest glade.

I am call'd where the vales are dreaming
    In golden, celestial light,
With the gables of castles gleaming,
    And village roofs steep and bright;
With distant spires set slimly
    Over tangles of twining boughs,
And a ribbon of river seen dimly
    Thro' fields that the farmer ploughs.

I am call'd where a twilight ocean
    Laps the piers of an ancient town,
And dream-ships in ghostly motion
    Ride at anchor up and down;
Where sea-lanes narrow and bending
    Climb steep thro' the fragrant gloom
Of chimneys and gambrels blending
    With orchard branches in bloom.

And when o'er the waves enchanted
    The moon and the stars appear,
I am haunted—haunted—haunted
    By dreams of a mystic year;
Of a year long lost in the dawning,
    When the planets were vague and pale,
And the chasms of space were yawning
    To vistas that fade and fail.

I am haunted by recollections
    Of lands that were not of earth,
Of places where mad perfections
    In horror were brought to birth;
Where pylons of onyx mounted
    To heavens with fire embower'd,
And turrets and domes uncounted
    O'er the terrac'd torrents tower'd.

I am call'd to these reachless regions
    In tones that are old and known,
By a chorus of phantom legions
    That must have been once my own—
But the spell is a charm swift fleeting,
    And the earth has a potent thrall,
So I never have known the freeing.
    Or heeded the springtime's call.

To an Infant

They have captured and chained you, my brother, from Aidenne be-
    yond the blue,
The Fates and the vast All-Mother, to laugh at an hour or two.
They have envied your wings dilated, beating heedless of age or clime,
So they snared you and cast you weighted into dungeons of space and
    time.
And now as you newly languish in the quivering bonds called flesh,
Unknowing as yet the anguish and gall of the long-felt mesh,
They smile as they find you comely, and gloat on their ancient power
To twist you and drive you dumbly for the sport of a listless hour.
They have given you joy but to take it, and youth but to snatch it away,

They have made you a will but to break it, and hope but to lead you
    astray;
They have bound you to objects inutile, and senses that shut out the
    light,
That themselves, who are bitter and futile, may laugh as you grope in
    their sight.
But you, if you will, can cheat them, and join in the mocking mirth,
For you have that to defeat them which could not be chained at birth:
Though your heart they have trussed and tethered, and your soul they
    have stricken drear
Yet a spark from your dreams has weathered all the whirlwinds that
    swept you here.
It has slipt by the onyx portal that holds you to earthly things,
From the crystalline gulfs immortal, that sounded once to your wings.
It will flame through the mists of morning and lighten the hours of
    your youth,
Till the blaze of its bright adorning will banish the clouds of truth.
But foster it well, young dreamer, lest the covetous Great Ones call
On Time, the malign Arch-Schemer, to gather it into his thrall;
For dreams, as they are most precious, are most fragile of all we prize,
And the powers of earth that enmesh us would sear them out of our
    eyes;
Would marshal the years to slay them, and summon the flesh to teach
Our hardening brains to betray them, and drive them beyond our reach.
They are all that we have to save us from the sport of the Ruthless
    Ones,
These dreams that the cosmos gave us in the void past the farthest
    suns;
They are freedom and light surviving as a flicker in cells of ill,
As against the Dark Gods' contriving we must harbour and guard them
    still.
So may you, in whose eyes serenely so much of the old lore shines,
Grow valiant, and battle keenly the envious Gods' designs;
Dissolve when they seek to bind you; fling worlds at their clanking
    chain;
That never their noose may find you, and never their whim restrain.
Weave magic against their weaving, dream out of their sly duress,
Till the prisons of their deceiving shall crumble to nothingness.

Mock back when they storm your reason, and hold you from all you
    crave,
For your body alone they seize on—no dream can be made a slave.
Deride all their empty offers, and sneer at their specious lure,
Enriching your fancy's coffers with gold that is always pure.
Your dreams are yourself, so tend them as all that preserves you free;
With all of your strength defend them, nor grant to the years a fee;
Let never a daemon buy them with pleasures that flash and fade,
Nor sophistry's tongue defy them, nor dogma diffuse its shade.
For these are your own, my brother, and hold in their boundless sweep
The wings that the Gods would smother, and the key to your native
    deep!

To George Kirk, Esq.,

Upon His Entertaining a Company in His New-Decorated Chambers
18th January 1925

Gay, gen'rous host whose faultless taste is shewn
Each day in volumes bought for worth alone,
On this bright evening in thy freshen'd nest
Receive the praise of those who love thee best!
Graceful the walls that now enclose thee round,
Eternal beauty hovering profound,
With classick urn and graven image join'd
In one vast whole to please the tasteful mind.
Light touches here, and bits of colour there
Lend pleasing charms and animate the air;
And not a prospect but impels the eye,
Rejoicing, to confess its majesty.
Drest thus in style, these scenes must needs distill
Keen lively judgment from thy pliant quill;
In style piquant of thee a critick mould
Refin'd in manners, but in matter bold—
King of them all, inform'd and agile-soul'd!
                      —L. Theobald Jones

To George Willard Kirk, Gent., of Chelsea Village in New York, upon His Birthday, Novr. 25, 1925

Watchman, attend! Which feast is this which lights
The village street that should be dark o' nights?
Say, what strange rapture brings ecstatick fires
Where rural CHELSEA rears its peaceful spires?
Unwonted streamers deck the antique walls,
And o'er the green, confetti mounts and falls:
Scholar and cit as one resign their work
And shout in mingled joy, "Long flourish KIRK!"
Health to the sage whose natal night we sing;
Whose praises loud from ev'ry trumpet ring;
Health to the sage, who has with skilful pains
Led learning back to CHELSEA'S verdant lanes.
Each loyal cotter beams with brimming eye,
And studious swains promote the minstrelsy:
For KIRK'S Egyptian art, with spells of yore,
Lights once again the long-quencht lamp of MOORE!

How long ago that pleasing minstrel sung
The Yuletide lines alive on ev'ry tongue:
"Night Before Christmas," which our fancies took
From lips maternal, or the picture-book!
These spacious acres form'd our MOORE'S domain
Ere CHELSEA'S rows of brick involv'd the plain;
But as the village proud and prosp'rous grew,
The Muse for want of nourishment withdrew:
Southward to GREENWICH she her footsteps train'd,
Where tho' scarce worshipt, she was shrewdly feign'd.
Thus pass'd the years, when lo! auspicious Fate
Our CHELSEA spies, and mourns her lost estate;
Scours the broad West for some heroick hand
To throne Apollo in a twice-born land,
And finds skill'd KIRK, of letter'd knights the head,
By AKRON mother'd, and by CLEVELAND bred!
See now the conqu'ror stride with shining lance,
Boetia trembling at his bold advance;
See frighten'd Dulness in far caverns hide,

Whilst fleeting Vanity discards her pride:
Grim lines of sombre mansions smile anew,
And vanisht splendour climbs once more to view;
Learning, long exil'd, claims her ancient seat,
And led by KIRK, troops stately up the street!
His mellow tomes, to all the town display'd,
The scholar's treasure, and the Muses' aid,
Gleam in the windows, while his festive door
Welcomes a throng that knew not books before.
But not content with what the great have writ,
Vivacious KIRK must needs have living wit:
Like Will's or Burton's must his threshold glow
With the sage sermon and the quick *bon-mot:*
Wise in his time, he draws from meads around
Bright courtly balladists, and bards profound;
Poets and pedants, scholiasts and seers,
Midst whom he sits, the first among his peers!
Reviving CHELSEA heeds, and from her shores
The grateful birthday paean lovely pours:
Each ancient wharf, where restless vessels ride,
Responsive sings, and tells the roving tide.
Sequester'd quads, where piety is nurst,
Wake from their hymns, and into tributes burst,
Whilst envious GREENWICH o'er the southern fields
With envy sighs, and all her laurels yields.

KIRK, may thy life be happy, wise, and long,
With learning blest, and bright with Delian song;
May Virtue be no stranger, and may joy
Perpetual reign, and all thy care employ.
Few are thy years, as yet, but as they fly,
May genial mem'ry gild the hours gone by,
Till all about thee shine with waxing ray,
And doubled treasures greet each natal day!
                                November 24, 1925

Two Christmas Poems to G. W. K.

1

Since Chelsea is old SANTA's very home,
I trust he'll call before he starts to roam,
And find in KIRK a worthy youth to crown
With all the fame that MOORE of old laid down.

2

Where Chelsea's cluster'd steeples climb
    And peaceful hearths at Christmas glow,
Let simple age direct a rhyme
    To sing the praise of long ago.

With wholesome boons may all be blest
    Who bide within thy happy door!
Charlie, small Oscar, and the rest—
    And thou, whose Art can highest soar!

A Year Off

Had I a year to idle thro',
    With cash to waste and no restriction,
I'd plan a programme to outdo
    The wildest feats of travel fiction.

On steamship guides I'd slake my thirst,
    And railway maps would make me wiser—
America consider'd first
    To please the local advertiser.

O'er England and the Continent
    I'd chart a course to shame the sages,
In each cathedral town intent
    To catch the colour of the ages.

Paris and Rome I would not miss;
    Without the Rhine I'd be no planner,
For one must make a jaunt like this
    A Grand Tour in the ancient manner!

But Europe is a trifle trite,
    So I would spare no pains in learning
How best to scan in casual flight
    The East, where sheiks and sands are burning.

I'd look up ferries on the Nile,
    And 'bus fares for the trip to Mecca;
Have chemists test in proper style
    The drinking-fountain of Rebecca.

The route of ev'ry Tigris barge
    I'd note, and find how much they'd ask us;
What good hotels in Bagdad charge,
    And yellow taxis in Damascus.

And I would surely have on hand
    The folders of that great excursion,
The Golden Road to Samarcand,
    Thro' Bahai bow'rs and gardens Persian.

Beyond the Pullman rates I'd get
    For Kiao-chan and Yokohama,
Arranging passage thro' Tibet
    To dally with the Dalai Lama.

In tropic isles I'd plan to stay
    Till South Sea melodies would bore me,
And for the North Pole book a day,
    Where only Peary went before me.

Thus might I scheme—till in the end
    The year would slip away unheeded,
My money safe with me to spend,
    And the wild outing scarcely needed!

In Memoriam: Oscar Incoul Verelst of Manhattan 1920–1926

Damn'd be this harsh mechanick Age
    That whirls us fast and faster,
And swallows with Sabazian Rage
    Nine Lives in one Disaster.

I take my Quill with sadden'd Thought,
    Tho' falt'ringly I do it;
And, having curst the Juggernaut,
    Inscribe: OSCARVS FVIT!

                —L. Theobald, Jun.

Samuel Loveman

SAMUEL LOVEMAN
(1887–1976)

Samuel Loveman, at thirty-seven, came to New York in August 1924 to work in the book trade. It helped, of course, that his old Cleveland friends George Kirk and Hart Crane were already here, and that his new friend, Howard Lovecraft, was here also. Aside from a short stint in World War I, which he spent largely in a U.S. hospital, it was Loveman's first time of living away from Cleveland.

Steeped in the classics and Elizabethans, with a refined poetic sensibility, sensitive and intelligent, Loveman was by far the best poet of the Kalems. He had been trained as, of all things, an accountant. Like Rheinhart Kleiner, Loveman loved music, and in Cleveland he and Kirk had co-sponsored several performances.

Loveman and Lovecraft first corresponded in 1917, when Lovecraft praised Loveman's poetry. They met in April 1922, when Sonia Greene invited them both to New York. During that visit, Rheinhart Kleiner, Frank Belknap Long, Everett McNeil, and James Morton guided them around the city. So taken with Loveman was Lovecraft that he soon visited him in Cleveland, where Loveman lived with his mother and brother in the Lenore Apartments. Lovecraft admired Loveman's erudition and his aesthetic sensibilities. During that visit, Loveman introduced Lovecraft to his bookseller friend, George Kirk, who, in November 1922, published *Twenty-one Letters of Ambrose Bierce*, edited, and with a note, by Loveman.

In New York, Loveman moved into a fourth-floor apartment at 78 Columbia Heights, Brooklyn, with a spectacular view of the Manhattan skyline. Hart Crane lived just down the hall. Soon Loveman found employment at Dauber and Pine, booksellers, at Fifth Avenue and 12th St.

Loveman had a pleasant, open face, and was handsome, despite premature balding and large ears. In photos, he looks dapper and well-dressed. Somewhat formal, courteous, and steady, Loveman was also an enthusiast, although Hart Crane saw him as inhibited and frightened. Loveman was kind and generous. Whenever possible, he helped Lovecraft with employment, and he wrote a generous introduction to Long's first book of poetry. Although Loveman never married, through the years he lived with several partners.

The Kalem years were a happy time for Loveman. As a sophisticated, well-read man, with many artistic sensibilities, he probably felt at home in New York. He had almost daily contact with dear friends. And these years were productive poetically. He published widely in the amateur press, and in 1926 *The Hermaphrodite*, his best-known and longest poem, came out, dedicated to George Kirk.

Loveman and Lovecraft remained friends and visited each other several times through the years. Loveman stayed in New York and later worked at the Gotham Book Mart; he owned the Bodley Book Shop, publishing several books under its imprint. In 1936 the Caxton Press published *The Hermaphrodite and Other Poems,* a substantial volume, and in 1944 *The Sphinx,* a lengthy prose drama, appeared.

Although Loveman's work was highly praised by many, he never achieved wide recognition as a poet. His classical themes and formal meter probably seemed old-fashioned, even archaic, next to Eliot, Pound, and Crane. He remained a romantic writing in an age of modernism. Loveman never tried to collect his poems, seemingly content to publish in amateur journals. (Hippocampus Press has now issued his *Out of the Immortal Night: Selected Works by Samuel Loveman.*)

Interestingly enough, Loveman maintained close friendships with both Lovecraft and Crane. After the death of Crane's mother, Loveman became the executor of Crane's estate. Loveman died in the Jewish Home and Hospital in Cleveland in 1976, at the age of eighty-nine. His last poem, written a month before his death, is "John Clare in 1864."

A Letter to G—— K——

Here, in the night, are winds that cry and keep
Their frozen clangor on the wall of sleep;
Autumn, in pyramidal splendor pales,
But in her heart the joy it is that fails
And fades. Not all her sun, rain, wrath, her cries,
The red lustration of a soul that dies
Uncherished and regretful, still'd in bronze,
Under the year's immortal gonfalons—
Dare keep her with us. To her clarion call,
Is whispered moaning the confessional
That precedes Winter, when by way and flood,
Steals as a doom, the whiter brotherhood,
Unshriving and unshriven with a speech,
Deeper than heartache in the depth of each,
Alone, yet muted.
                    O my dearest friend!
Never the day that does not reach an end.
Never yet in the wild symphonic din,
But there came subtler the cry within;
Give up . . . give over! I am he who said:
Until this disquiet heart be quieted;
Not even a winged vestige shall remain,
Save the one prophesying voice that spells,
Rebellion for this nethermost of hells;
Protest against the blind, the dumb, the driven,
Beggar'd on earth yet still denied their heaven:
Not until thither as a torch at tryst,
There perish in my soul the mutinist,
Shall I be silenced! I have heard it told,
Of a vast tower of perfume and of gold;
About a wayfarer as in a dream,
Who saw the molten spire and windows gleam,
Heard cry a voice in the enchanted night,
From lips like music, laughter and delight;
Something that pealed: Enter! for here at feast,
Thou, that of mankind art accounted least,
Shalt as a god sit, strange, imperial, lone,

Tremulous and sublunar on thy throne. . . .
And entered in huge silence, but at dawn,
One who beside him stood, cried: Now begone!
A shadow art thou henceforth, even as these
That wrought so cruelly thy destinies—
Call thyself Pity, ever after! I
Must be that wayfarer until I die;
Shall seek, and always seeking never find
Wisdom in hearts, beauty in eyes stone-blind,
Then pass to one who passed before me. . . . He
Who so loved life, who so loved liberty,
That all the darkness in eternal space,
Shone golden on us with his godlike face,
In still, saturnian largess. We remain,
Never to know his druid self again;
Nor on the water's perilous rise and fall,
To hear soft-brimm'd, that voice of voices call
Lines from the sonnets he so loved to speak,
Shakespeare, Stagnelius, or some purple Greek,
Who sang to lyres by the Ionian Sea,
Forgotten, save by him alone. But we,
When Spring begins out Dover-way, shall find
The butterflies again upon the wind,
And see in all the blue sky, pink and white,
The apple blossoms in their downward flight,
Hearken the birds upon the boughs that bend,
To sing the song that only Spring shall end,
And hear his soul, the cry in flowers and leaves,
Love me—but love me not, who pines and grieves!

To George Kirk on His 27th Birthday

Still do I hear where hillside winds are shaken,
    When the long daylight ends;
From one whose lips shall never re-awaken:
    "Be friends, and always friends."

Friend, to one friend—we only and none other,
    This lustrous vigil keep—
The memory of our violet-laden brother,
    Bound fast in Roman sleep.

For the Chelsea Book Shop [1]

Walk into Chelsea where each street
  Climbs down to take a tug or wherry;
Never a rose-tree shall you meet,
  Never a lilac near the ferry.

By mast and spar and silhouette
  The ancient ghosts cling each together;
The city streets are chill and wet—
  They vow 'tis only fine Spring weather.

Yet when the winter, vast and pale,
  Beckons with snow and wind at riot;
They seek a shelter from the gale
  Within your realm of books and quiet.

And see your shelves stand row on row,
  And hear the world move by with laughter—
More than the living ever know,
  The wisdom of the dead knows after.

For the Chelsea Book Shop [2]

The night is over Chelsea Town,
  But far below the houses lie;
Mute, mute is all the city grown,
  Stiller than silence now, am I.

Who saw the yellow moon that climbs
  To flood the purple, Attic night;
Then gave the cry of ancient times,
  Half ecstasy and half delight.

Come with me now, as one believes
  That when the dawn begins to stir;
The birds must sing among the leaves,
  While hedges break with lavender.

And heed no more the city's ache,
  Than he who sang the age of gold
Within a heart that needs must break
  Seeing the tired world turn old.

For a Cat

Oscar, when your eyes of light,
Face the vast abyss of night,
And on ghostly stairs you crawl,
In your paradisal hall,
Take a lighted doorway where
A sign reads: "Chelsea Book Shop here";
Enter, if you care to play,
Sleep by night and dream by day,
Tarry till your eyes grow dim,
And you meet the feline Him,
While He hears when shadows fall,
Your immortal caterwaul.

For a Book of Poems

The nightingales that sang in their Asian garden
    Are mute, and the Tyrian dreams
No longer of sultry wines that made him their warden,
    Drifting in dyed triremes.

But come, I have never grown old and if you but hearken
    My song shall give you release;
Far, far from these eyes that shiver and darken . . .
    I can take you back to Greece.

Admonition

Fever and heartache, joy and grief,
    Take pause, for the end must come;
Beautiful songs so frail and brief
    From beautiful lips long dumb.

Fasten your heart to the cherry-bough
    That touches the light and wakes;
All that is dark and secret now
    Will bend when the blossom breaks.

Limbo

There was a moth that took the flame at even
    Against the sunset sky,

And saw with wings that covered half of heaven,
  A vaster butterfly.

So far within the moonlight, fluttered deeper,
  The wings that could not scale;
A night that takes the dreamer and the sleeper
  And all brief things that fail.

To H. P. L.

In Providence, at fringèd eve,
  Old Theobald takes his cap and cane;
And where the antique shadows grieve,
  Dreams his colonial dreams again.

Sees the pale periwigs that pass,
  Pause delicately by, then fare
Past balustrades that shine like glass
  To find his Eighteenth Century there.

Dream, Theobald—close your tired eyes,
  Forget the ruder world around;
Only these bygone folk were wise,
  Only the vanisht world was sound.

Hold them an instant if you will,
  Shadows of perfume, light and flow'rs—
We never knew their grace until
  You, by your genius, made them ours.
                    21 September 1924

[Inscribed below: "For George who also loves H.P.L., from Sam."]

Genesis

Half the world was chaos
  In the golden deep;
God blew on the waters,
  And murmured: Let them sleep.

Blew upon the daybreak,
  And hid within His wings;

Men awoke in sorrow
    At the memory of things.

Spring at El Retiro

Spring comes this way on bud and briar
    With birds that wing in sun and light;
And deep within her dreaming fire,
    She yearns again for space and flight.

Hold her, O master and her lover,
    Keep her beside you all her years,
Blue as the bluest sky above her,
    Her eyes are often filled with tears.

Arcesilaus

Never again shall I come to you in Spring divinely drunken
    The god who came to you;
With the lore of Greece on my lips and eyelids sunken,
    Heavy with dreaming too.

O beautiful! I sang as a bird that sings—as a bird that sings its fill
    While crescent Summer wakes;
With laughter and love, with the joy of singing until
    The burning heart of it breaks.

John Clare in 1864

Here, in the shadows of the creek,
Sits Clare, the gentlest of the weak.

Across the tethered portico,
The shadows come, the shadows go.

He sees the blue skies overhead,
But at his feet the flowers are dead.

Once only are his eyes alight,
An effort less of lark in flight.

John Clare stares up, his dull eyes bright.
Someday I'll follow in his flight.

[Written in the spring of 1976, when Loveman was 89.]

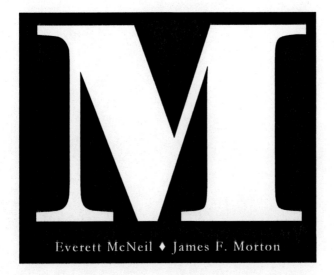

Everett McNeil ◆ James F. Morton

ADVENTURE
▼ PIONEER ▼
▼▼ INDIAN ▼▼

From the jacket design of "For the Glory of France"

STORIES for BOYS
by EVERETT McNEIL

McNeil's For the Glory of France *(1927) tells the story of Samuel de Champlain through the eyes of fictitious stowaways Noel Bidoux and Robert de Boville, "two French boys."*

EVERETT MCNEIL
(1867–1929)

By 1924, Everett McNeil, at sixty-two, was well past his prime. As the author of sixteen adventure books for boys, he had achieved some financial success, but in 1924 he lived in poverty in a hotel on West 49th Street, the area of Manhattan known as "Hell's Kitchen." His diet was canned soup and crackers. Things had been worse: at times, according to Lovecraft, McNeil subsisted solely on sugar water.

McNeil was born and raised on a Wisconsin farm. As a young man— undoubtedly with literary ambitions—he had walked and hitchhiked to New York, where, through the years, E. P. Dutton published his books. As far as we know, McNeil never married or had children. Were his middle years more prosperous? We can only hope so, but by 1924 his was a meager, lonely existence.

We must credit McNeil for starting the group that became the Kalem Club. For several years prior to 1924, James Morton had visited McNeil's small, neat rooms weekly, sometimes joined by Rheinhart Kleiner, Frank Belknap Long, and perhaps Arthur Leeds, who lived nearby. Probably these friends made his life bearable. When H. P. Lovecraft visited New York in April 1922, McNeil graciously acted as a guide.

Although all the Kalems were fond of modest, genial McNeil, they may have been somewhat bored by his company also. He was, after all, writing romanticized adventure stories for boys, and according to Kirk's letters, did not have to talk down to his readers. According to Kirk also, McNeil was a born storyteller, but even storytellers can be tiring. Simple and direct, he was no match for sophisticated Lovecraft and Morton. When a rift arose between McNeil and Leeds over borrowed funds, McNeil refused to attend meetings if Leeds were there, and instead held his own meetings. At times Lovecraft was his only guest.

Small, slightly stooped, with white hair and a kindly face, McNeil was a square peg in a round hole, a misfit in New York's complex, harsh, competitive, rushing society. Perhaps he was oblivious to his surroundings, with his head in a different world, dreaming of Wisconsin and his early days— sunshine, maples, and hay. Simple and wholesome, he preferred coffee and milk to muscatel, and books to women. He should have been rocking by the fire in a Wisconsin farmhouse, telling stories on a snowy evening.

During the Kalem years, McNeil spent his days writing—slowly and painstakingly, about 200 words a day—and doing research, probably at the New York Public Library, about a mile walk from his hotel. Even at that, he was the most prolific of the Kalems. He didn't participate in the all-night walks, the Sunday promenades in Brooklyn, or the afternoon coffees, having neither the time, the money, nor perhaps the energy to do so. He was working on the story of Daniel DuLuth—a voyageur who discovered the city in which I live—

and in 1927, Dutton published his book on the story of Champlain, *For the Glory of France.* All McNeil's books are set in other times and places than twentieth century Manhattan: Colorado, Texas, Minnesota, or Virginia.

McNeil was not to live much longer. He died at sixty-seven, in 1929, in Tacoma, where he had been living with his sister.

From *Tonty of the Iron Hand* (1925)

The story begins in a garden in France, separated from the public
highway by a tall iron fence, wherein the spikes were like great iron
lances, such as I had seen certain of the King's soldiers carry on gala
days. I remember these lance-like spikes distinctly, although the garden
and the great house set well back from the highway form but a dim picture in my memory. I was then but a boy of some ten years and unimportant things will fix themselves in a small boy's memory to the
casting out of more important matters.

Presently, as I played in that garden, with my eyes turning ever to the
broad highway beyond the iron spikes of the fence, whereon might pass
many wonderful and mysterious things in so small a boy's eyes, I heard
the galloping of a horse and ran swiftly to the fence, thrust my small face
between two of the iron spikes, and looked down the road eagerly in the
direction of the sound of the galloping horse. I saw first a cloud of dust,
then from out the cloud burst a great black horse, and when the horse
had come nearer, I saw on his back the figure of a tall man, with a great
scarlet-lined cloak floating out behind his broad shoulders and a great
black hat with a long scarlet plume encircling its brim and fluttering out
behind, on his head. A most gallant figure he made as he came galloping
down the highway, the scarlet-lined cloak and the great plume fluttering
in the wind of his coming; and great was my astonishment when, at sight
of my face thrust between the spikes, he suddenly jerked his horse to a
sliding halt directly in front of me and looked down at me out of a pair of
the blackest and most piercing eyes I have ever seen in human head.

For a time he sat motionless in his saddle, like a stone man, his bold
eyes on my face, and I, boy-like, stood entranced, admiring the great size
of the man, the richness of his dress, the long sword, with its jeweled hilt,
which hung by the side of one long leg, the curls of his black hair, and
the masterful way in which he sat the saddle of that great horse as if a
part of the beast's body. I have no distinct remembrance of how the face
itself then looked, save that a peculiar scar puckered the left cheek directly under the eye and gave a queer, but not unpleasant, squint to the
eye itself, as if it could see two ways at once, and that I was greatly
amused thereby. My childish eyes saw only the external splendors of the
man and these fascinated and awed me, for into my quiet boy-life never
before had come riding such a man and horse. Even to this day the picture of that great swart man sitting on the back of that great black horse,

with the scarlet plume of his great hat falling alongside the curls of his
black hair, his scarlet-lined cloak thrown back from his shoulders, the
jeweled hilt of his sword glittering at his side, his black eyes searching my
face, that picture, as seen through my boyish eyes on that warm June day,
still remains the most vivid scene in childhood's memory.

"This must be the very boy!" he at length cried out, and I felt that
for some unknown reason he was surprised and glad to find me standing there staring up at him. "Now, my young cockerel," and his voice
sharpened and his eyes went quickly from my small figure to the great
house in the far background, then came swiftly back to me, "if I mistake not you are named Edmond, Edmond de Leon, and you live in
that big house there," and his hand went out and one gloved finger
pointed toward the house.

"Yes, Monsieur," I answered, trembling a bit in my body and staring
up awesomely into the face beneath the wide brim of that great black hat.

"Then, by the bones of St. Catherine! I am in right good luck!" and
the two lips beneath a long black mustache came into a smile that showed
two rows of teeth, whose even whiteness was broken by a single great
fanglike tooth, which protruded from the upper jaw directly beneath the
puckered scar under the left eye. I know not why, save that its protruding
ugliness, suddenly showing in so handsome a face, hit my boyish fancy,
but that great fanglike tooth bit so deeply into my memory that even now
it is one of the most distinct things I remember about that face.

"Yea, by the bones of the good St. Anthony! I am in luck to find you
standing here, as if your good angel had bade you come hither to await my
coming. Now clamber you quickly to the top of that fence, wherefrom I
can swing you to the saddle in front of me, for I have come to take you to
your Lady Mother who, by an evil mischance, fell from the horse she was
riding and has been so grievously hurt that she bade me ride in all speed
and bring you to her. She lies, attended by two surgeons, in the house of a
friend not far from here. Quick, my lad, up to the top of the fence. There
is not a moment to waste if you would see your Lady Mother living," and
the look in the black eyes became peremptory and compelling.

Had I been in all of my wits, even all of my boy-wits, I would have
noted the uneasy glances of the man in the direction of the big house in
the far background as he lifted me from the top of the fence and swung
me with cruel haste, regardless of the tenderness of my young body, on to
the saddle in front of him, but the thought of my Dear Lady Mother lying
hurt and in pain and calling for me, and the chill of the great dread that

came into my young heart at the words of the man, made me blind and thoughtless of all else save the getting to her as speedily as possible. Not an hour before she had kissed me good-bye and, mounting her horse, had ridden away, the most beautiful and lovesome lady in all France, or so she seemed to her young and worshiping son. Now—I shuddered.

"Make haste!" I cried and then my throat choked.

"Grip the pommel of the saddle tightly and hold fast!" the man cried. "We are off!" and the great black beast beneath me leaped like a suddenly released spring, almost out from under me at the deep thrust of the spurs.

Even in that dread moment I could but exult in the swift movement of the horse, in the push of the wind against my face, in the thought that I sat the back of this great horse; but, presently, again came thoughts of my Dear Lady Mother and her hurt and I partly turned to make further inquiry. Then, suddenly, before a word came from between my lips, the man behind me uttered a deep curse and I felt the thrust of his legs as he drove the spurs deep into the flanks of his horse, and I would have been unseated by the sudden forward leap of his steed, if his great hand had not gripped me by the shoulder and thrust me back into my place, with a rough strength that jarred every bone in my body.

"Sit firm and hold tight the pommel of the saddle and utter not a sound, or by heaven! I'll hurl you from me with a force that will break every bone in your body!" His voice had suddenly lost all its softness and was harsh with purpose, and yet, even in my young ears, I heard an exultant thrill in it, as if the man joyed in that mad ride and the danger of it; for danger, I knew, had driven so suddenly the spurs into his horse.

"What is it?" I cried out in alarm, again partly turning in an effort to look back.

But before he could answer there came a swift spiteful hiss and rush of air past my right ear, instantly followed by the sharp, crack-crack, of two pistol shots. I shuddered and bent close over the pommel and clung there tightly. What meant those pistol shots?

"That was well-aimed," and the man in the saddle behind me laughed grimly. "But 'twill take more than pistol shots to stop the Black Rover," and I could feel his body turning in the saddle so that he could look backward.

"But one! *Peste!* I'll not flee from one! Better to stop his tongue from telling what his eyes have seen," and I saw the reins tighten in the grip of the one hand that held them in front of me and I felt the speed of the horse slacken.

"Hold, hold! Stealer of babes! Hold! My blade will give you worthier work to do."

My heart jumped at the sound of that voice coming from out the distance behind, the voice of my Dear Lady Mother's most trusted and bravest friend, since the death of my father, Raoul de Ligny. He had ridden away with my Dear Lady Mother that morning when I had kissed her good-bye. Then, if harm had come to her, he must know of it!

"Hold, it is Raoul!" I cried. "He rode with my Dear Lady Mother and will know of her hurt. He——"

A hand clapped rudely and forcibly over my lips stopped the words in my mouth.

"Shut up and keep shut up!" a voice hissed in my ear, "or I'll spit your tender body on my sword, even as I am about to spit the body of this Raoul of yours, whose voice challenges so boldly. Speak but again and——"

I felt the sharp point of his sword prick into the small of my back, and, had not the greatest fear of my life paralyzed my tongue, I would have screamed, with the terror this sudden change in the behavior of the man gave me. What could it mean? I clung desperately to the pommel of the saddle with both hands, for a great dread of I know not what was sucking the strength from my trembling body.

By now the road had dipped into a small valley, where trees grew close on both sides of the highway, and here, under the low branches of a great oak, the Black Rover—for so the swart man had called himself—turned his horse about, pulled him to a standstill, and sat silent and grim in his saddle, his long sword in one hand, to await the coming of Raoul. Nor had he long to wait. In a whirlwind of dust Raoul came to a halt not six paces in front of him, his bare sword shining in his hand.

"Yield yourself my prisoner, you base stealer of babes, or my sword will free the child with your life," Raoul cried, his eager sword thirsting in his hand.

"That I will not," answered the Black Rover coldly. "Now dismount and out with your bodkin. I'll be at your service presently, as soon as I bind the wings of this young cockerel, so that he will not take flight. And while you await me, make your peace with God, for I am about to spit your heart on my sword."

There was a cold finality in his voice that sent a chill of dread to my heart, for I loved Raoul. Then I recalled, with a rush of warmth and hope, that I had often heard the skill of Raoul de Ligny with the sword sung loudly, that it was said he had never met his master.

"Do you likewise make peace with God, stealer of babes, for on my sword's point lies the key to your grave."

I felt pride in the scorn and cold harshness in Raoul's voice and I knew that there was no fear of this great swart man in his brave heart.

Now these two men, without more words, began to prepare for the grim business before them. Raoul dismounted and took his station a little way from under the great oak, where its shadows did not fall and the light was better; and I could but wonder at the pleasant smile that came on his lips, as his eyes sought mine. The Black Rover bound my hands tightly behind my back, thrust me about in the saddle, and then firmly tied my hands to the pommel. As he did this I heard him humming a gay tune joyously to himself, like a man with a delightsome task before him—and I shivered.

I shudder, even now, as I recall that fight to the death, the first my young eyes had witnessed. The Black Rover turned from me, swept the great hat from his head, and holding it against his bosom, bowed low.

"My sword is now at your service," he said and flung hat and scarlet-lined cloak to the ground and with naked sword in his hand, strode to where Raoul stood awaiting him. A moment later I heard the clicking of their swift swords. Even my boyish eyes saw at once that Raoul had met his match, possibly his master, and a great fear began gathering in my heart.

Then was fought, I am sure, a marvelously skilled sword-fight. My memory tells me this, and I have since learned that the Black Rover was one of the most famous swordsmen of his time; but I was only a boy, with my heart chugging in my mouth and my eyes watching those swiftly moving points with a greater intensity than I have ever watched anything else in my life, dreading the moment when I would see one of them thrust into a human bosom.

Raoul fought with a cold, deadly fury. The Black Rover fought as if he were exhibiting the finer points of his skill and even as he fought, I heard that gay humming tune, as if he were keeping time to the lightning-like play of his sword.

Then, suddenly, his sword leaped straight out, like a thing of life, and the next instant my horrified eyes saw the blade for half its length sticking into the bosom of brave Raoul——

From that moment of horror and for many hours after, my memory is a blank.

Frank Belknap Long, H. P. Lovecraft, and James F. Morton
at the Poe cottage, New York

JAMES FERDINAND MORTON
(1870–1941)

In 1924, it seemed as if James F. Morton, at fifty-four, would never marry or find adequate full-time professional employment. A confirmed bachelor, he lived alone in Harlem—thus supporting one of the causes he espoused—and pieced together a living as lecturer and essayist on causes that inspired him: Negro rights, tax reform, and Esperanto. His many areas of expertise also included mineralogy, amateur journalism, genealogy, and puzzle solving. As a reformer, Morton was the social conscience of the Kalem group.

Certainly Morton was the most cosmopolitan—and vied with Lovecraft for being the most erudite—of the Kalem members. Born in Littleton, Massachusetts, of old New England stock, he earned an M.A. from Harvard, had been a Rhodes Scholar, traveled to Europe twice, lived in free love colonies, been a news reporter and social speaker, and had been in much financial hardship, surviving in Boston on nothing but crackers for weeks.

Morton was first "introduced" to Lovecraft through their mutual friend, Maurice Moe. They met in person at an amateur journalists' conference in Boston, in 1920, and thus began a long and close friendship. Morton had been in New York for several years and was in the habit of visiting Everett McNeil's rooms weekly for literary talk, occasionally joined by Rheinhart Kleiner and Frank Belknap Long. This group was to form the nucleus of the Kalem Club.

Stocky, portly, with graying red hair and a moustache, Morton was a central figure among the Kalems. They highly valued his opinions, appreciated his erudition, and reveled in his witty repartee. George Kirk wrote: "If Lovecraft is a prince, Morton is a King."

Morton's life changed dramatically during the Kalem years. In 1925 he married Pearl K. Merritt, a member of the Blue Pencil Club. That same year, he became director of the Paterson (New Jersey) Museum, and left Manhattan for Paterson. Morton asked Lovecraft to be his assistant, but somehow that never materialized. He held this position until his retirement at seventy, in 1940.

In New Jersey, Morton, an enthusiast with high energy, became active in the Paterson Hiking Club. Often Kirk, Kleiner, and very occasionally Lovecraft joined him and others on Sunday hikes. After Lovecraft's return to Providence in April 1926, although the Kalems met only sporadically, these Sunday hikes became routine.

Morton published tracts and articles during his lifetime, on Negro rights, Esperanto, and tax reform. He wrote some occasional poems and, late in life, wrote a series of genealogy articles for the Boston Evening Transcript. In 1940, shortly before he and Pearl began their retirement in New Hampshire, Morton, at seventy, was struck and killed by an automobile. He left behind no book and no children.

To G.W.K. on His 27ᵗʰ Birthday

Another year has sped. Mourn not its flight.
   Though restless time stays not at our command,
Its gifts of larger wisdom, keener sight,
With pleasures snatched at envious Fate's despite,
   Are amply scattered from its lavish hand.

Another year has sped. A year of note
   It is to us, your friends, who greet you here.
It brought us you, at date not long remote;
It anchored in our midst your welcome boat,
   And nobly graced our lives with added cheer.

Another year has sped. And though the days
   To come perchance hold many a lurking care,
Be sure, dear George, if Fate our will obeys,
Success will march with you in all your ways;
   And all your fortunes will be bright and fair.

From *The Curse of Race Prejudice* (1906?)

> "For the hope of every creature is the banner that we bear;
>   And the world is marching on!"
>   William Morris: Song of the Workers.

Our rapid survey of what is termed the race question must not be
deemed to have exhausted the subject. Race prejudice is not an
isolated phenomenon, but a single phase of the old tendency to fetish
worship, which our civilization has not yet outgrown. Full mental
emancipation is a discouragingly slow process, and beset with many
backslidings. Even among the most broadminded, there are strange
survivals of antiquated and grotesquely superstitious beliefs. Voodoo-
ism, in some of its aspects, is far from being confined to the wholly or
mainly illiterate classes. Men and women of high standing in the business and social world, and even possessed of what passes for an excellent education, actually shiver at the thought of dining in a party of
thirteen, of walking under a ladder, or of beginning a journey or launch-
ing a ship on Friday; and the United States government itself is weak

enough to cater to the last-named absurdity. And yet the very people who are such fools with relation to these particular survivals of barbaric ignorance, are thoroughly intelligent on ordinary topics. In like manner, race prejudice is to be found among many high-minded persons, otherwise endowed with splendid mental traits. The severe language employed in some parts of this pamphlet is not to be construed as a personal attack, but as an exposure of the clay feet of the blindly worshipped idol. There are millions of men and women, South as well as North, who are absolutely honest in their delusion. They are too good to be forever deceived by the shallow catchwords and base appeals to passion, wherewith unscrupulous politicians and merciless labor-exploiters seek to beguile them. When the truly honorable and chivalrous sons and daughters of the South realize that through a mistaken sense of honor, they have been made catspaws for the dirty work of a horde of conscienceless grafters, that magnificent section will shake off the nightmare of race prejudice, and enter upon the most glorious period of its history.

To make the issue perfectly plain, and to sum up the positions taken by the opponents of race prejudice, the following theses are subjoined:

1. All social, economic, religious or political discrimination based solely on color or race is wrong in principle and demoralizing in practice.
2. To treat a race as inferior is the surest way to make and keep it so.
3. It is a disgrace to any association of any sort to draw a color line.
4. A mere difference in color should debar no person from holding any office or position which is fit to be held at all.
5. Immigration into this or any other country should be open to all races on precisely equal terms.
6. The question of racial amalgamation is not involved in the demand for equal justice, and may be safely left to nature, without any present attempt to decide on its merits or possible evils.
7. The present status of a race in no way proves its permanent or even long continued superiority or inferiority as compared with any other race.
8. The inherent possibilities of a race are to be measured by the highest individual it has produced.

9. It is unutterably mean, as well as heartlessly cruel, to refuse to extend the hand of fellowship to an individual who is our equal in intelligence, refinement and character, simply because his family or race as a whole is on a much lower level.

10. An individual who has succeeded in rising superior to his racial environment deserves not only full social recognition at the hands of his equals in culture and intelligence, but exceptional regard on account of his splendid achievement in surmounting the obstacles of birth and early environment.

The hope that civilization can finally banish race prejudice from the Anglo Saxon mind is not a foolish dream. Looking through the course of history, we can trace the ultimate disappearance of delusions as deeply rooted and of as ancient origin. Belief in witchcraft has gone, with a host of other medieval superstitions. Slavery has disappeared, though only in our own time. No false doctrine, however powerfully entrenched in the human mind, can boast of an everlasting tenure. The process of clarifying the minds of men is slow, but sure. Already, there are many hopeful signs. The better element in the South is forging its way to the front, and making its influence felt. The "inferior races," and preeminently the colored race in America, are making their mark in every walk of life, and compelling a reluctant admission of their progressive qualities, even in circles where race hatred has been most assiduously cultivated. The future is full of promise. The law of social progress is irresistible. It will triumph here, as in every other department. The pity of it is that men and women should be found, who deliberately set themselves against it, and seek to block its movements. The ideal of a universal human brotherhood is the grandest which it has been given the mind of man to conceive; and there is unutterable sadness in the thought that there should be thousands of men and women in this fair land who have neither part nor lot in this divinest vision of the future, but instead turn from it with horror and aversion.

The great peace movement must sooner or later recognize its most insidious enemy in the doctrine that some races are inherently and eternally inferior to others. The disappearance of race prejudice will deal a final death-blow to jingoism. The sense of a common humanity must be rendered universal, before the giant crime of war can be made impossible. Until this fundamental psychological change is brought about, the success of Peace Congresses will be relatively insignificant; and their trifling barriers will continue to be broken down by every mad outbreak of inflamed national vanity or greed. International justice, enlarged human sympathy, a deeper regard for the sacredness of human life, all flow as of course from a full recognition of the unity of mankind. This is the lesson which the lovers of peace will do well to teach with the utmost emphasis, wherever they carry their most commendable propaganda; for in no other way can they render so effective service to their noble cause.

The presence of a mass of human ignorance and brutalization, white or black, is indeed a sore trial for any people to endure in their very midst; and the South deserves the deepest sympathy in the difficult problem with which she is compelled to grapple. But she in her turn must learn to look facts in the face, and not multiply difficulties for herself by seeking a wrong way out. Race prejudice only makes matters worse. Injustice breeds revenge. Hope stimulates aspiration and progress. No doubt a thousand faults of the undeveloped Negro race are unpleasantly apparent, and fearfully hard to endure. A world of patience is needed. Yet the South has only to open her eyes, in order to see a multitude of encouraging facts. Instead of keeping the Negro severely down, let him be stimulated to rise as high as he proves capable of rising. Instead of a competitor with the white race, let him be adopted as a partner; and both races will reap the benefit. Break down the artificial barriers, which compel an unhealthful herding, and breed ill feeling against the white race.

There is no other solution to the problem. Race prejudice is merely destructive. It offers nothing but a hopeless warfare and a blank pessimism. It has no future, but clings to a dead and decaying past. It has no constructive plan of any sort. The present condition is intolerable; and race prejudice, so far from suggesting a way out, proposes merely to intensify the worst features of the existing evil. Its overthrow must precede the general application of any effective remedy. The issue cannot be dodged. "A nation divided against itself cannot stand." Two races cannot live side by side at daggers' points with one another, and protect civilization, or maintain a healthy state of progress, in either. The perpetual feud destroys what is best and most hopeful in both. Race prejudice must die, that each of the races now cursed by its envenomed influence may truly live.

One other word must be spoken. In relation to the Negro, we of the North and South are prone to forget that we have a debt to pay, which has been accruing for many generations. Why should we who have sinned against the Negro throw all the burden on him, and expect to escape without making any sacrifices? He did not come here of his own accord. The problem was created by ourselves, not by him. The North, the first to sin, was also the first to repent. The South, so long the beneficiary of the original crime, has also a responsibility which cannot be evaded by cursing the victim. For good or for evil, we cannot shirk the results of our ancestors' acts. The Negro is what we have made him; and it is only fair that we should bear the consequences. The ascent to the supreme heights of civilization is not the matter of a day or a generation with any race; and no people is to be inexorably judged by its actual achievement at some particular period. Our ancestors were the rudest savages. They have had time and opportunity for development; and they have reached a relatively high stage of culture, though marred even yet by many crudities and unfortunate survivals. The Negro is today far in advance of the Saxon and Norman brutes who fought over the claims of William the Conqueror; and he has not yet had anything like an opportunity to develop the best that is in him. The highest of his race already stand on a level with the best of ours; and the supposition that the rank and file must forever remain inferior to the average of the white race is purely gratuitous and without scientific or historical justification.

The pettiness of race prejudice is unworthy of a great nation. Our very pride of race itself may fittingly be invoked to calm our fears of successful rivalry. The Anglo Saxon is not such a weak incompetent, that he must trample on the rights of others, in order to maintain his own position. We can afford to be foremost in exemplifying the principle of unlimited fraternity. The theory of our institutions demands it. The very definition of democracy involves it. The development of our own finer instincts compels it. The poor dreams of empire appeal to the heartless conqueror; and the glories of bloodstained conquest turn to apples of Sodom in his grasp. Infinitely more worthy of a true man or woman is the sublime vision of a day to come when the common good shall be the supreme law of all mankind, and when all nations and races shall be welded together into one great brotherhood. To all human appearance, that day is still far distant; but the measure in which we approach it marks our stage of development. The only function of race prejudice is to block the road; and no man can in any way render greater service to mankind than by devoting his energy toward the removal of this mighty obstacle to our highest hopes. Speed the hour when the Anglo Saxon and the African, the Latin and the Mongolian, the Slav and the Semite, bathed in the sunlight of the great reconciliation, shall be found side by side, laboring in brotherly love and friendly emulation for the achievement of loftier results than the world has yet conceived. The destruction of race prejudice is the beginning of the higher civilization.

APPENDIX

AFTER A DECADE AND THE KALEM CLUB
Rheinhart Kleiner

The Kalem Club flourished in New York City a decade ago. It was an extremely informal organization, and never definitely allied with amateur journalism. Nevertheless, among its members were a few amateur journalists of sufficient note to justify this brief chronicle of past glory by a self-appointed historian.

James F. Morton, Howard P. Lovecraft, Samuel Loveman, and Belknap Long were among those who found the club a congenial place for the completest and most untrammeled expression of opinion. Personal convictions, as well as the merest whimsies of thought, were here openly paraded and insisted upon, and there was no one too diffident to wage battle for the most astonishing paradox, if it happened to be his own.

James Morton had long been prominent as a writer and lecturer on controversial subjects, while amateur journalists knew him as a Moses who dispensed the law from Mt. Sinai. To Kalemites he appeared as the arbiter of literary taste, ready to quote chapter and verse from the most recondite classics, and prepared at any time to enter the lists in support of the Elizabethan dramatists.

Howard Lovecraft possessed a scholarly equipment of formidable thoroughness, aided by a memory quite incapable of losing anything which had ever been entrusted to it. He was regarded as the chief defender of Eighteenth century literature, architecture, and manners, but his versatility led him in many other directions, among which his ability in the art of writing weird stories deserved, and still deserves, conspicuous mention.

Samuel Loveman had just arrived from Cleveland with George Kirk, and the singing robes he wore about him seemed to trail clouds of glory as he came. His burst of lyrical power as a young poet in the National Amateur Press Association, followed by a long and inexplicable silence, had made him somewhat of a legendary figure. There was some uncertainly as to whether he should be regarded as a Chaucer or a Chatterton, but critical opinion agreed in considering him one of the few real poets to appear in amateur journalism. "The Hermaphrodite," which as recently found a handsome second publication at a western press, was then shortly to make its first appearance, in tasteful format, from the press of W. Paul Cook, in Athol, Mass.

Belknap Long, most youthful of the group, brought Shelleyan fire to his poetry and to his opinions. Rather more under the influence of extreme modernism—or what was such ten years ago—than the rest, he uttered convictions of a psycho-analytical cast which not infrequently non-plussed the representatives of the Elizabethan, Augustan, and Victorian ages. His inspiration as a poet was drawn from the true Pierian Spring, as readers of "The Man from Genoa, and Other Poems" (W. Paul Cook, Athol, Mass.) have discovered for themselves.

Among other members of note, was Everett McNeil, then at the height of his fame as an author for boys. His tales of adventure, published by E. P. Dutton & Co, filled an entire library shelf, and librarians reported that worn out copies of his books could not be replaced fast enough to meet the demand. His most popular story was "Tonty of the Iron Hand," published in 1925, which went into several editions. Some of his other titles were "The Totem of Black Hawk," "In Texas with Davy Crockett," and "Fighting with Fremont." He was easily the patriarch of the club, and, with his silvery hair and somewhat quizzical expression of face, presented a striking appearance. He was kindly of heart, and often entertained the club in his bachelor apartment of the west side. The complexities of modern life at times awakened a suggestion of the querulous in him, which none misunderstood. He died just when it seemed likely that the delayed rewards of a life of industrious authorship were about to be his.

Vrest Orton, another member, was the personification of "the man about town"—that idealized character of whom one so seldom hears today—and it was hardly surmised that a genuine bibliographer lay concealed beneath his air of dilitantism. He has since achieved fame as the bibliographer of Theodore Dreiser, and as the one who has been given credit by Bennett Cerf, and others, for the organization of The Colophon Club, whose publications are prized by scholars and bibliophiles the world over.

Wilfred B. Talman was one of the 'dependables' of the club. At the time, he was a reporter on a Brooklyn daily, with an amateur career as poet and publisher behind him. He had once conceived the idea of printing a book of his own verses on a hand press, and had set up two pages, facing, which fitted into one form. After printing many sheets, he discovered the omission of a word in the set-up, and forthwith scrapped the entire project. More fortunate in his professional ventures, he succeeded in selling stories and poems to magazines of national circulation.

Arthur Leeds, actor, story-writer, and authority on cinematic affairs of the day, contributed the accumulated experience of much travel and observation, as well as the knowledge gained from extensive literary browsing, to the deliberations of the group.

Most of the meetings of the Kalem Club, during the period of its greatest efflorescence, took place after business hours, at George Kirk's Chelsea Bookshop, on West 15th Street, near Ninth Avenue, New York City. George dealt in bibliophilic rarities and fine press books, and his magnificently stocked shelves reached from the floor to the ceiling, entirely around the room. He himself, possessed a finely discriminating taste in literature, and his equal as an amiable and generous host would have been difficult to find. In such an environment, and with such a host, it is not surprising that hearts were lightened and spirits soared.

George's ability and perseverance in brewing coffee, and his liberality with buns and sandwiches, left nothing to be desired. Nor need it cause wonder if certain individuals became so attached to proprietor and shop as to appear every evening, often with the expectation—which was never disappointed—of sleeping there. A host, whose bed in the rear room could accommodate five guests, if they did not toss too much, was never at a loss when visitors declined to go home.

What was said and done at some of these hilarious gatherings could never effectively be retold or reenacted. Our discussions and diversions were nothing if not spontaneous—and they were undoubtedly spontaneous. From some of our more serious sessions, the mind recalls a comprehensive appraisal of Walt Whitman's poetry, by James; a bit of amusing cynicism regarding Jane Austen's novels, from George; and a stout pronouncement that no woman over forty ever wrote a true lyric, on the part of Belknap. On one occasion, Sam read T. S. Eliot's poem, "The Waste Land," aloud, and those who did not succumb to torpor were aroused to torridity in the expression of opinion.

Recollection comes of a solemn evening when George announced that Otto, the house-cat—large, plump, and royally bewhiskered—had been killed in front of the door by a passing motor. Otto!—singularly gifted feline, with a genius for impromptu acrobatics on the hall stairway, and a benign imperturbability of demeanor in the face of false lures that were vainly designed to torment him! Lamentations and panegyrics became the order of the evening, and all poets present set to work upon suitable expressions of Kalemite grief. So far as can be ascertained, none of these notable productions was preserved, but the poems produced by Howard and Sam were regarded as masterpieces, that evening. Had these been spared from the maw of Time, it is not unlikely that so long established a favorite in this kind of poetry as Gray's "On the Death of a Favorite Cat Drowned in a Tub of Goldfishes," would have had its supremacy challenged.

Of a preliminary phase in the Kalem Club's history, involving Brooklyn, when George, Sam and Howard had rooms very near one another, on the Heights, much might be said, but who will say it?

Suffice it to conclude this incomplete and rambling record with the explanation—perhaps undesired—that "Kalem" was based upon the letters K, L, and M, which happened to be the initial letters in the names of the original group—McNeil, Long, and the writer—and of those who joined during the first six months of the club.

BARDS AND BIBLIOPHILES

Rheinhart Kleiner

Scene. A little coffee shop at the corner of Court and Schemerhorn Streets, Brooklyn. (The last-named thoroughfare, by the way, is known as "Skimmerhorn" to all true Brooklynites.)

Time. Approximately one a.m.

Half the lights in the shop are already out, but Lovecraft, Long, Kirk, and I are still looking over the first editions of the morning papers.

Young Long, wearing a carefully nurtured little mustache, a pearl-gray vest, and tie and spats to harmonize—it seems to me, now, that Marcel Proust, in his own youth, must have prefigured him—puts down his papers with a yawn, and says, "Well, I've read Don Marquis and F.P.A. Boredom begins again!"

There is a murmur of applause and approval from the others. Lovecraft beams upon his protégé. The correct attitude has just been summed up in a sentence.

As we leave the cashier's counter and move out into the street, there are sounds of a precipitous locking-up behind us.

Long, who has remained beyond his usual time, and now faces a

tedious train ride to his home in uptown Manhattan, makes brief fare-
wells and darts down the steps of a nearby subway entrance.

What now? Lovecraft and Kirk need not go far, since they have
rooms in an old three-story-and-basement brick house at the corner of
State and Clinton Streets, a three-minute walk from where we stand.
Loveman is close to the East River, on Columbia Heights itself, having
a similar room in this region of down-at-the-heels mansions, and
pinchback respectabilities. His lodging on the top floor offers a splendid view of the Manhattan skyline across the river, with the arching
lights of Brooklyn Bridge at the right, and the farther looming obscurity
of Governor's Island at the left.

(Ernest Poole, in his novel *The Harbor*, tells all about the past glo-
ries of this once aristocratic locality. Literary historians inform us that
Walt Whitman set type for the first edition of *Leaves of Grass* in a shop
at the corner of Cranberry and Fulton Streets—a little below the
Heights, geographically, but not far. Over in Bridge Street, Lucy Hop-
per, one of Griswold's "Female Poets of America," received visits from
John Greenleaf Whittier; and, in First Place, just off Clinton Street,
John Godfrey Saxe, once popular light-versifier, had his home.)

We decide to see Loveman to his door. It is true that I have a little
homeward journey of my own to make, to the Bushwick section, but as
a hardy "Borougher," and a fairly young one at that time, I think nothing of it.

It is a more than chilly night in late Autumn. A bitter blast from the
harbor strikes us as we emerge upon Columbia Heights, but the walk
will not be long.

A stray cat is sighted across the street, crawling close to the com-
fortless iron bars of a railing. Lovecraft and Kirk are professed cat-
lovers. For that matter, neither Loveman nor I am indifferent to them,
but there is a time and place for everything. The first two stop in their
tracks and make the customary wheedling sounds. The cat is obviously
flattered but inclined to be cautious; she starts to come over and then
changes her mind.

My hands and feet are already numb, and I am not sure but that my
ears are frostbitten. To get moving, I attempt to cut matters short by
interpolating a loud hiss into the proceedings. The startled cat, apparently about to yield, shrinks back to her railing. Indignant at such cal-
lousness from me, Lovecraft and Kirk redouble their coaxings and
blandishments. Moving closer to the curb, I hiss with such fury and de-

termination as finally to dispose of the cat, who disappears into the darkness of an alley. Loveman, from whom we have heard nothing, is found doubled-up in a doorway, not with the cold but with helpless merriment at what he has just beheld. We prop him up among us and get him home.

Trivialities, no doubt; but these are what remain of mind after a lapse of years.

There were other members of the Kalem Club, at this time, besides those just mentioned—the others being James Morton, Everett McNeil, and Vrest Orton. They were not given, however, to hanging around with us during the week. Other cares and preoccupations kept them from all but our regular gatherings.

Everett McNeil, silvery-haired and of a quizzical countenance, had all unconsciously acted as the center around which the club formed. Having made his acquaintance sometime in the early 1920s, through Ernest A. Dench at the Writers' Club, a professional group, I soon began visiting the old author at his tiny flat in West Forty-ninth Street, near Tenth Avenue, in Manhattan—an unsavory locality known at "Hell's Kitchen." McNeil, who had walked and hitched to New York from Wisconsin in his younger days, did not live here from choice. His small income, derived from royalties on his juvenile fictions, necessitated economical living, and rentals were not high in this part of the city.

It became his custom to read me the chapters he had written during the previous week, and in this way I acquired a familiarity with his last few stories for boys, among them being *Tonty of the Iron Hand* and *Daniel Du Luth, or Adventuring on the Great Lakes.*

Lovecraft, still in Providence, had been duly apprised of my acquaintance with the teller of tales, and it came about, somehow, that a "young Mr. Long" began calling at McNeil's. It was finally arranged that we should appear there together on a particular evening every week.

Something like an exodus of poets and booksellers from Cleveland taking place that year (1925), Samuel Loveman and George Kirk soon appeared in our midst. Then came Lovecraft. This group, meeting at McNeil's, decided that it ought to have a name. I don't know who thought of it, but since the patronymics of members began with K, L, or M, why not call it the Kalem Club? That was how the name came into being. Continuing to dwell for a moment on first causes, I do not know what it was that impelled Lovecraft to leave his beloved Providence for New York. If I ever did know, the reason has quite escaped my mind. Loveman and Kirk, in coming from Cleveland, were guided, understandably enough, by the hope of wider opportunities in their chosen field of rare books.

One of our milder diversions during the heyday of the club's Brooklyn period was the Sunday afternoon promenade in Clinton Street. This was traditional on the Heights, having been inaugurated by the landed gentry who first occupied the now dilapidated brownstone and brick mansions. Furthermore, Clinton Street was the time-honored setting for the observance of this custom.

For the purpose, we assembled in our best regalia either in Kirk's room or Lovecraft's, directly above. The occasion required the "wearing" of a cane, but the acquisition of this adjunct to our Sunday splendor proved no great problem.

Lovecraft produced an heirloom from Providence which was undeniably authentic, at once chastely severe and unobtrusively classical. Long appeared with a modishly tapered stick of timber which even bore his initials engraved on a silver band. Kirk carried a slender shining lance of some length, with a glass or quartz ball at the holding end. Loveman's affair was no less seemly than the rest, but it is not unlikely that his modest spirit shrank a little from such ostentation. Realizing that my own chances of cutting a figure in this aggregation were but slim, I had nevertheless made a choice from the stock of a pawnshop in Fulton Street, and felt that I might have done worse for the economical quarter involved.

These promenades sometimes wound up at a Spanish restaurant in Fulton Street—Loveman and Kirk having brought the tastes of cosmopolites from their Ohio home.

Occasionally, we visited a "speak-easy" in the Italian quarter of Greenwich Village, where a very thick soup might be had with a very sour wine. The Prohibition amendment having long since been repealed, it is probably safe to say that the place was somewhere near the drab center of that very drab thoroughfare, Downing Street. It had no name, for obvious reasons, and so we always referred to it by the name of the obliging Italian lad who waited on us, "Dominick's." Sixth Avenue has since been extended through the heart of this locality, and the obscure tenement which housed "Dominick's" is now almost at the corner of the new street intersection.

Lovecraft never touched the wine, just as he never used tobacco.

Loveman might make the gesture of taking a swallow—after all, he had the feeling, if not the taste, for wine!—but he was no tobacco user, either. The mere jollity of such an occasion was usually enough to suffuse his kindly countenance with a glow of "meridian splendor." Lovecraft may have felt that "Dominick's" was quite the sort of place which someone of his more rakish forebears among the English gentry might have frequented, and never expressed or implied any disapproval of the gay proceedings.

Mention cannot be overlooked of several expeditions, usually at night, into the Red Hook and Erie Basin neighborhoods, lying between the Heights and Bay Ridge, and fronting on the Narrows. This was a squalid area consisting mostly of docks, shipyards, freight depots, and decrepit tenements, and it swarmed with a motley population. An average visitor might have carried away an impression of a sordid shambles, but Lovecraft found it suitable for the setting of a "horror" tale. Upon its publication, the magazine's editor heard from a reader who said he had lived in Red Hook most of his life, but had never known of such goings on there. (Dorothy C. Walter, in her brochure "Lovecraft and Benefit Street," intimates that our author did something similar for a street in Providence. Lucky Red Hook and lucky Benefit Street, say I!)

An ancient Dutch cemetery in Flatbush, where moldering gravestones bearing early eighteenth-century inscriptions might still be seen, was frequently visited. Lovecraft was delighted with the "Hier Lydt" or "Hier leght begraaven" still plainly discernible on the pieces of scaling red slate. Long, to whom the whims of his mentor were not disturbing, would smoke a philosophic pipe while our horror specialist jestingly weighed the chances of getting a piece of the crumbling red slate home with him. Loveman, obviously in a state of apprehensive unease, would try to laugh the notion away. Truth to tell, there was a ghoulish gleam in Lovecraft's eye at such times which did not entirely belie Loveman's fears!

Something, but not too much, might be said of the club's expedition, on a bitterly cold morning in January 1925, to see the eclipse of the sun. Lovecraft, an amateur astronomer of note, could hardly have been expected to miss it. I was not there, but understood later from Kirk, whose participation in anything unusual or bizarre could be counted upon, that the experience almost proved disastrous for Lovecraft. The cold, on the exposed spot they had chosen, was so intense as to leave Lovecraft—lover of tropic heat—in a crippled condition for days afterward.

These, or similar frivolities, did not get in the way of the labor all of us had to perform. Lovecraft was loaded down with "hack" work of the dreariest kind. One of his clients, a minister of the gospel, paid a dollar a line for verse revisions, and since every "revision" was really a complete "rewrite," the money was not easily earned. Only his ability, real or fancied, to work all night when he chose, enabled him also to produce the stories dating from that period.

Loveman was preparing catalogues of rare books for one dealer or another, and rebelling at the drudgery, but his well-informed and conscientious efforts sometimes yielded unexpected rewards. Twice did Christopher Morley, with high praise, reprint in *The Saturday Review of Literature* the prefaces written by Loveman for current catalogues. Kirk spent the daylight hours in quest of desirable items, singly or in lots, for the bookshop he was soon to open in Manhattan. Long, just out of college, was meditating a career of authorship, and had already written short stories that were acceptable to editors. My own clerical job in a commercial house did not interfere too much with versifying, reading, and book-collecting.

Naturally, there was always much talk of books as we sat around together of an evening. Loveman, being in touch with the trade gossip concerning authors of the day, kept us posted as to the fluctuating market values of moderns who were then being "collected"—Arthur Machen, James Branch Cabell, Joseph Hergesheimer, or Theodore Dreiser. Lovecraft was primed with enthusiasms for little-known masters of the "horror" tale. He had a special feeling for Dunsany, who, while not a specialist in "horror," so far as I know, seemed to have made certain notable excursions into the realm of the fantastic. How often did we hear the name, enunciated with relish to the very last syllable, of "Edward John Moreton Drax Plunkett, Eighteenth Baron Dunsany"! I think the "Plunkett" was no inconsiderable part of the name's charm for Lovecraft.

Long followed Lovecraft quite closely in his own reading, but had found opportunity for a more than casual inspection of the poets of the "Yellow Nineties." Kirk, at that time, was giving much attention to the novels of a particular favorite of his, Anthony Trollope.

Sometimes, in the course of an informal session, there would be a little spontaneous versifying on the part of those qualified for such an exercise; or a "cross-word" puzzle might engage the attention of all for most of an evening. It must be stated that two of our most intellectual members became adepts in the matter of solving such puzzles, these being Lovecraft and Morton.

The former found it no distraction to do them even in the course of general conversation, but Morton carefully hoarded all that were given to him for a time when he might concentrate upon them properly.

Once in a while, a visiting amateur journalist from out of town might spend an evening or two with us. W. Paul Cook, great amateur and rare companion, was thus entertained on several visits.

Another guest, unique in his own way, was Adolphe Danziger de Castro, formerly consul to some Latin American country, and, more recently, author of a book on Ambrose Bierce, for which Belknap Long had written a foreword. One of Mr. de Castro's claims to attention was his collaboration with Bierce on a story entitled "The Monk and the Hangman's Daughter." Some unpleasantness between Bierce and de Castro had followed upon this venture, and the collaborator admitted that Bierce finally broke a cane over his head. These details naturally made us feel very close to the exciting source material of recent literary history. Mr. de Castro, moreover, was pleasantly plausible in conversation and provided an interesting evening.

Much more might be said of those vanished days on Brooklyn Heights, and it is to be hoped that Long or Loveman may yet feel the desire to contribute recollections to the Kalem Chronicle.

Some years ago—in Bradofsky's *Californian* for the fall of 1936, to be exact—I attempted to tell the story of the club in its Manhattan period, giving some attention to our regular meetings and going into more detail about individual members. We were a smaller and, possibly, more carefree group in our Brooklyn incarnation.

When the article appeared in *The Californian*, McNeil had already passed on, and Lovecraft was beginning to fail. Since he died in March of 1937, it is possible that he did not see my effort to revive the recollections of old days. Morton, a regular and ever dependable Kalemite, has left us more recently.

"Even such is time," who

> "When we had wandered all our ways,
> Shuts up the story of our days."

SOURCES AND WORKS CONSULTED

A. Sources

Kirk, George. "Book Collecting: The Prince of Hobbies." Unpublished.
———. "The Kalem Letters." Unpublished. Excerpts in Mara Kirk Hart, "Walkers in the City: George Willard Kirk and Howard Phillips Lovecraft in New York City, 1924–1926," *Lovecraft Studies* No. 28 (Spring 1993): 2–17; rpt. in *Lovecraft Remembered*, ed. Peter Cannon (Sauk City, WI: Arkham House, 1998), pp. 221–47.
Kleiner, Rheinhart. "After a Decade and the Kalem Club." *Californian* 4, No. 2 (Fall 1936): 45–47.
———. "At Providence in 1918." *Conservative* 5, No. 1 (July 1919): 8.
———. "Bards and Bibliophiles." *Aonian* 2, No. 4 (Winter 1944): 169–74. Rpt. in *Lovecraft Remembered*, ed. Peter Cannon. Sauk City, WI: Arkham House, 1998, pp.188–94.
———. "Blue Pencil Anniversary Song." *Brooklynite* 19, No. 5 (March 1930): 9.
———. "Brooklyn, My Brooklyn." *New York Evening Post* (date unknown); rpt. in *The Bowling Green: An Anthology of Verse*, ed. Christopher Morley (Garden City, NY: Doubleday, Page, 1924), pp. 101–2.
———. "Columbia Heights, Brooklyn." Unpublished.
———. "Epistle to Mr. and Mrs. Lovecraft." *Brooklynite* 14, No. 2 (April 1924): 1.
———. "The Four of Us (Rondeau)." Unpublished.
———. "The Great Adventure." Unpublished.
———. "H. P. L." *Olympian* No. 35 (Autumn 1940): facing p. 1.
———. "If I Had Lived a Hundred Years Ago." *Brooklynite* 19, No. 5 (March 1930): 2.
———. "On a Favorite Cat Killed by an Automobile." Unpublished.
———. "[Prisky.]" Unpublished.
———. "To George W. Kirk, upon His 26th Birthday." Unpublished.

————. "To His Peculiar Friend, G. Kirk, Esq." Unpublished.

————. "What My Ancestors Were Like." Unpublished.

————. "Your Street." Unpublished.

Leeds, Arthur. "He Had to Pay the Nine-Tailed Cat." *Ghost Stories* 1, No. 4 (October 1926): 36–38, 83–85.

Long, Frank Belknap. "Come, Let Us Make." In *A Man from Genoa and Other Poems.*

————. "A Man from Genoa." In *A Man from Genoa and Other Poems.* Athol, MA: Recluse Press, 1926.

————. "The Man Who Died Twice." *Ghost Stories* 2, No. 1 (January 1927): 46–48, 52, 54.

Lovecraft, H. P. "In Memoriam: Oscar Incoul Verelst of Manhattan 1920–1926." In *The Ancient Track: Complete Poetical Works* (San Francisco: Night Shade Books, 2001), p. 171.

————. "Plaster-All." *Lovecraft Studies* No. 27 (Fall 1992): 30–31. In *The Ancient Track*, pp. 248–51.

————. "Primavera." *Brooklynite* 15, No. 2 (April 1925): 1. In *The Ancient Track*, pp. 56–58.

————. "Providence." *Brooklynite* 14, No. 4 (November 1924): 2–3. In *The Ancient Track*, pp. 302–3.

————. "To an Infant." *Brooklynite* 15, No. 4 (October 1925): 2. In *The Ancient Track*, pp. 167–68.

————. "To Endymion." *Tryout* 8, No. 10 (September 1923): [15–16]. In *The Ancient Track*, pp. 155–56.

————. "To George Kirk, Esq." In *The Ancient Track*, p. 162.

————. "To George Willard Kirk, Gent." *National Amateur* 49, No. 5 (May 1927): 5 (as "George Willard Kirk"). In *The Ancient Track*, pp. 169–70.

————. "Two Christmas Poems to G. W. K." In *The Ancient Track*, pp. 49, 63.

————. "A Year Off." In *The Ancient Track*, pp. 165–67.

————. "Waste Paper." *Books at Brown* 26 (1978): 48–52. In *The Ancient Track*, pp. 252–55.

Loveman, Samuel. "Admonition." *United Amateur* 25, No. 3 (July 1926): 5.

————. "Arcesilaus." In *The Hermaphrodite and Other Poems*, p. 56.

————. "For a Book of Poems." In *The Hermaphrodite and Other Poems* (Caldwell, ID: Caxton Printers, 1936), p. 58.

———. "For a Cat." In *Out of the Immortal Night: Selected Works by Samuel Loveman* (New York: Hippocampus Press, 2004, p. 111 (as "Oscar Redivivus").

———. "For the Chelsea Book Shop" [1]. Broadside, bookmark, n.d.

———. "For the Chelsea Book Shop" [2]. In *Out of the Immortal Night*, pp. 119–20.

———. "Genesis." *United Amateur* 25, No. 2 (May 1926): 2.

———. "John Clare in 1864." In *Out of the Immortal Night*, p. 122.

———. "A Letter to G—— K——." *Rainbow* 2, No. 2 [sic] (May 1922): 15.

———. "Limbo." In *The Hermaphrodite and Other Poems*, p. 97.

———. "Spring at El Retiro." In *Out of the Immortal Night*, p. 121.

———. "To George Kirk on His 27th Birthday." In *Out of the Immortal Night*, p. 112.

———. "To H. P. L." *United Amateur* 25, No. 3 (July 1926): 8 (as "To Mr. Theobald").

McNeil, Everett. *Tonty of the Iron Hand.* New York: E. P. Dutton, 1925, pp. 4–13.

Morton, James Ferdinand. *The Curse of Race Prejudice.* N.p., [1906?], pp. 65–69.

———. "To G. W. K. on His 27th Birthday." Unpublished.

B. Works Consulted

Cannon, Peter. *H. P. Lovecraft.* Boston: Twayne, 1989.

———. *Long Memories: Recollections of Frank Belknap Long.* Stock Port, UK: British Fantasy Society, 1997.

———, ed. *Lovecraft Remembered.* Sauk City, WI: Arkham House, 1998.

Davis, Sonia. *The Private Life of H. P. Lovecraft.* West Warwick, RI: Necronomicon Press, 1985.

de Camp, L. Sprague. *Lovecraft: A Biography.* Garden City, NY: Doubleday, 1975.

Faig, Kenneth W. *H. P. Lovecraft: His Life, His Work.* West Warwick, RI: Necronomicon Press, 1979.

Hart, Mara Kirk. "Walkers in the City: George Willard Kirk and Howard Phillips Lovecraft in New York City, 1924–1926." *Lovecraft Studies* No. 28 (Spring 1993): 2–17; rpt. in *Lovecraft Remembered*, ed. Peter Cannon (Sauk City, WI: Arkham House, 1998), pp. 221–47.

Joshi, S. T. *H. P. Lovecraft: A Life*. West Warwick, RI: Necronomicon Press, 1996.

Kleiner, Rheinhart. "Howard Phillips Lovecraft." *Californian* 5, No. 1 (Summer 1937): 5–8.

Long, Frank Belknap. *Autobiographical Memoir*. West Warwick, RI: Necronomicon Press, 1985.

———. *Howard Phillips Lovecraft: Dreamer on the Nightside*. Sauk City, WI: Arkham House, 1975.

Lovecraft, H. P. *The Annotated H. P. Lovecraft*. Annotated by S. T. Joshi. New York: Dell, 1996.

———. *From the Pest Zone: The New York Stories*. Edited by S. T. Joshi and David E. Schultz. New York: Hippocampus Press, 2003.

———. *Lord of a Visible World: An Autobiography in Letters*. Edited by S. T. Joshi and David E. Schultz. Athens: Ohio University Press, 2000.

———. *Selected Letters*, Volumes I and II. Edited by August Derleth and Donald Wandrei. Sauk City, WI: Arkham House, 1965, 1968.

Talman, Wilfred B. "The Normal Lovecraft." In *The Normal Lovecraft* by Wilfred B. Talman et al. Saddle River, NJ: Gerry de la Ree, 1973, pp. 5–17. Rpt. in *Lovecraft Remembered*, ed. Peter Cannon. Sauk City, WI: Arkham House, 1998, pp. 212–20.

INDEX

Only the introduction and the Kalem Letters have been indexed.

Printed in the United States
53362LVS00002B/553-570